POINT NEMO

MAJESTIC FILES - BOOK 4

ANDY BRIGGS

TANGLEBOX
BOOKS

POINT NEMO

Copyright © 2021 by Andy Briggs

Cover art: Shutterstock

www.andybriggsbooks.com
Twitter: @abriggswriter
Instagram: @itsandybriggs

POINT NEMO

a lonely place to die

"We have salt in our blood, in our sweat, in our tears. We are tied to the ocean. And when we go back to the sea ... we are going back from whence we came."

JFK

UNTITLED

"We have salt in our blood, in our sweat, in our tears. We are tied to the ocean. And when we go back to the sea ... we are going back from whence we came."

JFK

ONE

4.299224 N, **73.012527 E**

WARM JADE WATERS stretched to infinity, a gorgeous emerald enhanced by Scott Bowers' polarized Maui Jims as he basked in the luxury of another Maldivian day.

Booking the last-minute trip had been Ruth's idea after a rough couple of months back in London. Escaping the bleak grey weather had been akin to bring freed from a hole, not just in their spirits but their relationship which had become as monotonous as the London weather. Mobile phones switched off for the week; in an ocean villa, perched on stilts above crystal waters of the Indian Ocean. It had taken a fifteen-minute sea plane ride to reach, and was the perfect choice to get away from civilization. A welcome feeling of near-isolation.

He rolled his head to the side, studying Ruth draped on the other wooden lounger, dressed in a simple black bikini, the arc of her back and legs perfectly contoured to the chair.

A figure he had forgotten to admire for so long. Was he solely to blame? He had never been easy to live with, passionately wrapped in his work and – after a couple of years therapy – now accepting that he was just on the autistic spectrum. When he spoke to others, it made him sound emotionally hard, distant, uncaring – all the usual incorrect assumptions people made about ASD. Even himself.

He learned that it was his own inability to identify his own emotions, a condition called *alexithymia*. Normally suffers are limited to their own emotions, but Scott wasn't able to judge other's either. Without paying close attention to non-verbal cues, particularly facial expressions – and unless they were extremes of emotional expression, from laughter to floods of tears, it would be like reading a blank slate.

Ruth was tolerant, in fact she was the one who urged him to seek a therapist in the hope it would improve things between them. Whereas all it had done was make Scott aware of just how miserable he was making others. A head load to bear that just made him sad, in turn, distant. Something he had simply termed the spiral.

The first few days had broken the spiral. They had been bliss, packed with rare physical connections that had been absent from their lives for far too long. But since yesterday Ruth had retreated into the distance, leaving Scott unsure what he had done to trigger it. In a day, she had become attached to her mobile phone, and they sank back into monosyllabic routine that had threatened their relationship. To add insult, the eczema that gnawed his forearms when he was stressed made an unwelcome return despite the healthy tan he was building.

Christ, he thought, *I'm falling apart both inside and out...*

He cast his gaze back to the water and the lone speed

boat that had appeared to blight perfection. He pondered prying into the cause of Ruth's mood and wondered if she was a fellow undiagnosed ASD suffer. A successful surgeon, such a detachment from emotions would be a blessing. He stopped that train of thought; it was nothing but ill will. As usual, her mood would be down to something he had blindly said and concluded that it would only lead to a series of snappy retorts, and he wanted nothing to further ruin their break. He only hoped he'd brought enough new novels from the airport book store to keep him entertained for the remaining time and deeply regretted leaving his Kindle behind.

"The wi-fi keeps dying." It was the first comment Ruth had made in the last hour.

Scott watched the boat circle in the atoll's direction. "What do you expect, we're in the middle of nowhere."

Her muttered reply was barely audible. "No reason to disconnect from the world."

Like you connect with it normally, trolled a bitter voice in Scott's head. An unfair comment as she was the more gregarious of the two of them. He closed his eyes and tried to quell the negativity with a nap. The shuffling from Ruth's lounger betrayed she had finally moved. He opened one eye and peered at her.

"If you're getting up, call for another Mojito." He smacked his lips to indicate how parched he was, hoping a little levity would help. His therapist had told him it would.

She ignored him. Now sitting upright, she was gazing out to sea. "That boat's coming this way."

Scott jolted upright in his seat. Now he could see the boat was not the usual tourist vessel, but a sleek black yacht that was heading towards them at full clip. He had heard the stories of pirates kidnapping people in the Indian Ocean, but that was much further south. Surely the Maldives was a tame paradise...

Ruth stood moments before Scott noticed the small Stars 'n' Stripes flying from the stern and the bobbed haired blonde woman, dressed incongruously in a black business suit, clinging to a rail on the bridge, just behind the burly shade-wearing captain.

"Scott...?" Ruth's voice trailed off as the boat cut its engine and coasted towards them, turning on its axis and sending a bow wave splashing over the deck of their raised bungalow.

Scott stood and removed his shades. The blonde and the flag had reassured him they were not pirates. Or at least, pirates in the traditional sense. The woman locked eyes with him and gave a subtle nod of recognition as they drew closer.

"Doctor Bowers?"

"Yes," Ruth and Scott replied in unison.

The blonde cast a glance at Ruth before turning her attention back to Scott. "Doctor *Scott* Bowers?"

"Uh-huh."

"I'm Sienna Lutz from United Salvage." Scott merely gave a puzzled shrug, so she continued. "You name was passed to us by Frisco Dynamics."

Scott glanced at Ruth, more puzzled than ever, although the name was familiar. He'd been employed by Frisco Dynamic some three years earlier. Based in San Francisco, they had commissioned him for an impact assessment report on plastic toxins in the marine food chain and its adaptive effects on life. Marine Biology, in particular extremophiles, was his specialty. A career he felt that Ruth never quite understood.

Sienna stared at him, her fingers impatiently drumming against the support rail. Now he could see that her hair was damp with sweat. Under her suit, her shirt was open in an almost respectable V, but the dark patches betrayed the fact she had obviously taken the wrong clothes for the tropics.

"That's me," was all he could think of answering.

"Your services are required."

He exchanged a look with Ruth, then gestured around. "I'm on holiday," he stated not quite believing she hadn't worked that out.

"This is an emergency."

Ruth laughed. "What kind of emergency requires an extremophile specialist?"

"Clause forty-four," she stated matter-of-factly.

It took a moment for Scott to make the link to his own impact paper. Part of the assessment was the formation of specialist teams should an environmental disaster strike the marine ecosystem. Anything from an oil spill to seismic activity, such as the incident that caused the terrible Boxing Day tsunami of 2004, so that the impact on the ecosystem could be studied in real time and measures could be placed to stem the damage. Saving money had been the goal, not protecting the environment. The eleven-million gallons of oil from the Deepwater Horizon spill had polluted over thirteen hundred kilometers of coastline in the Gulf of Mexico, costing BP over four-billion dollars just to contain – and wiping out swathes of marine life and, along with it, people's incomes.

"Has there been an oil spill?"

"I'm not at liberty to say. I'm authorized to pay you fifty-thousand dollars a week for your services if you come with us."

All thoughts of asking for reimbursement for the interrupted holiday dissolved. He reached for Ruth's hand in a pointless gesture of permission.

"Ruth..." he began in barely a whisper.

She nodded, and to his surprise, smiled. "Go. We could do with the cash."

He frowned as she held up her phone. He saw an email on-screen, although the text was blocked by her fingers.

"My obstetrician. I'm finally pregnant."

Scott skipped a breath and felt as if he'd been punched in the gut. A calm area of his mind was surprised by the unexpected emotional response - another part was screaming at him that there was something bigger at stake here than his own feelings. He gaped wordlessly, noticing Ruth's smile had been replaced by a frown of concern.

"I didn't know... how you'd react." Her eyes scanned his face for an honest answer.

"It's... that's... Ruth. That is wonderful news."

He kissed her. Again, a gesture lacking any fiery passion of old, but when he parted her lips were twisted into a relived smile. She flicked a glance at the yacht.

"So go and save some exotic sea slug and get back to me. We have a lot of planning ahead of us. A whole new start."

Exactly what they needed, Scott thought. A fresh injection of life. It was an invigorating revelation and now he hesitated, not wishing to suddenly leave his pregnant wife.

"Will you be–?"

Ruth waved her hand dismissively. "Will I be fine for a few day's contemplation in five-star tropical comfort? I'll struggle on somehow. Go."

She leaned in and kissed him again, this time pushing against his mouth. He felt a small thrill of excitement. The next few minutes were spent dressing and hurriedly packing.

Other than the jeans, jacket and trainers he'd worn for the flight, he'd only brought a couple of casual shirts and trousers for evening dining. He double-checked he had his vital travel accessories: his phone, passport, wallet black Omega Seamaster Planet Ocean watch that Ruth had bought him as a fifth anniversary gift. He still regretted that he'd only bought her some cheap flowers from a petrol station in return, failing, as usual, to register the significance of the date.

He kissed Ruth again before boarding the yacht, helped aboard by a stony-faced captain who was the only other person he could see on-board. Almost instantly they peeled away from the bungalow, surging to full speed within seconds. He waved at Ruth who stood motionless on the bungalow's deck. He forced a smile at Sienna.

"I'm going to be a dad." Sienna nodded without interest. "So now we're alone, where are we going?"

TWO

31.181349 N, **121.442095 E**

TRACKING anybody down in the sprawling metropolis of Shanghai should be difficult, but the Chinese facial recognition network was one of the biggest in the world, with London coming a close second. Within minutes City Brain had identified its target. It also helped that Eric Dong was a creature of habit.

From the outside, Shanghai Stadium looked closed, with most of the shutters pulled tight over the entrances and the car park empty save for several Geely cars, two dozen scooters packed close together, and a couple of vans parked on the Tiyuchang Ring Road. A single side entrance was open, allowing direct access to the under-stand areas containing the player changing rooms, multiple storage areas packed with grounds maintenance tools and tunnels leading directly to the track and pitch.

It was on the pitch that Eric was enjoying a high-speed

race around the arena, soaring meters above the ground at speeds of 125 mph as he ducked through neon hoops, pulled a sudden stop as he flipped a ninety-degree turn before accelerating down a curved enclosed pipe.

Eric vicariously experienced every second of his racing drone's flight through an Oculus VR headset that focused the image with high-definition clarity. His thumbs deftly juggled the sticks on the radio control unit in his hands and he tried to filter out the chorus of rising cheers as his drone narrowly avoided a collision with another and slid into first place.

The two-dozen people gathered to play in their amateur racing league had placed a series of obstacles around the arena: hoops, pipes and had even adapted the corridors under the stadium to be part of the flight path.

It was this leg of the circuit that Eric entered, sharply banking his drone and dropping to five feet above the grass before accelerating into the concrete tunnel – and on a collision course with an unexpected hurdle.

A pair of shade wearing men were striding straight towards his drone. He was going too fast to make out details, but saw the leader's hand raise to swat the brick-sized aircraft away, obviously mistaking it for a bird. Eric jinked the control to the left – straight into a third man. The man's head loomed like a giant's in Eric's visor before the image blacked out as the connection was terminated.

Eric swore as he pulled off his headset as he raced to towards the tunnel. A direct strike even from a small racing drone could cause severe injuries, and the last thing he needed was to be up on an assault charge. From the tirade of swearing from the three other rival pilots, Eric knew they had literally flown into the same problem – one crashing into the wall.

By the time he reached the tunnel, a man staggered out clutching his bleeding forehead. Eric shuffled to a stop and felt a growing surge of panic. The man was built like a slab of muscle that was barely contained by his blood-spattered designer suit. At least he was alive; Eric's more logical side was trying to figure out the medical costs in a country with no real insurance schemes.

"I'm so sorry..."

The other two figures stepped out. One a woman, clutching her bleeding hand from swatting a drone, the other a man in his late fifties with neat grey hair who flashed Eric a warm smile that put him further on the back foot.

"Dong Chen?" the man asked, addressing him formally, although Eric preferred his adopted western moniker.

"Yes, sir."

The man extended one hand to shake, which Eric belatedly did. Then he nodded to his injured companions.

"Quite a weapon you have developed there."

"Uh? Oh, no, not a weapon. Drone racing. This is our... Shanghai league," he added lamely under the injured goons hostile glares.

The older man was amused. "I apologize for getting in the way of your *game*."

It only now dawned on Eric that they were looking specifically for him. Like anywhere else in the world, thugs in suits were never good news. The man continued as his gaze swept across the stadium. The other racers were rushing over to help the injured. The two thugs wordlessly stepped across the pitch to intercept them. Eric was conscious that they'd now effectively herded him away from the safety of his friends.

"You are working on the Yinghuo-2 project?"

On autopilot, Eric was about to agree before he stopped himself. His work for CAST – the Chinese Academy of Space Technology - was classified, especially when it came for their next planned Mars mission. The man flashed him a smile and held up a laminated CNSA ID held in a leather wallet.

"I work for the Chinese National Space Administration."

Eric took the ID and scrutinized it, aware the man – who according to the ID was named Keung – was carefully studying him. It looked authentic, but on the other hand Eric had never heard of the CNSA's 'Special Project' division the ID claimed he belonged to.

"You worked on the Tiangong-2?"

Eric nodded. It had been his first major assignment with the Administration, launching the second Chinese space station had been a moment of national pride. It had been a careful stepping stone for China to establish a presence on the moon. The first station had deorbited in 2018, burning up in the atmosphere in an act of controlled obsolescence, the second came down a year later.

"That is correct," again Eric was careful not give anything away.

Keung checked everybody was still out of earshot on the field before continuing.

"I am here to tell you that your work on Yinghuo-2 is suspended." Eric left out a gasp of surprise, but Keung continued talking before he could get a word in. "You are being reassigned. Immediately. We require your expertise on the Tiangong."

Eric shook his head, bewildered. "Why? It burned up on re-entry..."

Keung turned back to the tunnel and beckoned for Eric to follow. "Come."

"I don't see what the hurry is."

"We have a long way to travel."

Eric cast a look back at the drone racers who were having a heated conversation with the suits. Nobody was looking his way and, as he followed Keung into the dark tunnel, he wondered how long it would take them to notice he had disappeared.

"Where are we going?"

Keung's voice echoed eerily from the drab walls.

"Point Nemo."

THREE

48.2536 S, **123.2336 W**

"ALMOST THERE, SIR."

The radio's sharp click that preceded the announcement roused Scott Bowers from the vague slumber he had been snatching throughout the journey. They were words he'd thought he'd never hear after the thirteen hour flight from Malé to Wellington, New Zealand. Then ninety minutes in the back of a truck to some military base before another six and half hour flight to literally the middle of nowhere.

The Chinese built AVIC AG600, with its four massive turbo-props didn't look particularly special when he boarded, and the Kiwi pilot and Chinese co-pilot appeared blasé during take-off. It was only midway through the flight when Scott discovered that his new ride was not only still a classed as prototype aircraft; it was also the largest amphibious plane currently flying. That was, with a tremor of trepidation, how Scott had also learnt how they planned to land.

The aircraft could easily fit fifty people, but aside from the two crew, he shared the ride with a petite blonde Australian woman who had spoken only to introduce herself as Doctor Maya Johnson before donning noise-cancelling headphones and reclining in her seat to read; and a Chinese man called Eric who had popped a sleeping pill and snored his way through the journey. Beyond the five rows of seats, the rear of the aircraft was packed with silver flight cases secured in place by canvas webbing. Several times he had stretched his legs and examined the cargo, which mostly seemed to be vaguely labelled as fragile scientific equipment.

Scott sat up in the aircraft's wide military seat and cracked the tension from his neck as he yawned. He peered over the pilot's shoulder. It had taken almost a day to get to their destination using the fastest means possible.

The most remote place on the surface of the earth.

A Geographic Pole of Inaccessibility.

Point Nemo.

A whole bunch of nothing except the Pacific Ocean in every direction. Scott had been expecting tall seas with white-capped rolling waves, not the turquoise almost millpond still waters that stretched to infinity, blending sea with sky.

"Nobody gave me any detailed answers as to why they wanted me out here, and this isn't making things much clearer."

"They don't tell me either, mate," said the pilot, scanning the horizon from behind his polarized aviators. "They just pay us to as a taxi service." After a moment, he pointed ahead. "There we are."

Scott couldn't see anything against the glare of the sun from the water. He motioned to release his seatbelt, his hand on the metal buckle, just as the plane shimmied from turbulence. He wasn't afraid of flying, but the turbulence unsettled him greatly. Perhaps the general strangeness of the situation was getting to him. He had worked in many remote locations during the course of his work, that's where most extremophiles lived. But never in such a cloud of secrecy, and never had his research budgets stretched to what he saw before him.

He noticed Maya standing in the aisle to his side. She let out a low whistle.

"They sent out the welcome armada." She gripped the seats either side of her as the plane shimmied again. "Looks like we've found the only party in town."

Two massive aircraft carriers sat half a mile apart. A huge freighter - equipped with a helipad, was almost cleaved in two by an enormous moon pool – sat between them. A hundred-or-so meter battle-grey frigate that resembled a deadly dart, patrolled around the fleet.

As they drew nearer, Scott saw fluorescent green dots in the moon pool – even from this distance he recognized them as submersibles. The air was busy with choppers buzzing from ship-to-ship and three UAV drones circled the area. To his surprise, he noted the aircraft carriers sported flags from the USA and China. The lone Frigate flying the Stars and Stripes, while the freighter flew Kiwi colors.

He glanced at Eric, who was still deeply asleep. "What the hell's going on?" He was slightly gratified to see Maya gentle shake her head.

"Okay, folks. Strap in. We're landing shortly."

Maya's brown eyes were wide with excitement as she dropped into the seat opposite Scott and buckled up without taking her eyes from the flotilla ahead.

"This has gotta be something huge."

Scott swallowed his reply as the monotonous pitch from the engines changed and the aircraft sharply lost altitude as it lined up for a steep landing. He closed his eyes and gripped both arm rests tightly. He wasn't aware he was doing it until he felt Maya's hand briefly squeeze his own. He glanced at her, determinedly trying to avoid the view from the windows which all seemed to be ocean. She smiled at him, looking relaxed.

"Don't like flying, huh?"

"Flying yes. Turbulence, no. Or taking off. Or landing."

"Sounds like flying to me."

"And seaplanes... I just had to endure that in the Maldives."

"Oh, my heart bleeds." He couldn't tell if she was joking; that was another of his problems. Humor and sarcasm were wasted on him.

Landing on the water sent a jolt along Scott's spine. With closed eyes, he had been focused on the rumbling engines, but now the entire plane shuddered as it repeatedly hit the water, which, to Scott, felt very solid. In his mind's eye he couldn't cut out the image of the aircraft flipping tail-over-nose and smashing apart. He would normally expect to feel nothing more than detachment from such imagined dangers... but now, something unexpected.

A tremor of fear. Just the surfacing tendrils of a worry that were almost alien to him, goaded by the very thought of not seeing him unborn... daughter? Son?

As his therapist instructed, he examined the new emotion at arm's length, trying to understand the cause and effect. An impossible task as the aircraft thudded into the water again, this time the sudden water-resistance jolted him forward. The fuselage vibrated as it powered through the water, the sound of which almost drowned out the engines as they now whined to slow the aircraft. Scott swore they must have skipped another five or six times, each accompanied by a yelp of delight from Maya, before they finally came to a stop.

Scott leaned forward, putting his elbows against his knees as he sucked in a deep breath. The silent aircraft was now gently rocking in the water, enticing him to throw up.

He heard a sniff, then a yawn from behind. He glanced back to see Eric stretching in his seat and peering sleepily through the windows.

"Oh, we've landed?"

SCOTT FINALLY FOUND his sea legs once they had boarded the aircraft carrier, the USS Gerald R. Ford, and sat clutching a steaming mug of tea, which he was surprised to find served on an American Naval vessel.

A zodiac had picked the three of them up from the seaplane and ferried them to the American Arleigh Burke-Class combat ship, the USS Paul Ignatius. A gangway docked with the tender and they were marshalled quickly onboard. Led up a series of stairwells to a helipad, a chopper had then ferried them across to the colossal US aircraft carrier, the USS Gerald R. Ford.

They'd been assigned berths in the C deck of the massive floating city, where they'd had a chance to freshen up before a stern-face Puerto Rican yeowoman, who identified herself as Alanis, summoned them to a large windowless briefing room. They had no sooner been given drinks and an assortment of pastries, which Maya and Eric demolished, before the Captain strode in.

"Gentlemen, lady, I'm Captain Peers. Welcome aboard the Gerald R. Ford." The accent was unmistakably Bostonian. In his fifties, Peers stood six two and packed a muscular frame. Piercing eyes darted beneath eyebrows that were slightly too bushy. He gestured to the table in the center of the room and glanced at his watch. "Apologies for the lack of, well, lack of anything resembling an answer for the questions that you all no doubt have. I aim to rectify that shortly. Please take a seat. I trust on the long flight out you all got to know one another?"

They took their seats around the table, Peers on one side giving a very definite them-and-us vibe. Scott noticed the captain's thumb nervously drummed an iPad he clutched in one hand.

"Not really," Scott replied. "It was all of a blur, and the flights were rather uncomfortable."

"Not up to your usual five-star expectations. Doctor Bowers?"

Peers smiled, prompting Scott to answer curtly. "Not at all." He heard Maya give a short snort of laughter, before realizing the comment had been sarcastic. The tea wasn't helping cut through the lack of quality sleep and severe jetlag. Before he had time to explain, Peers held up a hand.

"I know all about you, Doctor Bowers, and that there was sarcasm. Relax, I'm just fucking with you."

The captain placed an iPad in front of him, fussily angling it so that it was square to the desk. "To orientate yourselves, the time here is still the day you left. You crossed the International Date Line, not like that's gonna help with the jetlag. You are now part of a joint US-Sino operation."

He indicated to Scott and Maya. "You both worked with Frisco Dynamics who in turn are contracted on a lot of... sensitive government operations." His finger made a small circle in the air. "They will be taking the lead on the operation." He pointed at Eric. "And your expertise is with the Chinese Space Administration."

Scott and Maya exchanged a puzzled look.

"Space administration?" said Maya. "I specialize in salvage operations."

Scott frowned. "I deal in extremophiles. Captain, are you sure you have the right people?"

"You are exactly the right people." The clipped reply came from an American woman marching into the room wearing a gray jumpsuit and flight boots. Her hawkish features were crowned by a blossom of frizzy black hair complete with grey streaks that looked as if lightning was coursing through it. "I'm Professor Jan Raven from Frisco and I personally requested the three of you." She sat at the table, tossing her own iPad carelessly down. "Coffee?" Her head darted around until she caught the eye of a crewman standing at the door. "Coffee. Keep it flowing."

Scott didn't recognize the rank of the crewman, but he obviously floated high above coffee intern, however he nodded helplessly before ducking out of the room. Scott flinched as Professor Raven slammed both palms on the table to get their attention.

"I'm afraid answers are going to beget more questions, which you're going to have to figure out along the way. What you need to know is that everything, from the hour before you were picked up, is now top secret."

"Meaning...?" Maya raised a questioning eyebrow.

"Meaning, no communication to the outside world until

you return. And even then, if your refer to this operation as anything more than a fishing trip then, trust me, incarceration would be the mild punishment." She allowed the threat to hang in the air. It was so on the nose that even Scott understood it. "We are on the doorstep of a historical moment. And when we cross through... who knows where it will lead."

FOUR

PROFESSOR RAVEN UNLOCKED HER IPAD. A few quick taps opened Google Earth, and she zeroed in on their location in the southern Pacific Ocean.

"We are seated at what they call the South Pacific Ocean Uninhabited Area, but I prefer to call it Point Nemo." Eric reacted to the name, but Scott and Maya looked non-the-wiser.

"This is the furthest point on the planet you can be from land. Ducie Island is to the north." Raven expanded the map; nothing but blue ocean, until some land finally appeared – nothing more than a fragment, a kilometer-and-half of an uninhabited toenail in the ocean. "Moto Nui, northeast, and Maher Island to the south. Right next to Antarctica. They're all about fifteen hundred nautical miles from us right now." She circled her hand in the air, taking in all points of the compass. "Hell, if the fleet wasn't outside, the nearest human beings to us are aboard the ISS when it passes two-hundred fifty-eight miles overhead."

Scott stared at the map. Nothing but the ocean surrounded them.

The true scale of their remoteness was just striking him, despite the epic voyage it had taken to get here.

"And what could possibly be of interest out here?" asked Maya.

The crewman entered and handed Raven a coffee in a paper cup. She examined it disparagingly and answered between sips, her lips puckering at the bitterness.

"We're well away from commercial shipping lanes, air corridors and good coffee. This is as isolated as it gets on the planet. The middle of the Sahara is a party hotspot by comparison. That makes it a very interesting place if you're trying to dump stuff."

Scott was fighting a head that felt it was swaddled in cotton wool. He hated his own mind at the best of times and all the travel was making him feel irritable. "What sort of stuff?" Raven pointed straight up, an answer that silently infuriated him. "Tell us, don't make us guess!"

"Space debris," said Eric, leaning forward curiously. Raven nodded. Eric took a pen from his jacket pocket and held it up for the benefit of Scott and Maya. "A satellite," he indicated to the pen, "can lose orbit for any number of reasons, potentially running the risk of falling on habitable areas."

Maya nodded. "But they burn up in the atmosphere."

"Not all the time. The larger they are, the more likely fragments can make it to the ground. Like Skylab."

"Never heard of it."

Raven gave Maya an appraising look. "Before your time, my dear." She finished her coffee. "It was a NASA space station launched in '73. It suffered a decaying orbit and in

'79 it fell to earth." She slammed the cup down for emphasis, crumpling it and causing Maya to flinch. "Mission Control adjusted its course over the Pacific and figured the eight-five ton monster would burn up on entry. They were very wrong. Parts of broke up just ten miles up. Fragments scattered down over West Australia, mostly near Perth. Lesson were learned and Point Nemo became party central for anything re-entering. With luck, it all burns up and gives us a fancy firework show. Worse case it splashes down. Kills a couple dozen fish."

Scott caught Eric's eye. "That explains the 'here'. But..." he left the unspoken question hanging.

"The Tiangong-2." Raven turned her attention to Eric.

Maya frowned. "The *what*?"

Raven's eyes stayed on Eric. "The Heavenly Palace. It is a Chinese space station. Tiangong burned up during re-entry last year. I worked on its construction," he added for Scott and Maya's benefit.

"That was the plan. Alas, best laid plans and all that... It didn't. It splashed down right here in the spacecraft ceme-tery." She smiled when Eric shook his head.

"You're mistaken. It was on the news..."

"Sorry, but whatever you heard was wrong." She winked at Eric. "Don't worry, it wasn't government censorship. NASA, the ESA, CNS, Roscosmos, JAXA... everybody saw it splashdown. They just toed-the-line and lied. It was in everybody's interests."

Eric was offended. "Why would they lie?"

"Because of why it came down in the first place." She held up her hand to stop him from asking any further ques-tions. "Stow that for later. Trust me. It's down there. I've seen it with my own eyes. Doctor Bower," she swept her gaze cross

Scott, "is a leading oceanographer. He wrote a report for Frisco on the impact of marine environs from extreme pollutants, primarily–"

"From volcanic and seismic activity," he finished.

Raven closed her eyes and rolled her thumb against the bridge of her nose, a sudden exhaustion washing over her. "Exactly. Beneath our collective asses, the seabed is active. Very active. Especially near the Tiangong. We are currently in a race against mother nature to recover the wreckage."

Once again, a puzzled expression crossed Eric's face. "Recover? Why would you want to do that? The... intention was to allow it to burn up. What could be left?"

"Not everything burns up. Titanium alloys, complex carbon fibers..."

Captain Peers had sat through the entire conversation with folded arms, silently studying the scientists with a hint of disapproval. His body language didn't shift as he spoke up.

"You have to understand, whatever is left, it's of national interest. To us, and your government, Professor Dong."

Eric had worked in enough government secrecy circles to know when not to pursue a line of questions. Scott, however, hadn't.

"Then I assume that it was carrying something toxic. A nuclear reactor? A payload that poses a contamination risk?"

Peers held up his hand to stop him. "Speculation is not helpful."

"Neither is secrecy." Peers' eyes narrowed momentarily. He wasn't a man used to being spoke back to, and Scott was simply blasé to the subtle cues. "Why else would you want me here?" Scott focused on Eric and Maya. "My paper for Frisco Dynamics was on the impact on extreme life forms from pollution risks, including radioactivity, and its impact on the larger biome." He ignored the captain's weary sigh and raised a questioning eyebrow at Raven. "So the basic conclusion is that it has to be something pretty unusual for you to drag me to the remotest spot on the face of the earth."

"Jeez, you sound like Spock," Maya said with a grin. Scott frowned at her. "From Star Trek?"

"Oh. No. Just..." he shrugged. One basic rule his therapist had reinforced was not to apologize for other people's discomfort.

Raven regarded him for a moment, toying with the crushed paper cup. Then a broad grin brightened her face. "I knew you'd get it." She flicked the cup into the middle of the table. "You're all going to be learning on the move. So let's move."

FIVE

ONLY THE OCCASIONAL flare of fluffy snow indicated that the otherwise black monitor wasn't broken. After the clock ticked just over thirty-three minutes, more snow gradually appeared, gently streaming past the camera in what became a blizzard.

"Marine snow," said Scott.

"Looks beautiful," commented Eric.

"The decomposing waste of everything above it. Fish, squid, whale..." Scott stopped when he saw the look on his face. "Nutrients that are vital for deeper life to flourish."

Eric pulled a face and sat back in his chair. "A soup of dead shit."

Maya couldn't repress a grin. The subtle beauty of nature always belied a darker truth.

Scott looked between them and decided not to turn it into a lecture. He took another sip of his tepid black coffee, the second he'd had since they had relocated to a control deck somewhere in the ship's island tower. Since the remote controlled drone entered the bathypelagic zone, the screens had been plunged into darkness, lit only by the drone's searchlights.

The drone's pilot, a man whose uniform name badge revealed Hernandez, and a stern Chinese officer, who had only been introduced as a 'liaison', were in the room during the descent. Only when the drone's pinging sonar began to actively increase tempo did Raven enter with uncanny timing.

Scott had been in many submersible command centers before, but for some reason the pulsing sonar ping was adding an irrational sense of tension that had slowly been gripping him.

Was it the news Ruth had imparted? Now he was out of communication, a flood of questions occurred to him, all of which he kicked himself for not asking her as would be expected. How long had she been pregnant? They had been trying for a year and he suspected their lack of success was another destabilizing factor in their relationship. A gynecologist assumed she had known or suspected for several weeks before they'd left.

Would his condition be passed to the poor kid? Was that something that had concerned her? He didn't even know the basics – did she want a boy or girl? A simple question that had never occurred to him to ask.

"Two hundred meters to seabed," Hernandez said.

The tone increased, derailing Scott's thoughts as he focused on the task at hand. He glanced at the others who were enrapt with the monitor. Even the stoic Chinese Officer's brow had creased in anticipation.

The sonar screen began picking out a rugged landscape the drone was descending into.

"One thirty..."

The screen seemed to lighten. At first Scott assumed it was his eyes compensating for the darkness until Eric spoke up.

"Is that a light?"

It took a moment for hints of red to coalesce to a definitive line on the screen.

"One hundred meters."

Scott let out an involuntary 'mmm' of intrigue as the red lines gained definition. A spider's web of red veins radiating from a central column of white.

"It's a smoker," he exclaimed with a trace of glee. He glanced at the depth gauge, which now read minus three-thousand six hundred and twenty-five meters.

"A what?"

"A volcano." He tapped the screen, tracing out each point. "We are seeing it at a high-angle. The red lines are rapidly cooling lava flows, radiating out from this point." He ran a finger up and down the white column. "The smoker. Super-hot sea water boiling in the frigid waters. The smoke is actually particle-laden sulfides. Four hundred centigrade. The surrounding water is only about two. It's not really white, it's black smoke caused by iron sulfide. The submersible lights are just highlighting it."

"Incredible. It's melting the seabed," Maya's voice was filled with wonder.

"No, no, no. Smokers are a haven for life. It evolves there, adapts... each one we have discovered harbors previously undiscovered species."

"You're kidding?"

Scott shook his head, eyes wide with anticipation. "They're a haven for extremophiles. This is the primordial soup all life on earth could have evolved from."

"I can't believe anything could live at these depths." Eric sounded doubtful.

"Trust me, we're just skimming the surface of what's down here. We've found microbes seventy meters below the sediment. Alive. Do you want to guess how old they are?"

Eric glanced at him. "I know you're going to say something ridiculous, like a thousand years or something."

"Not even close. Seventy-five million year old microbes living on almost zero energy."

It was Maya who could conceal her skepticism. "Bullshit!" She glanced at Raven, who laughed and threw her a look indicating she sided with Scott.

"I assure you it's not." Scott's eyes were now glued to the screen. "Life always finds a way. If I were a betting man, I'll tell you the universe is teeming with the stuff. We just haven't been looking in the correct places."

Scott cocked his head to make sense of the sharp dive angle they were approaching from that made the volcano appear lopsided. He quickly got his bearings and leaned closer to the screen.

"What is that?" His voice was no more than a whisper as he tapped the screen. "Can you get closer to it?"

Hernandez gave a slight shrug. "I can zoom in." He obliged, and the faintest shape Scott indicated resolved into naked tree-like branches.

"Coral!" Scott breathed excitedly.

"You find that in a lot of oceans," Eric said dryly.

Maya leaned closer to the screen, watching with curiosity. "Not at these depths you don't."

Scott spoke quietly, as if his words would disturb what he saw on-screen. "Deep sea coral is a relatively recent biological discovery. Originally found in the deep silty channels where the Amazon meets the Atlantic. Most scientists had previously thought them to be lifeless voids. Now we've found entire ecosystems there." He glanced at Eric. "I was on one of the original teams." He turned to Hernandez. "Can we get closer to the smoker?"

Raven shook her head. "This isn't a safari, Dr Bowers."

"Life on smokers is unique, more-so out here."

"Why 'out-here'?" Maya asked.

"We're within the South Pacific Gyre. Any nutrient-rich waters are essentially parted away from this area. We're supposedly in one of the most lifeless areas in the ocean."

Maya looked at Raven. "Why does the South Pacific Gyre sound familiar?"

Raven looked thoughtful. "Maybe you're thinking of trash?" Maya's confusion made her smile. "The Pacific Trash Vortex." Maya gave a low 'oh,' of understanding, but now Eric was puzzled. "A collection of trash, plastic, wood, chemical crap, you name it has been found in the northern hemisphere. One between Hawaii and California, the other between Hawaii and Japan. One-point-six million square kilometers of non-biodegradable shit that's choking all the life it touches. As above, so below. In 2017 we found one in the Southern Pacific. Right around here. Two -point-six million square kilo-meters." She let the numbers sink in. "Imagine a void one and a half times the size of Texas that chokes all life it touches."

A moment of silence struck the room, broken finally by Hernandez.

"Thirty meters and the water temperature has spiked to fifty-six degrees." He banked the drone around the volcano, giving the superheated cone of water a wide birth. It would melt the delicate craft in seconds, and if the cable tethering it to the aircraft carrier was dragged through, then the drone would be lost in the murk forever.

Scott watched the image of the smoker pass across the screen and could only wonder at what treasures he was missing out on. Although he'd investigated such locations before, they had all been previously discovered locations. Never had he had the fortune to stumble upon a new find. Despite the nagging sense of loss he was experiencing, he remained silent as Hernandez circumnavigated the obstruction and continued decent as they soared into an unmistakable valley.

The sonar ping suddenly changed.

"Picking up contact," Hernandez reported with almost casual indifference. Scott wondered just how many times he had made this trip so that it had become mundane.

"It that another volcano?" said Eric with a nod to the screen.

Ahead, a pale smudge resolved itself into another black smoker. From their low vantage point, it seemed almost twice as tall as the last. And beyond it to the right, another funneled out torrents of superheated water.

"The one on the right looks white to me," Maya pointed out. The two spewing clouds were of distinct contrast to one another.

Scott nodded. "Silicon, barium or calcium. It's a geological smorgasbord down here." He was reveling in just how clear the water was and surmised the geothermal activity was creating strong currents that prevented the marine snow from smogging up the water.

The sonar ping continued with renewed ferocity.

"Twenty meters."

"There it is," muttered Raven with a quick look to the Chinese Officer.

Using a thumb toggle, Hernandez pivoted the drone's search lights towards a target just to starboard. At first, Scott took it to be a vertical wall of rock, but as they drew nearer, he could see unmistakable metallic smooth patches between lumps of rock.

Eric muttered something in Mandarin, casting a look at the Chinese official. "The Tiangong," he said in English. He couldn't repress a smile and added with a hint of pride: "We built it so well it couldn't even burn up during re-entry."

Hernandez knew what was expected of him and brought the drone around and up a little so that it now faced the wreckage while drifting sideways to track along the structure.

Maya frowned and flicked a glance at Raven but remained silent. The professor's eyes were firmly on the screen. Scott noticed the exchange, but the sight of a space-craft laying on the seafloor had even impressed him.

"Remarkable. It looks as if it could take off right now." Nobody replied as Hernandez circled around the front of the Tiangong. Twisted struts that once held solar panels stretched from the fuselage, the fragile panels themselves would have been the first to disintegrate in the atmosphere. The rock continued around the space station's nose and up the other flank. A six-meter module poked perpendicular from the station, breaking its symmetry.

"That's a Tainzhou cargo module. The last addition to the Tiangong," said Eric, angling his head for a better look. "The docking would have been fully robotic controlled."

Scott had initially assumed the spacecraft had rolled into a narrow fissure in the seabed, but now saw the rock was somehow encasing it almost completely. "How heavy did you say that is?"

"Eight and a half tons," said Eric, his eyes glued to a screen. "Nine, including the cargo module. It would have made one hell of a splash down." His expression was grave, the previous pride now erased.

Maya picked up on what was bothering Scott. "Then it's nowhere heavy enough to gouge rock. Especially not in water. So how can it be encased?"

"I can't see any structural damaged in the exposed hull," Eric quietly reported. "And there is..." He stopped himself and looked at the stern faced official. If there was any communication between them, it was lost on Scott. Eric took a sharp breath and stared at Professor Raven. "What exactly is your plan here?"

"Recovery," Raven said firmly.

Eric rose from his seat for the first time since they had entered the room. He looked at everybody with equal puzzlement.

"Why on earth would you want to do that?"

"To discover what brought it down in the first place."

"Its orbit was decaying; the crew abandoned the station and..." he trailed off and stared accusingly at the Chinese Official. "Except they didn't, did they?"

"How can you know that?" Maya asked in surprise.

Eric tapped the end section of the Tiangong. "This is not part of the space lab. This is a Shenzhou capsule. Designed to carry the crew to and from the station. If the crew abandoned ship, why is it still attached?"

The Officer replied in rapid Mandarin, causing Raven to hold up her hand. "Remember, English, please," she said sharply, once again making Scott wondered just who was in charge.

Maya was horrified. "You mean they're still onboard?"

The Chinese Official folding his arms defensively. "The crew remained onboard and set the Tiangong to burn up in the atmosphere. They failed in their final mission."

"Why would they do that?" gasped Eric. Scott couldn't tell if the emotional strain was for the loss of life or the fate of his precious space station.

The Officer gave Raven an imperceptible nod of the head, which left Scott again confused as to who was in charge.

Her shoulders sagged as if in relieved from the burden she was about to share. "Because of what they discovered."

SIX

SCOTT FELT he had hit the wall, physically and, unexpectedly, emotionally. During the flight to Point Nemo, his mind had been cycling between the unknown assignment ahead and Ruth's surprise announcement that he was going to be a father. He tried to recall possible conception dates and came up with a hazy three occasions. One of which he was completely drunk.

Not a terrific start to a life of real responsibility.

His mobile phone had been hastily packed with his clothes and when he returned to his quarters, he wasn't surprised to find there was no signal to call home. It kept cutting out in the center of London so literally, the middle of nowhere, what chance did he have. There wasn't even a wi-fi network available for the crew, no doubt because the operation was so secretive – and the fact a Chinese aircraft carrier, the *Liaoning*, was parked a mere half mile away probably had them all running silent.

The two superpowers may have been working together on the Tiangong, but there was no escaping the undercurrent of mistrust between Professor Raven and the unnamed Chinese Official.

He promised himself, after the next briefing and a night's sleep, he would ask for a satellite connection to check up on Ruth. After a quick shower, the team had been ushered to another room, dominated by a boardroom table and long windows overlooking the endless ocean. The sun was kissing the horizon painted the sky with a honey glaze, although his phone, still on Maldives' time, had claimed it was in the dead of night. He watched occasional helicopter flutter between the freighter – whose name he could now read as *Ventura*, and support vessels. They were nothing more than fly specs swallowed by the view.

He felt a wave of isolation churn his stomach. It was an unfamiliar feeling, as he was a creature who preferred his own company. He had listened to Yeowoman Alanis tell Maya that the ship housed about twenty-five hundred personnel. Combined with the Chinese craft and the supporting ships, he guesstimated that there were over five thousand people surrounding him. Enough to fill a small town.

Yet the creeping sense of isolation never left him.

What an unfortunate time to seek counselling to get in-tune with his emotions. He wanted to ask Maya and Eric how they were coping with it, but both had left the RV control room, lost in their own thoughts. Eric looked almost distraught, and he was curious if he'd known the crew personally.

Maya entered the room, after a quick bathroom break, followed by Raven and the Chinese Officer. Eric had remained seated, lost in thought, as Scott paced the panoramic windows.

Raven was talking before she had a chance to sit down. "Okay folks, for the record, what are your first thoughts about the Tiangong?"

Scott took a seat next to Maya as Alanis led a pair of servicemen entered with trays of sandwiches, chicken drumsticks, cold sausage, coleslaw and vegetables, along with an urn of coffee and jugs of water. The young Yeowoman glanced around the room, sensing the terse atmosphere and quickly left, ushering her team from the room.

"It shouldn't be there," stated Eric.

"Let's take that for granted," Raven said, helping herself to a sandwich.

"What I mean is, what we saw was pretty intact. It was never designed to survive re-entry. Certainly not splash down. What, if anything, should be out there is nothing more than a trail of components littering the seabed."

As they spoke, the Chinese Officer switched on a monitor that played the recent drone footage.

Maya leaned to the food and came back with a fistful of celery which she rammed into a dip with a little more aggression than necessary, and Scott surmised she too had hit the fatigue wall.

Eric continued, emphasizing almost each word by stabbing his finger against the table. "And the rock should have ripped it apart. Instead, it looks like the damn thing sliced a groove through it."

Scott watched Raven carefully as she nodded thoughtfully, but offered no opinion. She was either playing dumb for some reason, or was just as foxed as the rest of them.

Maya gestured to the screen with a celery stick. "If that is new volcanic rock, then why the wreck hasn't melted into a lump of scrap?" She looked at Eric. "I'm hazarding a guess the body isn't that strong?"

Eric shook his head. "It's made from aluminum – about three millimeters is enough to keep the entire pressure for the life support. Beyond that, the hull is all protection: Kevlar and Nextel." He noticed her questioning look. "It's a high temperature ceramic used for insulation. All in all, it's about this thick." He extended his hands about thirty centimeters.

Maya stared thoughtfully. "I led a salvage off the coast of Borneo. A Japanese freighter sunk in the war. It'd suffered a major fire below deck when the furnace blew. Punched a molten hole straight through the hull when an American torpedo sank it. It went down quick. Anyways, some treasure hunters searching for Yamashita's gold had tracked it down. Paid me to scope it out. I found it in about three hundred feet of water. Thermal shock alone had weakened the hull; caved it in like a jackhammer to the side. And there was some gold there too. They found some. Bars had melted together. D'you know the melting point of gold?" She looked around the room. "A thousand and sixty-four degrees. I bet re-entry is a tad more?" Eric nodded. "Thing is, your Tiangong down there is in much better shape. And I don't care what new materials, Nextel or whatever, were used. I know that's not possible." She waved her hand to Raven as if to say *explain that*.

Raven nodded. "Exactly. It should have burned up or smashed up."

Scott stood and moved closer to the monitor. Something had caught his attention.

"Except that's not rock." He looked at the Chinese Officer. "Can you pause it?" The man did so and Scott indicated to a circular area on the screen. "Zoom in here." Again, the

Officer did so without question. Scott took a step back to take the whole image in. He looked at the others, who hadn't yet seen what had caught his eye. He indicated to the wispy edge of the rock as gave way to the tarnished silver of the spacecraft's hull. "Don't you see?"

Eric shook his head, but he noted Maya's eyes widen as she did.

"It's coral." He tapped the screen again. "This whole bank is coral."

Eric shrugged. "So? You said coral grows at depth. And that should have torn through the hull just as effectively."

"If the Tiangong had *struck* it. This coral has grown *around* the craft."

He watched with a glimmer of satisfaction as everybody shifted position for a better look. From the frown on Raven and the Chinese official's face, he guessed this was news to them.

Scott crossed to the video controls. "Can I...?" The Office moved back and gave a curt nod, his eyes not leaving the screen. Scott scrubbed back through the footage to show the drone's approach, then let it play. "So there is no gouge through the seabed or the coral, assuming that this is the front of the thing," he indicated to the Shenzhou capsule. "Even if it's not, it's quite clear as we bank around, there is no impact trench on the other side. This clearly hasn't cut through the coral on impact," he sliced his hand horizontally, "as you'd expect. It appears to have dropped straight down." He slammed his palm against the table for emphasis. "Which would have destroyed it anyway, even with water resistance taking the brunt of the weight."

Eric nodded. "So it may have cut across the planar to the

seabed," he copied Scott's horizontal hand motion. "Settled down, then the coral grew around it."

"That would account for the lack of any impact grooves on the seabed."

"Except there's a major problem with that hypothesis, isn't there?" Maya said, leaning back in her seat and staring at Scott with a gleam in her eye.

Scott nodded. "Coral doesn't grow quickly. I mean, you're looking at between five and twenty-five millimeters growth a year. To grow as large as this, we're talking... a hundred, hundred and twenty years."

"She's been down there for less than a month," stated Eric.

The three newcomers looked at the Professor for answers. She silently absorbed the information as she took another sandwich. After the first bite, she asked, "How do we explain that?"

Scott gazed at the setting sun for inspiration. "Some sort of accelerant? We would need to take samples. Study the coral. Did the spacecraft have a nuclear reactor onboard?"

Eric laughed and shook his head. "Like a science fiction movie? No. All electric. The solar panels gathered enough to power the station and connected modules."

"So, no radioactive seepage." Scott was already drawing a blank. He took a drumstick and slumped back in his chair, stifling a yawn. His mind may have been working overtime, but his body was beginning to crash. "You told us they positioned the station to burn up in the atmosphere." As he thought about it, a chill ran down his spine thinking of the crew. "Why?"

Raven frowned. "What do you mean, why?"

"You used the term 'positioned'. That means it wasn't coming down to begin with."

Eric and Maya sharply looked between Raven and the Chinese Official. Neither spoke. Eric snapped in Mandarin, then repeated in English. "It wasn't in a decaying orbit to begin with?"

Again, the Official remained silent and cast a pleading look at Raven. She took another bite of her sandwich and refused to meet their gazes.

Scott was the first to break the silence. "It was a suicide run." He noticed Eric react to his choice of words, but he blundered on. "What would scare somebody enough to commit a suicide run?"

#6A

Yeowoman Alanis Narvaez stepped from the elevator and finally blew a long breath of relief. She stepped into a corridor, wider than the usual passageways she had experienced on other carriers. She glanced at her watch and gave hasty goodbyes to the catering crew as they headed to the kitchen.

Since the Gerald R. Ford had been suddenly re-assigned from its scheduled tour close to the disputed Spratly Islands, the crew had been on high-alert, although the exact nature of the new mission had never been revealed.

She had been one of eight petty officers who had taken it upon themselves to learn Chinese and was surprised when she had been selected for intensive training during the ten-day journey, all under full power, to their current destination. The crew had been told they would be working with the Chinese on a recovery mission, but the usual layers of 'need-to-know' still made it a surprise when the crew were finally confronted by the Liaoning.

When Chinese officials had come aboard, it had placed her in a unique position with the Captain and senior crew to learn a little about the Tiangong-2 beneath the waves. Everything had become a whirlwind of meetings and quick debriefs every time the officials had left – focusing on any comments or nuances they detected amongst the Chinese crew that hadn't been officially translated. Either her Mandarin was worse than she thought, or the Chinese had been playing it pretty strait-laced. Whatever the full situation was, right now she was due some downtime and was determined to cash it in on a workout at one of the three spacious gyms the super-carrier boasted.

Alanis had always pushed herself hard. The middle-child of five she had always felt adrift at home. She approached her studies as a form of escapism and maintained top of her class in a rough San Juan High School, gaining top marks during her ASVAB test which gained her a scholarship at the Naval Academy. The first time she had set foot on a Naval carrier after graduation, she hadn't been able to hold back a tear of pride. Something she saw as a weakness and an embarrassment. That said, a number of male colleagues also had tears in their eyes.

Pounding the running machine, she upped the speed to match the pace of the Eminem song on her phone. The oldies were still her favorites. She ignored the muscle-pounding jocks around her, all good people who had never given her, or any of the other serving women onboard, a hard time. She had been fortunate not to experience the usual chauvinism reported by others. If there was going to be any screw-ups concerning conduct, then it would be on her own terms.

And boy did she screw up.

Jordan McLain had been one of the chefs onboard. Not

the usual sun-bleached testosterone that prowled the flight deck, but a wiry-haired red-head with a dozen more freckles than he needed, and a charming lopsided smile. The polar opposite of what normally attracted her. Yet there had been a spark. A massively unexpected spark.

Then shore leave in the Philippines had crystallized into a relationship. Not the best situation onboard the carrier, and certainly nothing they wanted to promote to others. Sure, their flirting had been picked up dozens of times, but they had so far deflected serious suspicion. A few dangerous liaisons in storage areas and, one time, the kitchen, had led to several near-misses which would have led to a possible court-martial.

Since the Point Nemo operation had begun, she had been so busy they had barely seen one another. The gym had become their de facto rendezvous during such situations, and she kept one eye on the door, via the full-length mirror.

Even as her legs began to ache, she upped the speed.

They had five more months on their current tour. After that, who knew? The Navy had been her lifelong ambition, something she wasn't willing to throw away. Jordan, however, wasn't so sure he wanted to stay. Somehow they figured they could work something out – an unexpected new future in which they both got what they wanted.

A flash of ginger in the mirror caught her eye. Jordan had entered and searched for her. He wasn't muscular like the other specimens in here, but he was shapely, like a panther she liked to say. She wanted nothing more than to leap on him with an energy sapping kiss – but that couldn't happen. She would have to settle for a fist-bump and some good old-fashioned close proximity.

Jordan almost made it to her side – before she was interrupted by a voice behind her.

"Yeoman Narvaez."

She turned to see the Executive Officer standing in her blindside. Bald, a decade older than the Captain, and now a couple of kilos heavier, Donovan Keller looked every-inch the man who knew further promotion was out of his league. The XO had a reputation for being spiteful and rumors persisted that his own command had been denied because of incompetence, but the exact nature of the ineptitude varied greatly depending on who was relating it.

Alanis killed the running machine and hopped off the slowing treadmill. She yanked her headphones out and saluted.

"Sir."

"The CO is looking for you."

Ordinarily cool under pressure, news that the captain was specifically looking for her couldn't be good. She glanced at Jordan – and immediately regretted it. The XO turned his predatory gaze on him.

"And I thought I'd find you here." His tone suggested he knew about their affair... or was she reading too much into the situation? To his credit, Jordan calmly acknowledge the XO's presence and took the machine next to Alanis as if that had been his intention all along.

The XO looked back at Alanis for a little too long, taking in her tight Lycra top that accented every curve.

"Come with me. You've got some new orders. Your babysitting duties have just become important."

SEVEN

THE SUN quickly sank over the horizon, leaving in its wake an overwhelming blossom of orange. On one hand it was beautiful and on the other, Scott couldn't help but think, an omen of the apocalypse.

Dark thoughts, he cautioned himself. The spiral... he scratched his forearm. The irritation had disappeared since leaving the Maldives, but now the unwelcome breath of stress was prickling his skin.

The Chinese Officer switched the video screen from the drone footage to a transmission from inside the Tiangong. One man floated in zero-g as he spoke with some urgency to the camera. The second crewman was inverted behind him, frantically typing on a laptop. A number of glass vials hovered around them. The words were a mystery to the Westerners in the room and the volume was just low enough so Eric couldn't distinguish words. The Officer paced as if working out his anxiety. He spoke in perfect English, with an accent that betrayed a Canadian education.

"Four weeks before re-entry, the crew reported problems

with the electronic systems. At first they were intermittent, but with each passing day the severity increased. A spacewalk was deemed necessary. They discovered a coating on the side of the Tiangong and one solar panel."

The screen changed to show pictures taken during the walk. A dark shadow covered the external wall, blotting out some of the Chinese characters written on the hull. Another showed a dusty covering across a solar panel, some thirty centimeters from where it attached to the craft. The rest of the panel reflected bright sunlight.

"Samples were analyzed onboard. And the conclusion was... startling."

The image changed to an ultra-magnified image of a green disc, comprising smaller yellowish-green circles surrounded by a thin white haze. A casual observer would be forgiven of thinking they were looking at a celestial planet, but Scott recognized it straight away.

"An algae spore?"

The Officer nodded. "That was the team's conclusion, too."

Maya snorted dismissively. "Algae? As in, the slimy crap that destroys every aquarium I've tried to own? It's a bastard in my tank, but surely it can't survive in space."

"That's not strictly true." Said Scott. Maya gave him a look that suggested he couldn't be serious. "In 2014, Cosmonauts found traces of marine plankton on the side of the ISS, along with several other microbes. They were thriving, out there, in hostile space."

Eric weaved his hand dismissively. "Impossible."

Scott managed a smile. "And yet, there it was. Not only that, but investigations also showed that it wasn't carried up there during lift off."

Eric sniggered. "Then the investigations were wrong. Maybe you find some microbes on a volcanic vent or a new species of crab, but—"

Scott's professional pride buttons were being pushed, and he didn't like it. "An experiment at the University of California swabbed three and a half thousand shoes and phones from the public. They found nine unstudied branches of life. *Entire* new branches. On a *shoe*."

Eric looked at the others, unsure if Scott was being serious. "So we're to assume a little piece of plankton, the food whales eat, just floated up from the ocean, entered orbit, and attached to the side of the ISS?" he indicated to the screen.

Scott felt Raven's gaze boring into him. "Precisely that. We're scratching the surface when it comes to understanding the diversity—"

"Despite there being no gravity. Oxygen. Cosmic radiation and temperatures fluctuating between -157 in the shade and 121 in the sun?"

Eric had touched on exactly the reason Scott had fallen into his area of expertise. "Extremophiles form in impossible situations. That's the point. Geothermal vents, in acidic or alkaline lakes. On the soles of your shoes. Look, worms and unrecorded arthropods have been recorded over two miles down in gold mines. A unique fungus has even been found living inside the remains of Chernobyl, feeding off the radiation. A third of this planet's biomass is estimated to be in the earth's crust... and undiscovered. Right beneath our feet."

That brought silence to the room. Raven plucked a drumstick and sat back in her chair, nibbling it, apparently satisfied with the explanation.

"May I continue?" the Officer said irritably. "The algae growth rapidly grew." A series of pictures tracked its progress along the solar panel. "Covering this panel in five days. The station's batteries were able to compensate for the loss of power, but unless the panel was cleaned or repaired, then the crew would only have weeks on minimal power to survive."

"A second spacewalk was initiated. It was then discovered that the growth had jammed the airlock seal."

"They couldn't get out." Eric's statement was barely a whisper of despair. The Officer gravely nodded and paused as Eric's next question formed. "Including the Shenzhou's docking mechanism?" The Officer nodded grimly. "They were trapped inside."

The Officer nodded. Then the slide changed, showing another patch of greenish mold. There was something odd about the surface that Scott couldn't quite put his finger on.

"The next day this was discovered."

"On the *inside?*" Eric's disbelief was clear.

They were looking at a close-up of the Tiangong's curved inside hull.

"That cannot happen." Eric slapped his palm on the table for emphasis.

"That's a helluva catch phrase you're working on," Maya said quietly, shooting him a look. "How about keeping an open mind?"

Eric glowered, but remained silent.

"Nevertheless, we're all looking at it," Raven said, indicating to the screen with the bones of her drumstick, before dropping them on her plate and sucking the tips of her fingers clean one by one. "Accept the facts so we can draw a solid conclusion about what is going on here. You helped build that vehicle. You know every inch. Every panel."

Eric signed. "Spores would require a way in. Think about that. Any entry point would destroy the hull's air-tight integrity. The ship would have simply exploded had there been a breach." He looked at Scott and Maya. "An algae spore isn't smaller than an oxygen particle, right?"

Scott nodded. "Right. The smallest is about 3 micrometers long."

The images changed again. This time the spores looked like a glutinous spiders-web stretching from one wall to another.

"And yet it grew inside." The Officer let them take that in for a moment. "Communication with the Tiangong became increasingly erratic. From energy readings onboard, it appeared the algae was feeding from the power."

Now it was Scott's turn to sound skeptical. "Feeding?"

The Officer continued. "An attempt was made to abandon the lab. That confirmed the Shenzhou module was firmly locked in position. There was no way out." He let that hang in the air.

Outside, the world had rapidly turned dark. Only the fleet's running lights pierced the veil. Scott caught his own reflection in the window. He looked jaded, haggard even. Nothing he had heard quite made sense. Extremophiles spent a majority of their energy purely surviving. The evidence he'd heard suggested this microbe was unnaturally aggressive. Destroying one's own ecosystem guaranteed a short lifespan.

"We need to analyze the craft," he said, although his own voice sounded distant as tiredness overwhelmed him.

"That's the plan," Raven confirmed. "We must know what brought the Tiangong down. And to do that, we have to recover her from the seafloor."

"That's quite a challenge," Eric said with a sudden yawn mid-sentence.

Maya pointed to herself and grinned. "That's why they shipped the big guns in."

Raven gave a tilt of the head. "Your name was top of the list. That's also why the Chinese came to us. We have the capability, but it's their vehicle." She gestured to the Official. "It gives the two great superpowers the opportunity to work together for a common goal."

Even Scott caught the thin, forced smile Raven threw towards the Officer as she stood.

"But to do so, we need you guys at your peak. I appreciate it's a lot to take in and a huge journey to the center of nowhere, so let's end the briefing here. Grab some sleep. We begin the salvage tomorrow. Any other questions you have, keep them until then."

SCOTT DIDN'T HAVE the energy for small talk as Yeowoman Alanis returned and guided them back to their cabins. His condition may have blunted his emotional range, but it made him acutely aware of change. Normally talkative, this time Alanis was taciturn and wore a pistol in a thigh holster. That had certainly not been present earlier, but he saw no point in drawing attention to it.

His quarters lay between Eric and Maya's. Goodnights were mumbled but by the time he had closed the door and noticed his bag was sitting next to the bed, he'd already forgotten what deck they were on. Unlike the stereotypical view of people on the spectrum, he had neither enhanced intelligence – he was just naturally smart – and definitely didn't have a photographic memory. Most of the time he struggled to remember names moments after he had been told them.

A shower would have to wait for tomorrow. As his head hit the pillow, his subconscious mind was molested by dark thoughts he couldn't quite put his finger on. The struggle between wakefulness and sleep was seized upon by an encroaching terror he could sense brooding around him. What its nature was, the presence was too devious to reveal.

Yet it was there, lurking on the edges of understanding, taunting on the fringes of primal fear.

It dragged him into a deeply disturbed slumber.

EIGHT

YEOWOMAN ALANIS NARVAEZ shoved Scott awake after pounding on his door for almost a minute. He'd fallen asleep fully clothed, and it took a moment for him to take in the cramped, windowless cabin. A bunk, desk and small shower area with a toilet and sink. The yeoman confirmed it counted as luxury onboard the aircraft carrier.

He quickly showered and changed into a blue polo shirt and black jeans. Rubbing the stubble across his chin, he decided to wait to shave as Alanis urged him to hurry. He joined the yeoman in the corridor where Maya, in a red sweat top, her hair pulled in a pony tail, and Eric, donning a smart black shirt and jeans, were already waiting.

Alanis led them to the officer's galley for breakfast and assured them she was to be on-hand for anything they required, before leaving them the eat.

"Why the hell was she telling us to hurry? I'm not even hungry." The poor quality of sleep had left Scott short-tempered. From the look of the other two, they had had a similarly bad night.

Guessing they may not have time for many meals, Eric forced some toast and scrambled eggs down. Small talk was made in the windowless galley, lit by hanging fluorescent tubes and suspiciously empty – indicating the crew had eaten earlier and eventually Eric produced photographs of the Tiangong on his phone and briefed them on the various sections and uses. He curtly answered their questions, but then remained quite subdued, only giving the occasional yes or no as conversation fillers, as Maya and Scott recapped the previous day.

After a particularly long lull in conversation, Maya pulled her mobile phone out and cycled through several useless options. "I don't suppose you guys found a Wi-Fi signal?"

"They'll be military encrypted," Eric said sullenly. Then added, "They don't want people like me listening in, do they?"

"I asked our lovely Alanis for a satellite connection," Maya lowered her voice. "She was evasive. I don't think we're gonna be talking to granny anytime soon."

Scott noticed Alanis was talking to one of the chefs through a serving hatch into the kitchen. It looked to be an animated conversation, but as usual he failed to pick up on the nuances. He focused back on conversations with his therapist and turned to Maya.

"Do you have any family?" He felt odd in asking. It was normally a question that would slide him by. She looked relieved somebody had asked; although he equally surmised that she could just be passing wind.

"I got a little boy. Thomas. He's seven. His dad's used to the heavy lifting when I'm away, even so, it's nice to hear their voices isn't it."

Scott looked away to mask his blank response. Was it nice? He guessed it must be. Hearing Ruth after a long period always made him relaxed. Had it been long enough? Was he over-analyzing a basic human response?

"What about you?" Maya had taken Scott's silence as a sign to move onto Eric.

Eric didn't look up. He just shook his head. "Not anymore."

Alanis returned to save the conversation from frosting over. She escorted them up several levels, ascending on hard metal staircases that echoed every footfall.

They were surprised to emerge on the deck. The flight deck cut before them, running some three hundred thirty-seven meters from stern to prow, and the command island rose five stories above. A gentle breeze raised goose bumps on Scott's arm. The sky above was clear blue, the seas around them an alluring flat azure.

"What a vacation hotspot," Maya said dryly, shoving her hands in her sweat top pouch for warmth.

Scott had never been on a ship so large before and felt as if he'd been temporarily miniaturized. He ambled around the tower, closer to the edge of the deck. His gaze was fixed the Chinese aircraft carrier opposite as a jet fighter sprang from its flight deck, afterburners blazing as it screamed over the ocean on some mysterious mission.

Fingers suddenly dug into his elbow and he felt a sharp yank backwards. It was Eric, who indicated downward.

"You better watch your step."

Scott followed his gaze. The deck suddenly ended without the courtesy of a safety rail, plummeting thirty-five meters to the ocean. From such a height, the impact with the water could easily snap his neck if he was so foolhardy to tumble head first.

Eric motioned back the way they came. "Our honor guard doesn't want us to wander off."

They re-joined Maya and Alanis midway down the flight deck. At the far end, a huge elevator, used for raising and lowering jets from the hangar below, swiftly rose with a high-pitch shrill of hydraulics. A dull grey V-22 Osprey aircraft was sat atop it. A pair of huge rotors positioned vertically from the wings allowing for vertical take-off, but in flight could turn horizontally, transforming the aircraft into a more traditional long-range airplane. As they approached, the rotors spooled up with a dull thump.

"Are we going somewhere?" Maya asked with a puzzled look around.

By the time they reached the rear tail ramp, the rotors were thunderous, the downdraft enough to knock a man down.

"Just a short hop," Alanis shouted above the din. "Get on."

Eric took a ridged jump seat bolted to the fuselage. Maya and Scott were less enthusiastic.

"A hop to where?"

"The Ventura," Alanis said, guiding them both with a surprisingly firm shove in the small of their backs.

She checked they were all strapped in and had just taken her own seat before the Osprey leapt vertically upward with such ferocity, Scott's chin sagged against his chest. The pilot didn't even bother closing the tail ramp for the whole minute it took them to reach the Ventura. As the Osprey rotated in position over the ship's helicopter pad, Scott glimpsed a crane and a huge moon pool in the deck. It was the salvage ship he had spotted on the way in.

Another minute later, Alanis was ushering them back down the ramp and towards the grinning bearded face of a huge bear of a man.

"I'm Captain Vasilis, and welcome aboard the Ventura. *My* ship." His accent was Greek and his lack of uniform indicated he was a civilian, too.

"And a helluva ship it is too, Captain," said Maya with admiration.

"My father designed her." He automatically crossed himself at the mention. "The largest moon pool on the ocean. Fully configurable salvage deck. Polar certified. In fact, we were running Antarctic test before we were pulled for this. A new thermal-plasticized hull coating to present icing."

"Another one of your inspirations?" Maya asked with a smile. The Greek's charm was obviously infectious.

"Naturally."

He motioned for them to follow down a step of iron steps that circled down from the helipad. Several doors were open under the pad, offering glimpses of machinery and the engine room, all bustling with crew.

A catwalk took them around the Ventura's towering bridge, beyond which they could now see the moon pool laid out ahead of them.

A crane was maneuvering a fluorescent green submersible over the water, while a second crane at the far end positioned another identical sub close to the side.

The end of the pool was dominated by a large window poised just above the water level. Inside, Scott could just make out a crewman controlling the cranes.

They were joined by another tall handsome Greek

crewman who stood almost six-five and possessed a goatee, which he idly stroked as he studied the newcomers.

"This is my First Officer, Markus. He's going to take Baloo." Vasilis indicated to the far sub.

"We're going down?" asked Scott in surprise.

Vasilis looked surprised that he didn't know. "Of course. The subs are only kitted out for three. I pilot Mowgli, so you must decide who goes with who."

Eric spun around to Alanis and wagged a finger at her. "Why the hell are we going down there? Nobody told me. I don't want to do this."

"They're the orders," Alanis said firmly.

"Not my orders. I want to speak with my people." He indicated the direction of the Liaoning.

"This is a joint mission, Professor." Alanis' tone didn't brook any argument. "Joint orders. Professor Raven needs you to inspect the wreckage first-hand."

"Where the hell is she, then?"

Vasilis indicated to the Baloo. "She's already onboard, my friend. As should we all be."

"I could have done that with an RV!" Despite the cool breeze, Eric brushed his sleeve over the thin film of sweat forming on his brow.

"Are you okay?" Maya asked with concern.

"I don't know if I can do it..." he said haltingly. Then, after a considered pause, "I get claustrophobic."

Maya rolled her eyes and started heading to the far sub. "Well, I'll go with the good Professor Raven." She gave a jaunty wave and with a twinkle in her eye, added: "See you in Davy Jones' locker boys."

Scott silently cursed his lack of reaction for not volunteering for the other craft quick enough. Instead, he gave Eric an awkward pat on the shoulder.

"I've done this dozens of times on heaps of junk that don't look this good."

Eric shot him a cold look. "Is that supposed to make me feel better?"

As the sub was gently pulled to the edge of the moon pool, Vasilis indicated they should get closer. The front of the vehicle was an enormous transparent bubble through which they could see three chairs in a triangular formation.

"It's the latest generation Triton submersible." Vasilis gently patted the bubble. "State-of-the-art acrylic dome, depth-rated to 3,700 meter. You get a pretty amazing view, almost three-sixty. We have positioned repeaters all the way down to keep in constant communication."

He indicated to six gyroscopic thrusters mounted on the power unit that cradled the rear of the sphere, meaning the view behind them would be obscured. "Thrusters here, two at the front, means we can out maneuver any sardine out there. Batteries are there, everything's electric." He indicated to tanks positioned against the back of the hull. "Plenty of oxygen for ten hours."

Then he indicated to the front, just underneath the pilot's seat sat a circular mounting. "Robotic arm and a sample net, in case you see anything you want to take home as a souvenir." He laughed at his own joke, then his voice dropped solemnly as he turned to Eric. "I assure you, I've been sober for almost a day." He broke into coarse laughter as Eric paled then swore under his breath.

Technicians set up a ladder from the deck to the top hatch, a circular piece of green metal precision fitted into the acrylic dome. He gestured they ascend. "The Navy isn't paying me by the hour."

With that, Vasilis scrambled up the ladder with practiced ease. He reached the hatch and motioned for Eric to follow.

Eric sucked in a deep breath – then clambered determined up the ladder. Vasilis lowered himself into the sub, then reached up to assist Eric, who paused at the lip of the hatch as he dangled his feet in.

"Aren't we supposed to put on wetsuits or something?"

Vasilis grinned. "If you're planning to get wet, then we will be in big trouble, my friend."

For a moment, Scott thought Eric was about to change his mind. A few anxious seconds passed, in which he noticed Maya was eagerly lowering into her sub, then Eric dropped himself.

Ordinarily, Scott adored any chance to ride in a submersible – and this one was clearly brand new. Yet, Eric's apprehension had uncharacteristically rubbed off on him somehow. Each step up the ladder felt heavy and by the time he reached the hatch, his palms were sweaty. So sweaty that he almost lost his grip as he lowered himself into the sub. Luckily, Vasilis was there to break his fall.

"Welcome aboard Mowgli," he indicated to a pair of curved padded seats behind the pilot's chair. "Strap yourselves in, then we're away."

Scott took his seat. Because of the confined space, Vasilis had to wait until he had strapped in, before he could reach for the hatch. With a grunt, he lowered it in place, pneumatics taking the weight as it gently thumped closed, smothering sounds from outside.

Vasilis turned the hatch's screw handle until it stopped moving.

"There we go, dogs are down," quipped Vasilis as he took his own seat and thumbed a button on a control panel.

Air pressure thumped Scott's ears as if he'd been cuffed. He forced a yawn to equalize the pressure and gave Eric a sidelong look to see how he was coping. Eric looked uncomfortable as he held his nose and blew to equalize the pressure.

Vasilis took his command seat, just forward and between the other two seats, so everybody got an unobscured view out. He placed a headset over one ear and positioned a microphone close to his lips. Scott and Eric followed suit with headsets straddling on the arms of their seats.

"Mowgli to Baloo, you copy?"

Markus's voice came back over the headset, and Scott saw the pilot in the other sub give a thumbs up.

"Baloo reading you loud and clear. We're pressurized. Ready to drop."

"Roger that. Auxiliary lights on."

A flick of a switch activated four powerful spots angled out from the sub to maximize visibility. A flare of light from Baloo indicated they had done the same. A pair of strobing red lights flickered on the top and bottom of the craft, serving as collision warnings.

Vasilis checked the gauges with relaxed professionalism. "Pressure nominal. Surface, decouple in five, four, three..."

Scott braced himself as the countdown concluded and the straps to the crane detached. The sub dropped in the water a foot or so and he heard a strangled gasp from Eric as the craft bobbed on the pool's gentle surface.

"Purging tanks. Let's go."

A hiss reverberated around the sub, and bubbles flowed past the glass. Almost instantly, water inched up the window as the craft began to sink.

Scott realized his sneakers were resting on a circular section of black metal grating attached to the acrylic bubble, which continued underneath. The disc-shaped housing of the external robotic arm was positioned just under the pilot's seat, allowing everybody a glimpse through the slats directly below.

Fixed spotlights lined the moon pool perimeter. As they watched, the bottom of the pool opened up, powered by huge pneumatic rams. It was like something out of a Bond movie as the ship's keel slid in two, revealing the inky blackness of the ocean below.

"Ventura here. Pool doors open. You're go for seabed."

Both submersible pilots acknowledged, then Vasilis increased their rate of descent.

Out of the corner of his eye, Scott noticed Eric gripping the armrest with knuckles white. He didn't think and platitudes would be useful, which is just as well as he couldn't recall any. Instead, he enjoyed the experience of the sub dropping through the moon pool and into the ocean proper.

Looking up, a trail of bubbles led towards the ship. The square cross section of open hull was clearly visible against the sky and Scott marveled that the ship had enough mass to remain afloat. The Baloo quickly followed in a stream of bubbles, looking like nothing more than a toy. Scott arced around but couldn't see the rest of the fleet as the water clouded after some hundred meters.

"Rest a little, boys," said Vasilis, craning around to treat them to a grin. "It will take about ninety minutes to reach the site."

Eric bristled. "Ninety minutes?"

"It's almost two and a half miles to the seabed, so relax. Enjoy the trip."

Eric's expression made it clear that enjoyment was the last item on his agenda.

THE INITIAL DECENT through the epipelagic layer gave relatively clear views all around. What Scott noted most was the complete lack of sea life. Not a single fish swam past the submersible. Maya's voice echoed this over the headphones.

"This is the most desolate ocean I have ever seen. No nutrients coming in. No food. We're bathing the world's biggest trash soup. Particles are so fine, we can't even see 'em."

The light notably reduced as they entered the mesopelagic, the water becoming inky blue syrup.

"Say goodbye to daylight," Scott muttered.

The comment drew a sharp intake of breath from Eric. He had been calm so far, but with each passing minute the light ebbed away and his breathing became more intense.

Then the ocean turned inky black, as if they were swallowed by some mighty kraken. Particles illuminated by the spotlights as Mowgli continued its decent. Scott checked above and saw only the red flash and beams of Baloo as it followed.

Even light that could travel the infinite expanses of space couldn't make it this far. A voice at the back of his mind warned him that even the remotest spot on the planet could get even more isolated.

"Outside temperature, four degrees," Vasilis reported.

"Shit!" Eric tried to bolt from his seat, but his seatbelt yanked him in place.

"What?" Scott said. His voice sounded flat, but he was definitely alarmed.

Eric wiped a droplet of water from his face and looked up as another struck him. "We're leaking!"

Vasilis unclipped his harness and pulled a cloth from his back pocket to wipe rivulets of moisture from the roof of the dome.

"Fixed," he stated with a grin. "Condensation. Perfectly normal, especially if you're hyperventilating. Breathe easy, my friend. The air con will look after everything else." He took his seat, checked the telemetry, then sat back with his legs extended. "Want some music?"

Scott categorically didn't, but instead gave a vague shrug. Before Eric could object, tinny Europop reverberated from the speaker. To make matters worse, Vasilis joined in every other verse in a voice that would have frightened mer-people, had there been any.

Forty minutes in, Eric had completely calmed and gazed out at the marine snow flowing hypnotically past them.

"There are some amazing species at these depths," said Scott. "The frilled shark in particular. Like meeting a dinosaur. They're in this part of the ocean, too."

They both peered into the darkness.

Eric sniffed, the moment of anticipation suddenly dying. "I see just a whole lot of nothing."

Scott nodded. "I haven't been in a such a dead sea before."

It was another twenty-five minutes of intolerable music choices before Vasilis's control panel pinged for attention. He sat bolt upright, angled the control screens and killed the music.

He angled his mike as he spoke into it. "Sonar has found the floor. We have arrived."

NINE

SCOTT AND ERIC were fixated on the floor grating as the sonar warbling increased.

Scott found himself gripped with an unfamiliar anxiety as the first faint glow of the highest smoker appeared in the gloom. He had made such trips before, and each one had always been a thrill, even if he had had difficulty voicing that to others. Yet not this time.

Fine layers of anxiety, each easy enough to ignore, were building into something more tangible. The troubled sleep, jet lag and the odd pressing isolation surrounding them was all adding to the ill-feeling.

He wondered if Eric was rubbing off on him.

Vasilis's cocky cowboy persona was now replaced by acute concentration as he angled the Triton to circumnavigate the volcanic plumes. Scott stares wistfully as they bypassed the unique eco-system and could only hypothesize what amazing treasures were slipping him by in the tenebrous waters.

As the submersible banked, another pair of black and

white smokers appeared. Scott realized they were on the same path the RV had taken the previous day.

"There she is." Vasilis barely whispered.

Scott shuffled his position in the chair and craned forward as the Tiangong's coral cradle came into view. Vasilis used a thumb toggle to pivot the searchlights onto the length of the space lab. No matter how clear the drone's footage had been, it was no replacement for seeing the spacecraft through the flawless acrylic dome.

"Get as close as you can," Scott said.

Vasilis obliged, slowing the sub down as it came within a meter of the coral. Baloo soared overhead and twisted around to face them from the other side of the spacecraft.

Professor Raven spoke over the intercom. "I can't see any signs of a hull breach. Professor Dong?"

Eric was staring wide-eyed at the station, as if not believing the evidence of his own eyes.

"Eric?" Raven spoke louder.

"Uh? Oh, yes. Yes... one moment." Eric pulled a pair of black framed spectacles from his breast pocket and put them on. He used his phone to take pictures through the canopy. This close, the curve of the spacecraft's superstructure was almost flawless, as if it had been plucked from the sky by a mighty hand and gently laid to rest. The broken struts that held the brittle solar panels extended from the top like broken fingers, bent backwards and charred at the tips.

"I can see no breaches in the hull," Eric confirmed. "There is sediment on the hull's surface, but I am not certain that is from the reported algae." He used the cuff of his shirt to wipe perspiration forming on his brow. "The skin should have burnt off in the upper atmosphere. The shield was not designed to endure such temperatures."

"And yet here she is," said Scott under his breath.

"She shouldn't be." Eric pointed to the far end of the ship. "I would like to see the Shenzhou."

Vasilis obliged with a flick of the joystick. A few seconds of thrust from the propellers was enough to send the Triton drifting sideways. Scott leaned forward, focusing on the coral growth.

"The coral appears to have adhered to the side of the ship. Possibly using it as an anchor point." As the sub gently rotated a few degrees, the white smoker hove into view. The light from the geothermal vent flickered, distorted by the superheated water. Even from this distance in the gloom, he could just see white track marks down the slow, residues from whatever chemicals the volcano was pumping out. He noted some snaked their way in their general direction, but his attention was brought back to the craft as the Shenzhou module came into view.

It was almost ten meters long and, like the lab, its solar panels had been torn off. The closest part docked to the lab, the Tiangong's habitational module he recalled from Eric's lackluster briefing over breakfast, allowed a crew member to sleep and housed the only toilet on the craft. Unlike the hull of the Tiangong that he could see, the module had multiple panels and bumps extending from the body, with a pair of thrusters just visible.

"The descent module looks intact," Eric reported as they tracked over the next section, a slightly smaller bullet shape made from a darker material. It was impossible to accurately tell the condition of the unit, but all knew that should have been the crew's ticket out of their tomb. Instead, it was still firmly attached to the Shenzhou's cylindrical collar. The craft was pushed firmly against the coral growth. "The service module has no apparent damage either."

Raven spoke again. "What about the docking ring?"

Again, Vasilis nudged the sub forward without being asked, this time slowly moving down the spacecraft's longitudinal axis. It was so close that Scott felt he could touch it. He glanced at the depth gauge on the pilot's control screen: -3622 meters. He tried to recall what the sub was depth rated to, but it surely wasn't far off. Once again, he was struck by an uneasiness he hadn't experienced before.

A quick reverse pulse from the propellers brought them to a graceful stop. Ahead, Baloo swung around to join them, its lights focusing on the docking mechanism.

"I can see silt on it," Eric reported as he took pictures. "But that seal looks unimpeded to me."

"Meaning...?" Raven asked.

"Meaning I don't see why it couldn't detach and send the crew to safety."

Maya's voice came over the intercom. "The growth may have fried on entry. Or perished in the water, the salinity, pressure..."

Scott registered the disbelief on Eric's face. He turned his attention to the coral growth, which was now just half a meter away. At first glance it fanned out like regular surface-dwelling coral.

"Looks like a type of *acropora*," he said with a frown. "I need more light on it. It looks... almost..."

His frown deepened as he tried to make sense of what he was seeing. Vasilis was forced to drift the sub backwards in order to target the searchlights. Meanwhile, Baloo hovered over the middle of the Tiangong. A small, tethered RV popped from a recess underneath and lowered towards the spacecraft.

"What are you doing?" Eric asked.

"Maya wants to take a sounding to test its integrity," Raven came back.

The RV was essentially a pair of claws. Rather than being directly attached to the sub and offer limited dexterity, this simple engineering solution could go *anywhere*. A suction cup instrument was strapped to one claw, which was positioned flat against the hull.

Scott turned back to the coral as Vasilis negotiated the light. "It's black. The coral is black."

"You mean it's dead?" Vasilis said.

"No. Dead coral bleaches. Like you see on the surface. Here, the polyps are literally black."

"I've heard of black coral before," said Raven.

"Not like this. Black coral is known in deep reefs, almost as deep as this. But it takes its name from the dark the skeleton, the living tissue is usually brightly colored. This... everything is alive *and* black."

"So it's unusual coral then?"

"More than you can imagine. It grows an average of 20 micrometers a year. Reefs are often four thousand years old. They don't grow overnight like this apparently has. But that's not the kicker. They're spiraling." This time, even Scott's usual flat delivery peaked with astonishment.

He knew some genus of black coral grew in long twists, like a helter-skelter, but nowhere were the branches themselves wound as tight as drill bits, giving the appearance of long black claws slowly grasping the Tiangong.

"That's probably the second most bizarre thing about today," Raven said uncharacteristically quietly.

"What the hell's got the top spot?" Eric asked.

"We've just sounded the hull. It's not flooded. It's still airtight."

"That's impossible!" Eric snapped, throwing up his hands.

"You really need to stop saying that," Maya quipped.

"The hull is designed to withstand one atmosphere of pressure pushing from the *inside* into the void of space. <u>One</u>. We're at 300 atmospheres down here, pressing in. If the ship wasn't flooded, it would have been crushed like a paper cup."

"I'm reading this right, mate," said Maya.

"Then this can't be the Tiangong." Eric stamped his foot for emphasis. "I helped design her, and I wouldn't know where to begin on constructing something that would survive burn up or these depths. You're looking at an imposter!"

There was no mistaking the sincerity on his face. He slumped back in his chair, shaking his head.

"If you can't handle that, then you're going to hate this." Professor Raven sighed so deeply is sounded like a blast of static over the radio. "There's something *moving* inside. The crew maybe still alive."

TEN

"I WAS TOLD I'd be able to talk to my wife."

"You were given incorrect information."

"I don't understand. You have satellite uplinks, don't you? Even out here."

Professor Raven's pace was unrelenting in the gunmetal corridor as they turned left, then right in an increasingly labyrinthine network of corridors. Scott was almost breathless as he kept up. He cast a look at yeowoman Alanis following behind, who made a passable impression that she had never promised such a thing.

"That's not the point, Professor Bowers–"

"And we're not even on first-name terms yet?"

Raven shot him a look. "Are you serious?"

"It was a joke." Scott's monotone made her smile.

"Ah, the old on the spectrum thing. Sorry, *Scott*, but I am way beyond a charm offensive. I work for Frisco Dynamics, they work for the Navy." They stepped through an open bulkhead. "So since this is a military operation, you best bitch about it to Alanis right here."

Scott looked expectantly at Alanis, who gave nothing away.

"Captain's orders are that we are running silent. Just a hole in the South Pacific."

"She's pregnant." Scott immediately regretted playing that card and wasn't sure what response he was trying to elicit. Raven's eyebrows flicked up, and a genuine look of pleasure flashed across her face.

"Congratulations. Sooner we sew this enigma up, the better for you then."

And with one amiable response, Scott felt his argument evaporate. With the latest developments on the seabed, the scout mission had been scrubbed, and both subs sent immediately to the surface. Maya had argued that it was a counter intuitive move, but Raven was adamant that, if there was anybody still alive inside, there was nothing they could immediately do to save them and every second spent bobbing useless on the seabed was a second shaved off a possible rescue.

The two-hour ascent had grown into a stream of overlapping voices across the coms as Captain Peers and several unnamed US and Chinese analysts joined in the debate. It was almost impossible to get a point across, so Scott had tossed his headset off midway through.

He tried to catch Eric's eye, but he remained sullen and staring out of the bubble for the entire journey to daylight. Transferred back to the USS Gerald R. Ford, they had time to shower the sheen of cloying perspiration off them before assembling in the tower's briefing room.

This time it was packed. Captain Peers sat at the head of the table, with a bank of Warrant Officers behind him. The other side of the table sat Admiral Liu, who commandeered the Chinese aircraft carrier. Next to him was the ever-present Chinese Official. As Scott, Raven, Eric and Maya took their seats, he the officer was finally introduced as a liaison from the PLAAF – People's Liberation Army Air Force. A *Shang Jiang*, which Raven clarified under her breath as the equivalent of a general.

Monitors played multiple images of the Tiangong, which Scott realized were being transmitted live from RVs that must have been deployed the moment they began their ascent. The hubbub in the room came to a sudden silence by sheer force of Captain Peer's personality.

"As of a little over three hours ago, the mission changed from a salvage operation to a rescue mission. However unlikely that seems. Since your initial contact, no further communication has been established."

Maya had improvised with the RV claw to gently knock against the hull, but no reply came from within. Several minutes intensive listening picked up a couple of potential shuffling sounds, but then nothing but silence.

"Maybe the crew are barely conscious, pinned and unable to move... truth is we just don't know. Which adds to the long list of things we don't understand about the Tiangong. So we need an open and frank discussion. No ideas or concepts should be left off the table." He fixed Admiral Liu with a long steady look. "Admiral, for the sake of clarity, is there anything that may have been... accidentally... left off the lab's manifest. Toxins, biological experiments, anything that – when we crack it open on the deck – won't be a nasty surprise to us?"

The Admiral gave a short snort and stood, pressing both palms on the table. He slowly scanned the room. He spoke with a slight accent, but there was no doubting the integrity of his words. "The People's Republic of China as submitted Tiangong's manifest to you, right down to the last grain of rice. The last experiments taken onboard were stem-cell research, which I believe Professor Raven has had full access to."

Raven nodded. "Exploratory research in zero-G, but we're hardly talking biohazard."

Peers kept his gaze on the Admiral for a moment too long out of military ingrain mistrust. He looked around the room and gave a gesture that said over to you. "Does anybody know how they could be alive after almost two months at the bottom of the ocean?"

"There is plenty of food onboard. Drinkable water," said a Chinese Navy technician. Scott couldn't read the name badge from across the table. "Minimal power consumption could, possibly, keep life support running..." At that comment, he pulled a face indicating he didn't quite believe it himself.

"Professor Dong?"

All eyes turned to him. His fellow countrymen, in particular the Admiral, seemed to wait with bated breath. Eric gently tapped the side of his drinking glass, watching the ripple shimmy across the surface before he spoke up.

"There's nobody alive in there."

"We all heard movement," Raven pointed out. "The recordings–"

Eric held up his hand. "Movement. Certainly. Things move."

Raven drummed her fingers on the table. "And if the craft is intact, then it must have been onboard from the very beginning, right? There are no animals on the manifest. In fact, an aborted mission was to bring white mice up for the stem cell research."

Eric gave a shrug worthy of the surliest teenager. "That's irrelevant, because that cannot be the craft I helped build."

Nobody spoke. The tension in the air was almost electric as Eric avoided everybody's gaze and focused on the ripples across his glass. "The Tiangong didn't have heat shielding to protect it on re-entry. That object down there is unscathed. It was never designed to have 30 atmospheres pressing in on it, yet..." he flicked his fingers, not needing to state the obvious.

Admiral Liu gave a thin smile. "Then what do you suggest is down there?"

Eric was unflinching when he met his gaze. "Some sort of elaborate hoax, created for reasons I can't possibly comprehend."

Captain Peers' sudden laugh made Scott jump in his seat. He hadn't realized how tense he had been.

"We all tracked the Tiangong to Point Nemo. Every space agency read the same telemetry. Now assuming the US government is squandering millions on some obscure plan to confuse this gentleman," he indicated to the Admiral, "and cause a major international incident... and assuming the Chinese haven't dropped a huge rubber spacecraft in the ass of nowhere to lure us here, again for reasons too baffling for me... I ask you, who and why would such a hoax be perpetrated? We need to assume this is the real craft. That movement, which our audio team confirmed is consistent with a major mass moving within the hull – so let's rule out a stowaway mouse or genetically engineered monkey, but it is in fact some poor soul trapped."

"It circles us back around to the fact this is now a rescue mission. Theorizing clearly is something we can do when we bring the craft up. The question for me is how do we do that?" The question was aimed at Maya.

"We need to free the ship from the coral. That stuff looked razor sharp and could probably pierce the hull of our RVs. It's too deep for divers, so the Tritons will have to do it manually. But that will be like chipping a brick wall with a dentist drill." She glanced at Scott, who took the cue.

"Before we surfaced, I was able to cut a piece of the coral to study. I haven't had chance yet, but what I can tell you is that it took a lot of pressure from the sub's claw to break it off. That's some unusually tough coral."

"You mentioned it was spiraling in shape," said Raven. "Why is that significant?"

"Like a unicorn horn. It was a lefthanded spiral..." He drifted thoughtfully off. Most of nature's curves tended to twist the other way. Mutations occurred, but...

"Doctor Bowers?"

"Mmm? Oh. It looks sharp. Corals pose problems cutting harnesses and safety lines. But without further study, I can only guess if this will be an issue."

"We have a DSRV out there," said Peers, indicating to the window. "Docked to a Los Angeles class sub. Could that be used to connect to the Tiangong?"

Scott peered through the window in surprise. He had wondered if a DSRV – a Deep Sea Rescue Vehicle – was onboard the carrier, but it was the first time anybody had indicated the fleet also comprising nuclear attack submarines. He was certain if the Americans have one on patrol, the Chinese would certain have theirs prowling the crash site. He had the sudden unwelcome feeling that he had stumbled to the edge of a potential minefield. Two great powers circling one another, fueled by mistrust.

A captain at the far end of the table shook his head. "There are no docking points for the DSRV. If we tried to cut an access hole, there is no telling what that would do to the integrity of the Tiangong."

"So we need to cut the coral casing away to attach cables to lift the entire thing to the surface?"

"Anchoring cables could tear the ship apart," Maya said thoughtfully. "We're going to have to get several cradles underneath and lift the Tiangong and Shenzhou at the same time."

Uneasy glances spread around the room.

"Two things," said Peers. "Is it achievable? And is it achievable *today*?"

Maya puffed her cheeks, reminding Scott of a builder about to give a client an unpleasant estimate.

"Yes... and I don't know. We're gonna have to improvise like hell. I'll need everything the Ventura has."

Peers nodded. "Captain Vasilis will be under your command. I want solutions in two hours, people."

ELEVEN

IT WAS one of the most well-appointed labs Scott had visited in years, including several state-of-the-art NASA backed research vessels. Alanis had taken him into the forward bowels of the C-deck, at such a pace that he thought he'd never learn the layout of the ship.

The coral sat in a salt water tank, temperature and pressure regulated to match the conditions at the bottom of the sea. Inside, a robotic arm was covered in sensors, allowing him to make measurements without tampering the faux-ecosystem. The lights in the room had been dimmed too, although providing just enough for him to move around the lab without bumping into anything.

Alanis had left him to his research, while Maya and Eric had been separated to focus on their specialist tasks. The last face he saw was Eric's, and that was of a man who didn't seem to want to participate in something he couldn't explain.

Scott sat for a moment to gather his thoughts and found himself cycling through pictures of Ruth on his phone. A majority were taken more than two years ago during a walking trip through the Scottish Highlands. Powerful back-drops fading to obscurity by the happy faces peering back at him. A time that had never been replicated since...

He tried to figure out how many days he'd been gone – two? Three? With all the travel and tripping over the international dateline, his mind felt foggy. He'd been away for far longer stretches and barely missed her, so why was he so overwhelmed now?

The baby...

Fatherhood felt like a responsibility for people far older and wiser than him, yet here it was foisted upon him. If everything was okay, that is. Leaving Ruth alone meant that his imagination could run rampant. *Anything* could have happened to her, despite the statistical likelihood that every-thing was okay.

Unused to such emotional teetering, Scott wrapped his knuckles against the desk to break out of his morbid train of thought. Why would anything happen to her? He'd left her in a safe place, and she was more than capable of looking after herself.

An audio warning from the aquarium brought him back to the moment. He tapped the computer keyboard to wake the system and noticed a sensor had detected a slight decrease in the tank's salinity levels. A faulty sensor was the last thing he needed. His hand was halfway to the mouse to silence it when he noticed movement inside the tank.

The coral was growing, the entire structure spiraling with an audible crack. Then it stopped, giving no indication anything had changed except the finger of coral was an inch longer. Scott peered close to the glass, searching for the point the growth had occurred. The dark texture made it difficult to see detail, but the best he could judge it came from the tip which had a trace of gelatinous strands around it like spider silk.. The computer confirmed the salt level had dropped, but nothing else seemed to have changed.

Four years' growth in just seconds. Impossible.

He slid a long pipette into the tank and sucked up a sample of the mucus. He quickly deposited a droplet into a petri dish and slid it under the microscope. The macro cameras shifted focus and a pin-sharp image appeared on the monitor. A dark green blotch that put Scott immediately in mind of a fungal spore. Then again, it was so basic, without further testing, it was just pure speculation.

A knock at the open door made him look up. Maya was at the door offering a Styrofoam cup of steaming coffee.

"Turns out we're workshop buddies." She nodded to the side. "They put me next door, but the fools armed me with a coffee machine."

Scott smiled and stretched, the tense muscles in his shoulder cracking from the effort. "All caffeine is welcome."

Maya stepped over the lip of the watertight door and into the room, glancing at the equipment with an air of curiosity. She handed the coffee to Scott while peering at the coral.

"I always thought coral was supposed to be beautiful."

"It is. This one particularly. It just grew."

"Grew?"

"Maybe an inch in a couple of seconds, then it stopped."

"So we're talking weird coral?" She leaned against the bench and glanced at the microscope monitor. "My money's on some toxic gunk leaking from the craft. I asked Eric for a full breakdown of all the materials they used."

"And?"

"I'm still waiting. You ask him anything and he keeps

looking at whichever Chinese officer is in the room. The man's paranoid."

Scott sipped the coffee and gave a chuckle. "I don't blame him. He's probably signed a million NDAs in China and now we're asking him to spill his guts. So what about you? Aren't you supposed to be formulating a rescue plan?"

"Firstly, I disagree with Eric. Survivors have been found in the most extreme circumstances. No matter how remote, we can't dismiss the possible there's somebody alive in that thing. That's the real puzzle. Fishing it out is a piece of piss. Let's face it, there's only one way we can lift that thing up quickly. It took me all of fifteen minutes to work that out. Everybody's scattering to see what equipment can be magicked up." She flashed him a content smile that revealed the dimples in her cheek. Blue eyes sparkled with a hint of smugness.

"And your theories on how it got there?"

The contentment vanished. "I'm afraid I have to side with our boy Eric on that. I can't see how that ship hit the atmosphere, splashed down and sank with only damage to the solar panels. I've seen a lot of wrecks in my time and that is the best looking hulk in any ocean. Basic engineering says the weight of water alone should have crushed it."

"So what is it?"

Maya shrugged and knocked back the rest of her drink in one gulp. "I've salvaged crashed satellites from impact craters in Mongolia. Crashed stealth bomber from the middle of the Congo. I even brought up a prototype Russian sub off the coast of Finland from right under their noses, I might add. Each one had its own inherent problems, but they all had one thing in common. They were the real deal. This..." she studied his face for a few seconds before continuing. "Well, we won't know until we bring it up. But I wouldn't be too surprised if we crack it open and find it's some kind of surreal Russian practical joke. That's my take. You?"

Scott's gaze fell back onto to coral fragment. "Engineering problems aside. I think it is the Tiangong and whatever it was carrying has had a major effect on the surrounding ecosystem."

"They said there was nothing onboard, no nuclear material..."

"Onboard. But the fuel tanks, coolants, all the equipment housed outside the module then poured into a geothermal vent..." he shook his head, not convinced by his own arguments. "I agree. It shouldn't survive. But I also trust my own eyes. But as for survivors..." he shook his head.

"Says Mr Extremophile!"

"People are entirely another matter. We are so fragile. What we gained with intelligence, we lost when it came to durability."

"But you believe the line about that plankton they discovered?"

"Plankton in space." He smiled. "Oddly, that's the part that makes the most sense. Extreme microbes have been found in the upper atmosphere, carried on jet streams and thriving perfectly well." Maya raised a skeptical eyebrow. "I notice you believe very little of what I say."

Maya laughed. "That's because you're talking about life. We all know life, or think we do, so being told we actually know jack-all about it. It's difficult to accept. And I have a young son who loves making shit up." She wagged a finger at him. "And he comes out with crazy talk just like you."

Scott paused for a moment as he decided she wasn't being entirely serious. "It's documented. Not terribly well, but they're up there alright. Life finds a way. And it's conceivable that a growth spurt across a solar panel could easily disrupt the power, like they said."

"Killer plankton. I would love to read your thesis on that, Dr Bower."

Was there a flirtatious tone to that? Or was he just too tired? The latter, he assured himself.

"Scoff all you want. But that's not behind this," he waved to the coral. "It came from the sea, it went back to the sea if it didn't fry on re-entry. If you want to know where my money is, the answers lay inside."

An intercom on the wall suddenly squawked for attention, causing him to jump.

Maya grinned. "Talk about wound up."

It could have been Yeoman Alanis, but it was distorted a little by the overly-loud volume. "Doctor Bower, report to the meeting room immediately with Dr Johnson. Repeat, immediately."

Scott knocked back his coffee and put the cup on the bench. "I would if I knew the way."

Maya headed for the exit and causally waved his hand for him to follow. "Luckily, I have an excellent sense of direction. Follow me."

Scott stepped into the gangway and was about to close the door before wondering how they knew Maya was in his lab. His eyes quickly scanned the room, noticing a pair of small dark hemispheres in the deckhead. Surveillance cameras he hadn't noticed before.

He suddenly felt sympathetic towards Eric's paranoia, but then wondered exactly *who* was being the most paranoid. And he didn't care to find out *why*.

#11A

Alanis watched as the Osprey took off from the USS Paul Ignatius' helipad and circled the aircraft carrier. A gentle breeze caused goose-bumps on her exposed forearms, but she remained rigidly 'at ease', conscious the XO was by her side.

A new wrinkle in the recovery operation led to the Chinese demanding a face-to-face meeting. Due to the skeleton crew functioning on the Gerald R. Ford, she had been selected to accompany him. She'd rather be any place but by Donovan Keller's side, but orders were orders.

In silence, they watched the Osprey circle like a preying hawk before gently touching down at the opposite end of the flight deck from the Tiangong. The flight crew saluted the XO as they boarded, but the silence continued until they were airborne. Only then did Keller adjust his microphone and look Alanis in the eyes.

"Your relationship with Petty Officer Jordan McLain has been brought to my attention."

Alanis felt like a deer in the headlights; unsure how to respond. Each word carried a damming weight. *Brought to my attention* repeated in her head like an earworm. By whom? Immediately, her guard was up; somebody had a grudge against them. With all that was going on, why the hell was XO Keller bringing it up now?

"You know the rules, Petty Officer Narvaez." She refused to flinch from his piercing gaze. "And you have blatantly ignored them."

They both gripped their jump seats tighter as the Osprey performed a sudden stop and made a series of tight turns as it descended.

"Maybe when we get out of this hell, you'll regret it."

They touched down with a jolt, and the old bastard was already out of his seat and heading for the ramp as it whined down. Alanis felt frozen for a moment, before quickly following.

They were greeted by the PLAAF liaison and four Petty Officers who stood to attention, a position that ensured the Americans could see they were carrying sidearms. It was an obvious, subtle sign, and the heavy steel of the sidearm in Alanis' thigh holster pressed against her leg with every step, reminding her they were playing the same game.

The Officer started walking before Keller reached him.

"Welcome aboard. We have much to discuss."

They quickly strode towards the bridge, where another two armed guards stood. Alanis glanced behind to confirm the honor-guard quartet was ensuring they didn't wonder off.

"We have picked up several data bursts from your ship."

The XO gave a gruff laugh. "I don't know whether to be surprised or insulted that you're monitoring our transmissions."

"I am sure you are too honorable to be doing the same to

us." Keller was smart enough not to deny it. "But this was not your usual frequencies or encryption methods."

They reached the door. Keller stopped in his tracks, forcing Alanis to follow suit.

"What're you trying to tell me?"

The Officer stopped and searched on how to frame his words. "This is the reason we extended this invitation. We two things have occurred and they carry a great urgency with them."

"I don't have time for riddles–"

The Officer talked over him. "Firstly, we have detected an anomaly with the Tiangong."

"You could have radioed that."

"Indeed. Which leads me to my second point. We believe there is a spy aboard your ship."

TWELVE

IT WAS A MUFFLED SOUND, akin to something sliding across the floor. The peaks and troughs of the graphic equalizer showed they came in a slightly rhythmic pattern that all who listened attributed to locomotion of some kind. The silence.

"Play it again," Eric said with his eyes closed as she leaned closer to the speaker of the laptop on the conference room desk. They had heard it almost a dozen times on loop – the noise rising from nowhere and stopping just as suddenly.

Maya waited until Eric had listened once more before she spoke up, finding that she had been holding her breath. "It puts me in mind of somebody trying to crawl across the floor."

One of the Chinese RVs orbiting the Tiangong had attached a microphone to the spacecraft's hull since the party had ascended. After hours of silence, it had suddenly picked the sounds up twelve minutes earlier.

"Is that evidence enough that somebody must be alive in

there?" Captain Peers looked around the crowded room, taking in the various nods of acceptance.

The Chinese captain's jaw clenched as he firmly nodded. "If there is any hint the crew survived, our priority is to save them," he said in a low voice that seemed to fill the conference room.

"Agreed," said Peers. "We need to put the salvage plan in effect right now."

Various voices in the room suddenly rose to make their points – forcing Scott to wave his hand and shout above them.

"Hold on, just wait – excuse me! Just wait a moment!"

The room fell silent as all eyes swiveled to him. Raven folded her arms and looked expectantly at him. Scott felt a flood of embarrassment, not used to being the center of attention.

"There are other explanations."

"Such as?" asked Raven.

"A leakage inside the craft moving things around."

"There was weight to that sound," said Maya.

"Only because we are all trying to anthropomorphize what we are hearing. The ground is seismically active. That could be moving, causing a resonance in the craft."

"Are we talking earthquakes now?" snapped Peers.

Scott was never one to be fazed by authority figures in uniform, and he swore there was a condescending tone to the Captain.

"It must be considered. And the coral is growing at an incredible rate around the craft. Perhaps that is creating noise." He saw indecision on most of the faces. "The fact we have only heard two sounds, quite random one, and nobody has attempted to communicate back tells me it's very unlikely that we're hearing a survivor."

Silence once again filled the room. The two captains exchanged a meaningful look, then turned to Raven. She shrugged, indicating Scott had a point.

"It could be crabs tap-dancing on the hull," she finally said. "Even stress on the structure itself. They're all possibilities." She looked levelly at Scott. "And amongst those possibilities, there really could be people alive inside. Correct?"

Scott reluctantly nodded.

Raven pursed her lips for a moment. Then sharply sucked in a breath.

"Okay. This is a rescue mission. Dr Johnson, take point. We move immediately."

FOR WHAT HAD OSTENSIBLY BECOME AN IMPROVISED operation, Scott was impressed by the team's smooth deployment of resources from both the Chinese and American vessels, who now used the Ventura as the base of operations.

Under the unchallenged authority of Professor Raven, snags and hitches were dealt with fuss or drama. Not for the first time, he wondered what hold Frisco Dynamics had over the military of both nations.

During a quick Osprey ride to the Trident submersibles, where he was once again teamed with Vasilis aboard the Mowgli, he was surprised to see hundreds of Chinese Naval personnel combing the decks of the Liaoning carrier, spreading out a huge inflatable cradle hastily designed by Maya to lift the Tiangong.

The actual practical details had been as sketchy as the

fleeting view he just had, before the Osprey sharply banked onto the Ventura's helipad and they were hustled into the submersible. This time he was a little relieved to see the beaming face of Maya in the jump seat next to him.

"Where's Eric?"

She jerked her head to Baloo, which was already maneuvering into the center of the moon pool. "Raven wants to keep a close eye on him. I think she's worried he'll have another meltdown."

"So you get the benefit of my company."

Maya smirked as she pulled her seatbelt tight. "That's why they're paying me danger money."

Rather than the previous serene descent, the radios were alive with communications, relayed through a network of repeater stations that had been lowered to various depths. Maya presented the salvage plan on her laptop, broadcast not only to the Baloo, visible yards away, but the surface team too.

Through the acrylic canopy, Scott could see the strobing collision lights of a dozen remotely piloted vehicles that were descending with them. The enormous cradle he'd seen on the Liaoning now resembled a hammock as it was strung between several of them.

In the depths, only the Tritons had free rein. An array of RV tethering cables stretched to the surface, restricting movement and increasing the risk of a possibly fatal collision. Even a modest prang could cripple an engine, leaving the submersibles stranded in the depths. Worse, a blemish in the acrylic canopy could easily weaken the hull's integrity and at these pressures, the vehicles would implode without warning. At least death would be instantaneous. Before leaving, Vasilis and Markus had repeated the safety warnings to their passengers and Scott had watched with detached interest as Raven became increasingly subdued and Eric's whole body language screamed 'unease'. Only Maya had flashed a lopsided smile, at ease with the risks.

His own internal dialogue, normally maintaining an emotional neutrality, had become slightly fraught. This would mark his eighty-sixth career descent, and the first time he'd expressed any apprehension. He tried not to self-analyze too much; he had a therapist he was paying to do that for him once he returned home...

Home. The word had literally meant the place he stored his possessions, slept and relaxed. Now it had emotional weight and, at the back of his mind, the image of Ruth waiting for him. It wasn't the distraction he needed right now, and he focused back on the briefing.

Eric was giving clipped responses to Maya's questions about the anchor points on the Tiangong and its ability to withstand being lifted from the seabed. Despite still insisting the craft couldn't be the one he built, her accusations had stoked a sense of pride and the Professor was becoming increasingly defensive. Although the schematics made it look fragile, the spacecraft had been built horizontally, positioned vertically as it was lifted to the top of a rocket and then endured massive G-forces as it was blasted into orbit.

In Eric's intermittent silences, Maya and Scott specu-lated Raven was giving him a hard time about his strained communication. Maya was a little more sympathetic than Scott, pointing out that something like the Tiangong-2 would be the culmination of anybody's career and now a bunch of strangers – foreigners - were dismantling his achievements.

Load-bearing weights, submersible thrust, rates of airflow pumped from the surface and pressure calculations... most of the technical details washed over Scott. Until they reached the actual site, his expertise was not needed. Instead, he stared into the void and in moments succumbed to a deep sleep.

A RIVULET of ice cold water on his forehead woke Scott immediately.

With a pounding heart he feared the worse – a leak. It took him several seconds to register that Maya and Vasilis were cool and focused on the view outside the canopy, and the water was merely condensation. He unclipped his harness and stood to wipe it clear, when he saw the view ahead.

"Ground floor, doc," said Maya with a grin.

The view of the black smoker outside vaporized any fatigued he'd been feeling. Under the powerful lights of the RVs above, he had a better view of it than ever before. Now he could just make out a moving mass on the volcano's flanks. Life – uninspected and most definitely unidentified.

Scott craned his head to watch it pass by, and noticed the RV drones, with their long tethers to the surface, were giving the smokers a wide berth. The superheated water added another complication to the rescue operation, drastically restricting the vehicles' mobility. Threading the tethering cables through the invisible corridors of boiling water required precision piloting from the operators safely ensconced on the aircraft carriers overhead. The spotlights all pivoted downwards, revealing the Tiangong.

"They're still acoustically coupled," Maya said, pointing to the moveable RV claw that was now clamped on the side of the spacecraft.

"OK, Mowgli," came Raven's voice over the headset, accompanied by a wave of static, "you're free to move into primary position."

Vasilis easily toyed the joystick, positioning them just several feet from the curving wall of black coral growing around the hull. As they sank lower, the twisting strands arced overhead like a menacing dark wave frozen in time.

Both Maya and Scott craned forward, the light from the RVs above illuminating the scene as if in broad daylight.

"The hull still appears to be intact," said Maya. She pointed to a spot several meters away. "That looks like the load-bearing axis."

Eric had described how the spacecraft had several load-bearing axis that sat on trestles in the hermetically sealed construction hangars in China. Far from being designed for what Maya had in mind, they still represented the strongest points to hook a harness under. Maya's simple plan was to inflate a rig directly underneath and scoop the space station from the seabed.

Simple, yet so many elements could turn it into a disaster. The harness had been constructed by the Chinese using parts cannibalized from the International fleet. One weak seam, a single tear, and the Tiangong would come crashing down. The thousands of meters of piping required to pump the air down had a similar problem. The Americans had worked on that problem, adapting the Gerald R. Ford's powerful generators to pump significantly more air than they'd been designed for. One slip in air pressure and the craft could come tumbling down.

While the calculations on paper indicated it was all possible, every member of the team was aware the real world was always on standby to throw a curve ball to make life difficult. Vasilis dutifully drifted to the spot.

Scott was more fascinated by the coral. It seemed to have curled around the hull, the dark razor-sharp fingers hanging crookedly over it like a gnarled claw. The pair of black and white smokers behind it added a Dante-esque dimension to the vision. He could see trails of some white sulfide material that had flowed from the smokers towards the base of the coral and could only speculate whether the exotic chemical had helped spur the coral's miraculous growth. He was so lost in thought, he almost missed movement in the darkness beyond.

"Dr Bowers?" Raven prompted.

"Just a moment. I think I saw..."

"We don't have a moment, Doctor. The clock is ticking. Lives are at stake."

Scott blinked and looked again. The superheated water around the volcanos flowed under the lights of the RVs, all adding to the illusion of movement. However, he regretted not insisting the seismic activity be monitored more closely.

"Doctor?"

He hated being rushed at the best of times. The fact he couldn't believe there was anybody trapped inside made the faux-urgency even more annoying. He tracked the crooked arms of coral that woven around one another, reaching down to the rocky seabed. Indicating to Vasilis which way to move, Mowgli was repositioned at the base of the coral.

"OK. I think we're good to go." He sadly shook his head at the pending act of wanton destruction. He wiped his sweating palms on his trousers, then gripped a small joystick that had been set up next to his seat. It controlled the robotic arm, and he'd had a whole five minutes to practice with it before they'd left; nowhere near enough for the challenging surgery he was about to perform.

The whine of servo motors vibrated through the sub as he slowly extended the arm.

"You're veering to the left," Maya pointed out rather unhelpfully.

He corrected his aim. The arm slowly inched towards the top of the coral. The tip of the arm was kitted out with a high-pressure hose designed to spray concentrated acid onto the coral base to sever the growth, allowing the coral to be pulled away. The corrosive acid would be diluted almost instantly, but the high-pressure spray would still be potent enough to slice the tough coral. Too close to the Tiangong and the hull would be pierced instantly. Scott had tried not to think about the tank of acid hastily clamped to the back of Mowgli, if that ruptured and dissolved the hull they'd be dead in seconds.

He glanced up through the bubble, watching as two small RVs moved into position, extendable claws clamping the top of the coral, ready to take the weight and guide it back, away from the spacecraft before it had chance to fall and puncture the hull.

"Ready to burn on my mark." Once again, Scott felt the unfamiliar prickles of anxiety. Dozens of things could suddenly go wrong. "Three, two, mark..."

He squeezed the joystick trigger.

If it wasn't for the camera mounted on the nozzle, they wouldn't have a clue if the acid was doing its job. The small screen bolted to the other arm of Scott's chair showed a discolored liquid striking the black coral. A plume of white material, smoke-like, sprung from the structure, obscuring the view. Scott continued slowly moving the joystick to the right, estimating its cutting progress, then–

"It's detached!" Raven exclaimed.

Scott released the trigger and looked up through the canopy as a thirty foot curved arch of coral broke free, tugged backwards by the RVs. It was like watching a mighty oak being uprooted, then defying gravity.

He flinched as the base of the spar dragged past the Triton so close that the displaced water caused an unwelcome shimmy. The RVs pulled it clear of the work site and unceremoniously dropped it close to the foot of the smoker, causing an enormous cloud of silt to be kicked up, obscuring its fate.

Scott examined his handiwork. The single coral arm had blossomed almost twenty feet in width, with hundreds of projections, so its removal had cleared a sizeable stretch from the Tiangong.

"Good work," said Maya, reaching over for a high-five. Against instinct, Scott slapped her hand before they moved back into position for the next felling.

Twenty minutes later, they had cut another four huge sections away without incident. Now they could see the spacecraft in all its glory, including the now revealed faded Chinese flag painted on the hull. The Baloo moved closer for Eric to give a visual inspection.

"Still don't think that's your baby?" Maya teased over the intercom.

"I can't see any further damage," came Eric's terse reply.

Scott had expected him to comment further,

"The man's not easily swayed," Maya muttered as they moved into secondary positions, ready to take her lead on the salvage operation.

Scott was taken by the now visible seabed. Silvery/white chemical tributaries from the smokers stretched down their flanks, mixing in the rock around the Tiangong and glittering in the light like slug trails.

Again, he caught movement just behind one smoker, on the very edge of the blazing lights. This time he was certain it wasn't an illusion. It was an enormous black cylinder slowly moving into the murk. His heart skipped a beat as he tried to process what he had just seen, before realizing it was a submarine. Impossible to judge *whose*, but an unwelcome reminder that the waters around them were silently observing them and bristling with weapons of war.

"All quiet!" Raven suddenly barked.

Scott and Maya froze, swapping alarmed looks. Everybody raised the volume on their headsets, bringing the constant hiss of white noise into sharp relief.

Random noise popped and snarled, hinting at whispering voices. Scott knew it was nothing more than auditory pareidolia, but it was nevertheless seductive.

Then a sudden loud noise caused them all to jump and quickly lower the volume.

A slow dull tapping.

Maya's eyes went wide as she looked between Vasilis and Scott for confirmation they were hearing the same thing. The Greek crossed himself. Scott frowned, closing his eyes to listen.

"It could be magma displacement..."

"Negative," Raven's voice had dropped to barely a whisper, as if wary of scaring off the source of the noise. "The RV confirms it is coming from *inside* the Tiangong."

The tapping continued with an uneven pace, sometimes

faster, sometimes slower, hinting that it wasn't something mechanical or a drip.

Against his better judgement, Scott couldn't shake the feeling that it sounded like flesh hammering for help.

"Is that, like, Morse code or something?" Maya asked.

Vasilis had been listening with increasing concern. Being trapped underwater must surely be one of his greatest fears. He shook his head. "No. It sounds like somebody with no strength... other than the will to live. If it were me in there, I would be screaming for my life."

Scott agreed with that sentiment, which begged the question, why weren't they doing just that?

Then it stopped. For a full minute, they all strained to listen to the steady hiss of background static over the radio. Then Raven broke the silence.

"OK, people, that's our cue to hurry and save those souls. Dr Johnson, it's in your hands now."

"Copy that," said Maya. A look of intensity drew a veil across her face.

The Triton suddenly shuddered as it was struck by an unseen current. Alarms squawked across Vasilis's dashboard. The external lights flickered for a moment, teasing the threat of utter darkness and the temperature inside soared, and they felt the skin on their faces prickle.

The sudden movement jerked Scott from his seat, and he cracked his head against the clear canopy. Through increasingly hazy vision, he saw the smoker nearest to them had ruptured its side, spewing a volcanic eruption in their direction.

Then blood stung his eyes, forcing them closed.

THIRTEEN

THE WAIL of alarms was disorienting as Scott blindly groped back to his seat. As the Triton shook again, his head painfully cracked, the underside of the monitor bolted to the chair arm, but it provided a firm reference point to enable him to drag himself back into the seat. He looped his harness around his waist to secure him in place as the sub lurched once more.

Sucking in an uncomfortably warm breath, he used his wrist to wipe the blood from his left eye and squinted around him. Vasilis was wrestling the joystick to regain stability. The thermal shock wave had rotated the submersible like a spin top, fortunately hurling it away from direct impact with the stream of superheated water.

Maya reached over as far as she could and squeezed his arm. "Are you okay?" She had still been strapped in place and rubbed her neck as whiplash twinged it.

He nodded, not at all reassured that her normally unflappable expression was blanched with fear.

Then everything fell silent as the power failed, and the

sub was plunged into near darkness. Only the lights from the RVs above allowed him to see Vasilis thumping the control panel over his head.

"Stay calm. I'm rebooting the system," he said in a massively distracted voice.

Scott raised his hand to stop being blinded as Baloo's search lights pierced the canopy to check on them. He felt nauseous, but had no desire to close his eyes.

With a whine, the power came back online and with it a torrent of radio chatter from the Baloo.

"–Systems down. Mobility zero! Mowgli, do you read?"

Vasilis turned to grin at his passengers and gave a thumbs up. "Only a little upsy-daisy! She is built like a rock." He patted the dash above his head, causing more condensation to drip off.

Scott repressed the urge to point out rocks don't float. He dabbed his forehead, his fingers coming back bloodied. "I'm bleeding to death." He glanced at Maya for confirmation and was surprised to see her easy smile had returned, although there was no mistaking the worry in her eyes.

"You'll live. It's only a scratch." She pre-empted the rebuttal on Scott's lips, and held up her thumb and finger millimeters apart. "Like this big. Scalp cuts bleed more. They like being melodramatic."

It took another few minutes for Vasilis to unclip a small first aid kit from under his seat and rub a stinging antiseptic wipe across the cut, before applying a plaster that would contain the bleed.

Baloo performed a visual check on them, while Vasilis ran a system diagnostic that claimed everything was fine.

"Hull integrity is a-okay."

The air con did an admirable job at lowering the temperature to comfortable levels. Baloo's final assessment that the acid tank bolted to the hull hadn't ruptured under the heat was the final seal of approval that the mission could proceed.

As Mowgli and Baloo took their positions with the other RVs around the spacecraft, Scott peered into the dark waters.

"How's the other sub?"

"What other sub?" asked Vasilis, locking his position centimeters over the sea bed so that Maya could take control of the remote arm to begin the salvage.

"The sub... the nuclear sub that was circling us."

Vasilis and Maya exchanged a look, and Maya shrugged. "I didn't see nothin'."

"There are no other support vessels close by," Vasilis said, shooting him a concerned look.

"I saw it. Just beyond the smoker." Scott hated the skeptical look on Vasilis's face. "Check sonar."

The Greek glanced at the sonar screen that was littered with targets. "Nothing that big is out there."

Maybe it was the blow to the head or the uncomfortable heat flush that made Scott feel annoyed. He keyed the mic.

"Raven, do you read me?"

"Go ahead, Scott," came Raven's reply.

"What's the status of the military submarine after the smoker vented?"

A pause. Then: "What sub is this?"

Scott looked away from Maya and Vasilis as they swapped uneasy looks. "I saw it. Raven, we know there is an American Los Angeles-Class sub somewhere out there."

"There is a Chinese sub and one of ours, both topside and on the perimeter. There is nobody else down here but us. Confirm you're in position."

Scott adjusted his mike, determined to insist he hadn't

imagined it, but hesitated. Perhaps it had been an internal reflection on the canopy? And if it was real, it wouldn't surprise him that one of the superpowers was keeping a paranoid eye on them.

He noticed Maya was giving him a thumbs-up. His fixation on what he may or may not have seen was distracting from the more-pressing rescue mission. He keyed the mike. "Maya's ready."

"Let's get this show on the surface. Baloo to Surface, position the cradle."

The large RVs moved with precision as they laid the cradle in front of the Tiangong. Tether cables crisscrossed within inches of entangling, but the skilled pilots never veered from their finely calculated positions.

Next, Markus positioned Baloo over the harness. Three small drones, mounted on an improvised cradle over Baloo's rear-mounted oxygen tanks, undocked. Now it was Eric's turn to show off his dexterous piloting as he gently guided one, then the other two in turn, to grasp nylon trailing lines from the harness.

He had remained silent about his drone racing passion, but it had turned up on his personnel file, leading two separate teams to victory in the *Drone Prix Beijing*. Merging the controls of all three drones, he edged them forward in unison, delicately threading the cords under the anchor points.

Everybody held their breath. If things went wrong now the entire operation would stop. Scott wasn't too thrilled that it all hinged on Eric.

Yet Eric didn't falter once. Sheltered from any currents, the three tiny drones passed under the Tiangong's anchor points and out the other side. Increasing thrust, the main arms of the cradle were pulled through. It had taken twenty-two minutes, but the cradle was finally in position and the nylon straps raised over the top of the spacecraft and secured so that it formed a tube.

Maya grinned at Scott. "A piece of cake." The stress on her face told otherwise. "Mowgli to surface. Inflation on my mark. Three... two – mark."

Nothing happened for almost two minutes as the air was pumped from the surface, two and a half miles above them, finally reached the harness.

The first sign of movement was a slow ripple through the cradle. The edges rippled like a sea slug fanning itself. Volcanic silt stirred, creating a black haze around the space-craft. The harness snapped fully ridged with a dull thud that carried through the water. Despite the generators working overtime to pump the air down at massive pressure, the rein-forced pipes still struggled to keep their shape in these crushing depths.

Raven's dry voice broke the tension. "We have lift off."

The Tiangong slowly rose from the seabed. 8,600 kilo-grams of spacecraft inched upwards, the silt giving the illu-sion of rocket smoke.

A flicker of a smile cracked Scott's face. It was an unusual sight to behold and proud moment. Eric had constantly stressed how fragile the craft was, insisting that it couldn't possibly survive the pressure. Every gentle move-ment or temperature change could be just enough to cause it to implode in an instant, rendering the entire operation pointless.

"Ten meters," chimed Maya. "Visual integrity remains A-Okay."

Searchlights from the orbiting RVs combed the hull as

they moved in a choreographed ballet. Vasilis edged forward, gently nosing towards the bottom of the inflated harness. The mass of the Tiangong filled the canopy above them and, with the seabed soon lost to the darkness, it was easy to imagine they were in orbit above the earth, ready to dock.

The Baloo banked under the Tiangong, mirroring Mowgli's position opposite. Raven extended the robotic arm towards the precious load; Maya following suit, keeping her eye on the depth gauge.

"Plus forty meters. Reaching out now." Her voice was tense with concentration.

Scott couldn't help but be impressed with Raven and Maya's coordination as the robotic arms gently gripped opposite sides of the harness in perfect synchronization.

"Contact," they both said at the same time.

"Twenty percent power," said Vasilis.

Scott felt the thrusters spool up and both subs pushed in the same direction. It was a gentle maneuver, but enough for the Tritons to perform their new duties as tugs, positioning the Tiangong further away from the smoker's superheated waters.

Vasilis flicked his attention between the hull outside and a thermal camera image that depicted the super-hot waters as red claws groping around them.

For ten long minutes, they slowly shepherded the craft between the corkscrewing thermals as they rose. With every meter the temperature plunged sending creaks of stressed metal from the Tiangong, through the arm, and vibrating everything within the submersible. The frequency rose, setting Scott's teeth on edge.

"Is that normal?"

"Normal is not a touchstone of this operation," Maya

barked over the noise. "Best I can do is assure you it's happening."

With less than half a meter between the canopy and the Tiangong, Scott could make out details on the hull, such as a pale yellow patina covering it. This close he could just make out fine wispy tendrils covering every inch that the HD cameras had failed to pick up.

Then the vibrations suddenly stopped.

Scott felt his heart in his throat. If the Tiangong imploded now, it would take the Tritons out with it. Speaking in rapid Greek, both Vasilis and Markus increased the rate of vertical ascent.

Around them the darkness was punctuated by the constant light and vigilance of the RVs as they checked the harness integrity.

Maya's voice broke the spell. "Four hundred meters. We've cleared the thermals and are picking up speed. Tell topside to put the coffee on."

Time seemed to stretch, metered only by the soft hum from the thrusters, the whirl of the air con and the Tiangong telegraphing occasional ghostly creaks through the attached arm. The pressurized recycled air was beginning to taste less fresh and more metallic.

The whole experience felt like being on the cusp of sleep. Protracted moments of nothingness, then the occasional shifting of constellations as the RVs switched positions. The monotony allowed the mind to wander.

Scott was struggling to think how somebody could have survived onboard the Tiangong. What isolation and despair they must have faced. Would the thought of salvation bring determination or madness should it fail?

Did they have family back home, anxious for news of

their return? Had they been officially presumed dead already? A tangible blackness tainted further questions – would he be missed should the shit suddenly hit the fan? He no longer had family, an only child and both parents gone within the last decade. Aside from several professional acquaintances he socialized with at seminars and Christmas, he had never really entertained close friendships. Ruth was all he had... her and a child who had only just begun to exist.

It was a crushing realization that he was as isolated inside as he was outside.

The welcome reappearance of marine snow gave them a sense of movement. Maya was asleep and Vasilis was alert in his seat, eyes fixed on their cargo.

Peering up through the canopy, there was still no hint of sunlight. At this speed, that lay hours away, so Scott attempted to relax back in his seat and closed his eyes as a wave of fatigue suddenly swept over him.

He was on the edge of soft warm sleep – when a fierce hammering jolted him awake. It was relayed through the RV's acoustic sensor still latched onto the Tiangong. It was not rhythmic, but staccato.

And not mechanical.

To Scott's ears, it was definitely organic...

FOURTEEN

THE SLOW CRAWL to the surface felt interminable, especially with more sporadic noises from within Tiangong which dropped to silence for minutes, before starting with the renewed fury of somebody scrabbling for their life.

After twenty-one minutes, the spacecraft lapsed into haunting silent once again.

Maya cranked up the speaker volume and the low hiss of static, broken by gentle creaks from the spacecraft, became a hypnotic lull. Every now and again they would swap glances at the faintest sounds. More than once Scott swore he heard a raspy sigh, but nobody else reacted to it.

Finally, light pierced the murk above. The Heavenly Palace bobbed to the surface with an almighty displacement of water that sent white frothy waves across Mowgli's canopy. A fleet of two dozen Zodiac speedboats swarmed around it as a pair of Chinooks hovered overhead, trailing steel cables. The crews of the Mowgli and Baloo were all but forgotten as divers attached lines to the inflated cradle and the Tiangong-2 was hoisted into the air, dripping water like a summer squall.

Scott lost sight of the space station as it was lifted up and over the immense grey wall of an aircraft carrier. Their job done, the Tritons re-submerged to dip into the moon pool. It was another forty minutes before the hatch was opened and the teams gulped in cold fresh air as they scrambled onto the ship's deck.

Alanis greeted them with the vaguest of nods and escorted them to a waiting Osprey. It was a relief to stretch the legs and Scott bound up the stairwell that circled the tower, catching up with Eric.

"Eric, hold on." Eric slowed his pace. "What's your verdict on the wreckage now?"

"I'm apparently a stubborn man. That's what Raven called me the entire journey back up." He shook his head but managed a thin smile. "I almost wished it was me inside."

A joke, Scott told himself. Despite the weight of the topic, he forced a chuckle. He saw Eric's eyes narrow as he looked at him.

"Are you taking the piss out of me?"

Scott held up his hand apologetically. "No. Sorry. I have this condition, sort of slight autism, and my therapist suggested I should respond with conventional norms so I don't come across as..."

"As a prick?"

"Yes."

Eric smirked. "*That* was a joke." He patted Scott on the back, the first friendly gesture he had demonstrated since they'd met. Behind the bridge tower Markus and Vasilis waved their goodbyes and entered the tower. Alanis marshalled the team up more metal steps to the landing pad.

Eric continued. "To answer your question... I don't know. It's still impossible. But I, for one would be happy to be the one credited with rewriting the laws of physics."

"Did you know the crew? Personally?"

Eric blew out a long breath and shook his head. "I only built the hardware. They don't let people like me near the software. I suppose we'll known when we open her up on the Liaoning."

Onboard the Osprey there was an exchange of theories, galvanized by the promise of forthcoming answers. They made the short hop to the aircraft carrier – but with no windows aft, they only noticed they had landed back on the USS Gerald R. Ford, not the Chinese carrier as planned.

"Why are we here?" Eric asked, with notable confusion.

His answer lay at the end of the three-hundred meter runway. The Tiangong had been set down behind a perimeter of cones nobody dared cross, right on top of the enormous '78' painted on the deck – CVN-78, the ship's official classification. Scott noted the ship had been positioned so that the foreign craft was downwind, a basic step to ensure any contamination didn't reach them.

Eric jabbed a finger at Professor Raven. "The Tiangong is Chinese property! It was agreed it would be placed onboard the Liaoning."

Raven feigned ignorance. "Circumstances must have changed while we were down there." They glanced at three Changhe Z-18 helicopters circling the carrier, keeping a steady distance. The Chinese were obviously not letting their space station out of their sight. "Don't worry, Professor Dong, we have all the facilities you need right here."

"This is a breach of trust! Theft!" he snarled, raising his voice.

Eric put a hand on his arm to calm him. "We don't know what has happened. But they're hardly going to steal this out here, are they?"

Eric flashed him a look that left Scott in no doubt he thought the Englishman was part of the conspiracy.

PLASTIC TENTS FILLED the hangar bay, now set up to be biologically sealed areas the team would use to inspect aspects of the space station. Scott had done his best to advise how they could seal the space off as tightly as possible, but at the end of the day, the aircraft carrier was simply not equipped to deal with large-scale biohazards. Hermetic isolation was impossible, and every measure was a token one.

The cavernous space had been partitioned in two, leaving access to only one of the carrier's three huge elevators, each large enough to lift aircraft to the flight deck. As many aircraft as possible had been moved into the second partition, but those remaining here had been pushed up against the white metal walls, wings folded to preserve space.

Every door was closed and sealed with plastic sheeting. The giant fuel tanks bolted to the walls had likewise been covered with heavy canvas sheets to protect against any possible corrosive substance the Tiangong may be carrying. Air conditioning had been securely isolated from the rest of the ship, here at least it had been designed with the perils of biological warfare in mind.

A single entrance through a succession of plastic corridors that led through an airlock that doubled as a decontamination stage.

Once through, Scott was uncomfortable as the hood of his hazmat suit sealed with a hiss and he felt the air pressure clamp his ears. His faceplate fogged for a moment as the temperature rose, but it cleared a few seconds later. A small bottle of oxygen on their backs would provide enough for forty minutes. Maya stood close to him, her eyes wide behind her visor. She was hyperventilating.

Scott lay a reassuring hand on her shoulder and angled her to face him. "Slow and steady. Deep breaths. It's uncomfortable at first, but there's nothing to worry about."

She followed his lead and was soon breathing normally. The corners of her mouth curled into a smile, but her eyes reflected her worry. Eric stood next to him in an identical day-glo yellow hazmat suit. He seemed more at ease than both of them.

They all fastened utility belts, a variety of tools hanging from carabiners. Eric checked his handheld camera was running. Intended for close up inspection, it would be backed-up by the smaller helmet cameras mounted in their hoods, which streamed the video back to the bridge, along with their radio chatter.

"Take this." Raven handed him a metal sample *case*. A range of swabs and tubes to collect samples were attached to the side. He flicked the lid open, checking the twelve sample jars inside were kept at a constant 4°C. Scott secured the strap over his shoulder and positioned the case behind.

"Let's go." Raven marshalled them through the airlocks with her usual bustle of overconfidence. "Okay, folks. The ship's doctor ran you through biological 101?" She accepted their small nods. "And Scott here added a few horror stories about infections..."

"They're hardly horror–"

Raven held up her hand to stop him. "My point is, this is about as ready as anybody can be in these exceptional circumstances. The priority, aside from our own safety, is not to contaminate the rest of the ship. Most of the crew are in lockdown until we can guarantee that. There's just a few of the crew assisting us from this point out. Understood?"

Again, more unenthusiastic nods.

"What do you expect us to find?" Scott asked, provoking a bemused frown from Raven. "What I mean is, Frisco Dynamics, you. What exactly are you looking for?"

She studied him, expressions hidden in the shadows of the suit. "You have been watching too many conspiracy films. We are a secretive company because we specialize in unique government assignments. The reclamation of the Tiangong and the causes behind its demise are just that. I expect answers, because I am relying on you to find them."

Further conversation was cut short by the force of a high-pressure chemical blast from overhead sprays. They endured fifteen seconds of buffeting before Raven led them onto a large hydraulic lift. Scott glimpsed a hazmat-suited technician behind a control window at the side of the hangar. Raven offered him a thumbs-up, then they rapidly ascended to the deck.

THE SUN SAT LOWER in the sky, almost blinding them as they emerged. Scott and Maya held their hands up to stop being dazzled as they looked at the Tiangong meters away. It sat on the inflated harness to protect it from the steel deck. Rivulets of seawater still trickled down the curve of the hull, pooling on the deck. Four F-35Cs sat on the edge of the deck, parked midway along the flight deck, the tips of their wings folded to save space.

"Eric, the visual inspection is over to you," said Raven, gesturing to it.

Eric raised a small camera and began circling the spacecraft. Maya walked by his side, but both remained silent over the radio.

Raven glanced at Scott, cuing him for his role. He extracted several medical swabs from his sample case. They felt overly small in his gloves.

Eric carefully studied the panels on the port side hull. "There is no visible damage."

Scott edged close to examine the filaments he had seen clinging to the hull. They were still there, like a fine layer of white cotton candy mere millimeters in length. In fact, they were everywhere. The entire hull was covered in them.

"Eric," Eric put the camera down and turned to him. "These fibers over the hull, are they from the protective coating, or insulation?"

Eric reacted as if he hadn't noticed them. He examined several areas of the hull. "This is not part of the vehicle. That is your department." He continued with his inspection.

Scott swabbed the material. The surface coating easily broke apart under the gentle pressure. It must be aquatic, he reasoned, too delicate to survive burning up in the atmosphere. A second examination showed a stubble-like root, almost too fine to see, remained attached to the hull.

Moving on, he took another sample of the material covering writing on the hull. It was just transparent enough for the Chinese red characters to show through. He noted with curiosity that the filaments had absorbed on the same color as the lettering.

"Bowers!"

The edge to Eric's voice made him quicken his pace to

join them. He was examining a twisted spar that held one of the great solar panels. A forearm of metal protruded from the hull, the ends of which were twisted, torn, and blackened. The spar itself was hollow, once containing cables that carried the change from the panels to the batteries. He could immediately see what had got Eric's attention.

Curving black cords, the thickness of a finger covered the opening of the spar, and twisted into the hollow. At first Scott assumed they were charred wires, but the cords branched out like tree roots, gnarled and twisted together. It was definitely organic.

"Coral?" Eric reached out to touch it – Scott quickly stayed his hand.

"No. Similar formation, but it's different." Scott wiped his visor. The faint sheen of moisture inside was enough to stop him getting a clear look. The spirals had the same left-handed orientation. Was it mimicking the coral? Or was some environmental factor at play?

He sensed Raven beside him, watching with curiosity. Wordlessly, she handed him a pair of pliers. He cut an inch of the material away. It was tough, and he wondered if the fierce re-entry temperatures had somehow helped preserve it.

With a sudden snap, the pliers sliced a section free. As it dropped, he caught it in his free hand and stowed it in the case. There was little time to study it further as Raven urged Eric on. If there were any crew alive, the external inspection could be nothing more than cursory.

Scott hurried after the team as they disappeared around the back of the hull – and stopped short as a huge, gnarled claw lashed out for his faceplate. His heart jack-knifed in his chest and his feet slipped on the wet deck. His hand automatically flailed for purchase, fingers raking down the side of the hull as he fell.

The inflated hazmat suit cushioned a little of the impact, but the hard deck still hurt like hell. A stab to his ribs expelled the breath from his lungs - he'd landed on his sample case.

"Scott!" it took him a moment to recognize Raven's voice. He reached for her, and had enough presence of mind to noticed that she didn't offer any assistance, instead she watched him with concern. "What happened?"

Scott didn't immediately reply he looked up, first noticing that Eric was more interested in examining the rake marks across the hull Scott had left. Then he noticed the claw was part of the station's robotic arm that now limply hung at an angle. The flayed fingers were extended and covered in a web of fibrous growth. He assumed it must have been obscured by the coral, which is why he hadn't noticed it before.

Raven still made no attempt to help him stand. "Has your suit been breached?"

Scott checked a sensor on his wrist, relieved to see the suit's pressure was stable. "Sure. All fine. I just slipped on the deck." He looked at his fingers, the yellow stains from the hull stained the tips. Raven mustn't have noticed, as her gloved hand was soon in his as she helped him up.

"You're sure you're ok?"

"I nearly headbutted that." He pointed at the claw.

Eric turned from the hull. "You didn't damage it," he said frostily, then joined Maya at the spherical docking section their path barred by the robotic cargo module lying at right angles to the main station. On the other side, at the tip of the Tiangong, the Shenzhou module was attached. Three free access points circled around it, one against the flight deck, another on top, and the last on the opposite side of the station.

Eric quickly walked to the end of the cargo cylinder. The multi-ringed docking point there had been chosen as their access point.

"There's a little growth in these seals," Maya pointed out. "Would that be enough to prevent the Shenzhou from leaving?"

Eric cast a quick gaze over it. "No." He paused, peering closely at the docking ring above it.

"What is it?"

"Nothing. It's clear too." He unclipped a power-drill from his belt. Engineers on the Chinese carrier had fashioned an attachment that would perfectly fit into the external lock to grant them access.

"Whatever external growth there was probably burned off on re-entry," Scott said as he joined them.

"Why is there some left on the hull?" Maya asked.

That was bothering Scott, too. "This could have grown in the water. Whatever it is, it appears to be bonded with the hull material."

Eric ran a hand around the docking ring. "This was used for their last spacewalk. They'd assumed the newest section might be the least contaminated."

For a moment, Scott wondered why the airlock hadn't been used for evacuation if they hadn't been able to detach the Shenzhou. Then he remembered that all the airlocks had seized. Besides, 393km above the earth, where could they go?

With the while world at their feet, they had been completely isolated.

The rasping whirl of the drill focused everybody back on

the hatch as Eric gave the lock a full turn. The clunk of retracting spars within the door resonated through the entire craft. When he stole a quick look at his companions, Scott could see apprehension marring Eric's face.

Then he slid the drill out and pulled the manual-release lever.

With a hiss, the hatch spiraled open, and they all felt the breeze from the darkness within expelled in one long mournful wail.

FIFTEEN

SPARS of fibrous growth crisscrossed the entrance like a spider's web, similar in appearance to the material coating the hull, but as thick as a wrist. The gaps beyond revealed nothing but pitch darkness.

Even through his hazmat suit, he felt the sharp rise in temperature. Condensation formed on the outside of his visor. Scott wiped it away as he knelt, the flashlights built into his hood revealed the spherical airlock beyond.

The passage leading into the cargo module was set at ninety-degrees preventing him from seeing further inside. "All the hatches are covered inside but," he squinted, confused by what he saw, "the central airlock is clear. As if..." he stopped himself, adding *as if intentional*. "The growth rate of this thing in here... it's incredible."

Eric waved a small phone-sized probe through the gap and looked at the screen. "38 degrees, 91% humidity. 20.95% oxygen..."

"It's like a rainforest in there."

Eric nodded. "And beyond the habitat's parameters. Should be 21 degrees, about 42% humidity."

Scott raised his voice. "Hello? Anybody hear me?" Within, his voice was dull, muted by the tangled growth inside.

He angled his head, aware his helmet would muffle any faint reply. He found it difficult to believe anybody could be alive in such a foul hellhole, but what had made the noises?

"Scott? Bowers! Let me remind you this is a rescue mission, not a sightseeing tour," Raven's reminder was aimed that their in-helmet cams were recording everything for later scrutiny; now was not the time to be delicate.

Scott tugged at the nearest tuber. It felt as if bolted in place. He unhooked a small circular blade power saw from his belt. The high-torque blade squealed as it bit through the growth, casting a fine mist of particles as Scott was forced to apply pressure to get it through. "It's like sawing through hardwood," he muttered as he cut the opposite end of the spar. It fell from the hatch with a clatter.

Scott was keen to examine the severed tip.

"This looks like *mycelium*. I can't quite make it out..."

He heard Maya over his intercom. "My-what?"

"Mycelium. That sort of fibrous growth you get in fungus."

"Doctor Bowers, please!" snapped Raven.

He was dripping with sweat from the constant warm flow from within, as he cleared another spar that blocked their path. He passed both back through the airlock for Raven to place on the deck for later analysis.

Once cleared, Eric positioned himself at the hatch and hesitantly climbed in. The tunnel leading into the main module was less that a meter in diameter. Ample room in zero-G, but awkward in a hazmat suit in full gravity.

On his hands and knees, he disappeared into the module. Only his grunts and sniffs filtering over the radio intercom could be heard. Then:

"The end of the module is clear of blockages, although that stuff is over the walls. Everywhere. It's damp too. Thin layer of water on the floor... covered in debris. It's like a steam bath in here. Temperature 41.7. Condensation on my visor's making... visibility is..." His words faded into heavy breathing.

Crawling into dark tight spaces was an inherent part of Scott's job. They were the favored home for extremophiles. His heartbeat rose with growing anticipations he clambered after Eric. Like most social cue, fear was an emotion he'd seldom experience – but he was approaching something close to it. The cargo module was willed with a fog that kept visibility to just a meter. He could barely make out the pale smudged from Eric's light.

"I'm coming in.".

The floor was littered with fragments, many unidentifiable, but amongst them broken glass, smashed cases, tools and implements, each of which had been shaken almost to destruction. It was a carpet of sharps, each a threat to the fragile hazmat suits. Scott's glove touched on a book, its pagers glued together by water, the Chinese writing undecipherable to him. Other personal positions poked from the carpet of junk.

"See anything, Eric?"

No response. The light ahead didn't seem to move. Scott's skin prickled from the excessive heat and he was already finding it difficult to breathe despite his self-contained breathing system being regulated.

"Feel like a boil in... the bag..." the words were almost too much effort to say.

Breathe and inch forward. That's all he seemed to have the strength for. Even though the Tiangong was palatial compared to the Triton that he'd visited the depths of the earth in, the mist added to the claustrophobia. He had never been prone to panic, but unwelcome pangs of agitation suddenly turned his stomach accompanied by an encroaching feeling of foreboding.

It was irrational, of course, but that didn't make it any easier to bear.

Rivulets of condensation trickled down the inside of his faceplate. He shook his hood, hoping to displace them, but that spread the problem. His head knocked something on the deckhead. He could just see more fibrous growths stretching across the side like biomechanical limbs bracing the structure together.

He suddenly became aware Eric's light had vanished.

"Eric?"

The long hiss of static was eventually interrupted by Raven.

"What's going on?"

"I've lost sight of him." The cargo module ended in another airlock section, this one spherical from which the Shenzhou and two branching modules were attached. "Eric, can you hear me?"

Still nothing.

With his own amplified breathing echoing in his ears, Scott edged forward, his light piercing the fog. More growths had spiraled around the rim of the airlocks, preventing them from closing. Again, the floor was littered with debris. He glanced down the length of both side modules. More enormous mycelium spars crisscrossed the access to the Tiangong's main capsule, meaning Eric couldn't have gone that way. The space to the left, into the Shenzhou, was clear. It made sense that if he was searching for the crew, he'd head straight into the life support module.

As his eyes adjusted, he thought he saw the pale glow of Eric's light through the moisture on his visor and the thickening mist.

Crouching, he crossed the airlock, things crunching under his booted feet. "I'm entering the Shenzhou."

Here the temperature was unbearable, and he found it difficult to speak let alone breathe. Hearing the sound of his own breathing caused him to breathe harder. The first time he had dived, he'd done the same thing, almost hyperventilating until his instructor had calmed him. He sucked in a breath and held it, forcing himself to slowly breathe.

Then he entered the Shenzhou.

White fangs loomed from the gloom – forcing him to duck. It was more growth that hung like stalactites halfway down to the floor. Scott had to drop to all-fours to see the back of Eric beyond, crouching half way down the Shenzhou. Straps and belongings hung from military netting bolted to the walls, still gently swaying where Eric had disturbed it.

"Eric?"

Eric said nothing. He didn't move.

Scott ducked under the hanging growths and straightened up as best he could. He slowly reached out to tap him on the shoulder – but froze when he saw what Eric was looking at.

The end of the capsule was a spiraling mass of thick growth, the surface damp from condensation. The material looked fibrous and veiny, with a large bulge at the center of the mass. Two distinctive humanoid forms... the emancipated forearm of one protruding from the husk.

They'd found the crew.

Eric slowly turned to glance at Scott. Even behind the fogged visor there was no mistaking the shock and horror on his face as he turned back in time to see the fingers twitch.

SIXTEEN

A ROLLING SERIES of images butted into one another with no recourse to logic.

Ruth's wails of labor echoed around the brightly lit Tiangong module, which had been kitted out as a surgical theatre. With the unfocused malaise of a nightmare, Scott watched as fibrous tendrils extended from the bed, wrapping around her wrists and ankles with such force he could clearly hear bone snap over her screams.

Then she abruptly give birth to their child. A hideous warped abomination that burst from her pelvis in a torrent of gore.

He sat bolt upright, breathing hard and soaked with a sheen of cloying sweat. It took several moments for him to recognize his cabin. His cabin light was still on. He hadn't the energy to extinguish it as he'd been asleep the moment his head had hit the pillow. After returning, and a thorough decontamination scrub with sharply bristled brushes and a cocktail of chemicals, he'd donned a loaned medical gown to return to his quarters. Even so, the room felt uncomfortably warm despite the air con being on max.

A quick glance at his Omega told him it was 4:30am. The orange decals on the buttons edging the bezel and fabric strap, appeared to glow from within until he rubbed his eyes, settling his vision.

The growth's apparent fungal quality had bothered him. On emerging from the Tiangong, Eric had complained the sunlight was too bright. He'd quickly adjusted, but Scott was all too aware of some fungus' psychotropic capabilities. Finally, he'd tossed the worry aside; the hazmat suits hadn't been breached, and the ship's doctor had put their symptoms down to stress combined with acute jetlag.

He rose from his bed and padded across to the sink to pour a glass of water. It had a vague chemical taste to it, having been pumped through the ship's desalination plant, but it was palatable and quenched his veracious thirst.

Despite the evidence, he had harbored real doubts about finding any of the crew alive. Let alone both of them. The other man had been completely covered by the material, but the occasional faint sounds of respiration could just be heard when he pressed his visor against it. Through a process he didn't understand, the cocoons must have kept them alive throughout the entire ordeal. Raven had led the paramedics through and he had been careful to instruct them to cut the entire cocoon mass around the bodies so they could be extracted as one mass.

A medical ward had been constructed in one of the pressurized tents set up in the hangar, and the large cocoon had been placed on three tables shoved together. Scott and the ship's surgeon – a woman called Maltese – reasoned that immediately freeing the astronauts – or *taikonauts*, as Eric kept correcting them - from the husk could endanger them. Who knew what symbiotic progress was keeping the men alive.

Blood samples were taken from the single exposed arm, an IV line had been inserted to deliver nutrients. The first examination of the blood sample under the microscope had showed some sort of infection swimming amongst the cells.

An infection for sure, but Scott hypothesized that the infection may be the very thing keeping them alive.

Maya and Eric had been quickly removed as they observed the proceedings. For all intents and purposes, it appeared that their job was over. Scott had taken several samples from the cocoon, then Alanis escorted him to his lab where several of the larger fibrous growths he had cut from the hatchway now lay in sealed inspection units.

Gloves, attached via air-tight cut-outs in the side of the units, enabled him to handle the specimens and take samples via an airlock to be analyzed in a Renishaw Biological Analyzer, a chunky desktop machine that would help him discover the growth's chemical makeup.

Time ran away with him as he sank into his routine. Every pass at the samples produced interesting yet contradictory data that gnawed deeper into his curiosity. One thing was clear, the biology at once both familiar and alien. Only when he left the lab to find a toilet, did he realize that an armed guard was standing outside.

Protecting whom from what, he wondered...

SCOTT FOLLOWED the yellow line on the floor that led him to the refectory. Aside from the guard, who remained at his door and only acknowledged him with a curt nod, he didn't pass a single soul. Every door he passed was sealed, leaving no doubt that he was confined away from the rest of the crew.

One of the several mess halls had been set up specifically for those on the active assignment. Which meant a single cook, a red-headed chef, served the five crew who sat in the corner. Coffee, orange juice, bacon, scrambled eggs and fried tomatoes were heaped on his plate before the chef turned back to a low conversation with Alanis, who gave Scott a quick greeting before resuming her conversation.

Scott joined Maya, who was alone in the corner, slowly eating a bowl of muesli.

"Mind if I join you?"

"As you can see, we're fighting for space." Her normal sparky persona seemed to have dimmed.

"Sleep well?"

She shook her head. From the dark patches under her eyes, he wondered if she'd slept at all. "I kept thinking about those poor men." Her voice was low, eyes darting around the room as if worried they'd be overheard. Raven hadn't explicitly told them not to talk to anybody, but there had been a suggestion they shouldn't speak until spoken to. "How is that possible?"

Scott prodded his eggs, but his appetite had suddenly deserted him.

"A ran a few simple tests," he hesitated, debating just how much he should say at this stage. Raven had supplied him with a satellite uplink to the US Army's Medical Research Institute for Infectious Diseases (USAMRIID), but so far the traffic had been very one-sided and his requests for information went unheeded. "The cocoon, the fibrous growths inside the Tiangong, in fact, that fine coating outside the hull, are all the same genetic material. I think the outside may have been covered, like the interior but it burnt off during re-entry."

"Raven said they identified the coating on the outside as plankton."

Scott couldn't suppress the flicker of doubt, and judging by her reaction, she saw it too. "Not exactly. Plankton is a collective term, these particular plankters appear to be phyto-plankton."

"Let me guess, that means they need light. Like plants?"

"They're photosynthesizing, yes."

"Which is why they flourished on the solar panel."

"Makes sense. What doesn't is how they survived at depth. I suspect the chemical makeup of the geothermal activity were the key to that. There's a lot of candidates, phytoplankton forms 1% of the earth's entire biomass."

"Jesus. We're seriously outnumbered." Scott smiled. Maya's deadpan humor appealed to him. "If these things are usually so small, why are we looking at some kind of giant mushroom?"

"I've seen similar fungal-like cell structures in phyto-plankton blooms..." He saw her shake her head slightly. "They happen in oceans across the world. You may have seen them on the news, changing the color of the water so as to be seen even from space."

"I think so. They stretch for miles and turn the water kinda pale blue."

"Sure. Colors change. You might have heard of red tides that choke life in the oceans?" She nodded. "That's a dinofla-gellate—"

"Dino? Should I be afraid?" She managed a flickering smile.

"Well, these dinos are real small algae, known as *Karenia brevis*. No known species grows in such a way we are seeing."

"You said you think the outer coating fired in the atmosphere. I've been thinking about the logistics here. How the station, which is as aerodynamic as a brick, could come down in one piece. And in such a way that the crew weren't killed."

Scott swirled the food on his plate. That had been the last thing on his mind before he had crashed out on the bed.

"And what were your conclusions?"

She thoughtfully stirred her muesli, but her appetite had vanished. "Okay, purely from a speculative engineering point of view Eric and I ran some numbers on the Tiangong's load bearing constraints, heat shield limits, and so on. Without doubt. It should have burned up on re-entry. The only way to avoid that is if it wasn't moving."

Now it was Scott's turn to flash a bemused look. Maya took a salt pot from the table.

"This is the Tiangong in orbit." She dragged it around her plate. "Moving at 4.7 miles per second. As it hits the atmosphere, air creates fiction which created heat."

"Got it."

She stopped moving the salt. "But if an object slowed to almost zero, it could drop into the atmosphere with no resistance and plummet to earth." She lifted the salt and moved it over the center of her plate. "That's the whole principle of a space elevator."

"But it would still be destroyed on impact."

"That doesn't matter because then it would be falling at

terminal velocity, which is 122 miles per hour. Air hitting the superstructure would easily rip it apart." She slid the salt shaker back across the table. "*Then* whatever is left would be destroyed on impact. Hitting water at that speed is like hitting concrete." She pushed her half-eaten bowl aside. "And the G-forces would have killed the crew, anyway. And without life-support systems, I don't see how they could survive for that long."

"That's where the phytoplankton comes in very useful. It sucks in CO_2 and pumps out oxygen extremely efficiently. The Russians used algae on Gagarin's first space launch. Theoretically, that could create enough oxygen for them to breathe." The idea was appealing on the surface, but riddled with convenient coincidences that provoked Scott's doubt. "But we're fragile creatures. They really should have died."

Maya slowly nodded in agreement. "Finding them like that..." she shivered at the memory. "It's hit Eric real hard. He feels as if it's somehow his fault."

She looked around, checking nobody was paying them any attention, and her voice lowered.

"He's been going nuts. They won't let him talk to directly to the Liaoning or to CAST. Everything has to go through Raven, and she is being a tight-lipped bitch. He's convinced they're not sharing information with his people. I was hustled out of the room when he went ballistic on Raven. He accused her of holding him captive."

"Shit."

"Yep."

Scott stared at the salt shaker.

"What if the Tiangong was cushioned?" It took a moment for her to realize he was still a beat behind the conversation. He grabbed the salt shaker and wrapped it in his cloth napkin. "If the growth covers the entire ship as it ground to a halt in orbit, then plummets straight down." He dropped the napkin on the floor, before picking it up and revealing the shaker was still in one piece.

Maya was on the back foot with the sudden conversation reversal, but she quickly recovered. "I suppose, but just how tough is that stuff? You cut through it with a saw."

Scott felt his fatigue ebb away as his mind raced. "Maybe it behaves one way in a vacuum, then differently when exposed to oxygen or water?"

Now Maya latched on to his train of thought. "So inside the craft it then acted as some sort of reinforcement?"

"Like scaffolding..." He recalled the lattice like structures inside the craft.

"That's... one hell of a super-material."

"Isn't it just," he mumbled as the implications surfaced.

"But how did it get inside?"

"The spacewalk."

"Possibly."

Then Scott remembered something. "The spars supporting the solar panels had the growth in them. What if... what if..." he trailed away, the idea seemed impossible.

"Keep me hanging," Maya said wryly.

"If at some molecular level it could use the wiring. The same way a virus can get through cell walls to spread an infection."

"I thought multicellular organisms were too larger to do that?"

"Yeah..." He signed. "And I suppose if the spacewalk even just the smallest amount got inside on a tool or the spacesuit. They didn't have any decontamination procedures in place."

Further speculation halted when Alanis hurried up to their table, her radio gripped in one hand.

"Professor Raven needs you to suit up. Something has happened."

SEVENTEEN

"WHAT THE BLOODY hell were you thinking?" Scott batted Raven's restraining hand from his shoulder. "We discussed this–"

"No Doctor Bowers, you gave your *opinion*."

Beyond the plexiglass screen, the patient's fingers tensed momentarily as if in pain. The most exposed taikonaut, who carried the moniker Patient One, had been partially cut from his husk. Now a layer, about a centimeter thick, followed the contours of his naked body with visible veins running his length, making him resemble a crude waxwork.

Filaments of the growth covered his eyes and ran into his mouth, nasal passages and ears. How the growth was allowing him to breathe was a mystery, but an EEG monitor supplying an up-tempo irregular beat indicated he was still very much alive.

"You were right. There appears to be a symbiotic relationship between the fungal growth and the man." Raven indicated to a monitor showed a computerized tomography scan of the man's entire body showing dark tubers riddling deep into his body. It had even infiltrated his skull, finer tendrils woven into his brain.

Despite his anger, Scott's scientific curiosity was getting the better of him. "The fibers aren't just helping him breath."

"No. Here they appear to have entered his veins like an IV." She swapped images to a close-up of the head. "These tendrils encompassing the whole brain and wrapped around the spinal cord, here. Our doctor is baffled by what's keeping him alive."

Scott was reminded of a spider cocooning its victim to savor as a live meal later. He slowly moved closer to the patient, irrationally expecting the growth to move protectively over its host. Kneeling for a closer look, he angled a table lamp close to the phytoplankton growth. Even through his hazmat visor, he could see it was covered in erect fine filaments.

"It's as if the husk is drawing nutrients from the air."

"Enough to keep him alive?"

"In order to keep *it* alive. Hosts generally serve as either food or a source of reproduction. Often both. The capsule was humid, damp. Maybe the perfect environment for it to thrive."

"Are you saying a fungus was terraforming a space station?"

"It's not uncommon for animals, even simple bacteria, to optimize their environment."

"But that would require some form of intelligence, surely?"

"Intelligence is subjective." From the look on her face Scott regretted choosing that moment to glance at her. He hadn't consciously intended it as a slight. "Old currency had it that communication was a sign of intelligence. Now we know even bacteria and plants communicate."

"Come on..."

"Studies prove it. Haven't you heard of the mycorrhizal network?"

"What do you think?"

"Okay, it's more commonly known as the wood-wide web. Trees communicate with each other using chemical releases, entangled roots and – importantly here – a symbiotic relationship with fungus that live on the root structures."

"That's..." she shook her head, clearly shocked. "You know I am a vegetarian, right?"

"I didn't. But these days that doesn't give you any moral superiority. They may not have brains, but Venus flytraps can *count*. They only close when five or more hairs are triggered by a hapless fly. Fewer, and the trap doesn't close. Not only that, they also have to be triggered within a set time period. Which indicates the plants also process *time*."

Raven stared at him, but said nothing more. She folded her arms and regarded the patient.

"So what exactly are we dealing with here? Some alien life that has just stopped at the Tiangong for a drive-by snack?"

As a medical doctor, Scott's wife has always claimed she maintained an emotional void between her and the patient. It was the only way she could treat them effectively. The moment she regarded them as a person, the burden of responsibility came crashing down on her. However, seeing Raven's detachment to the man before her spiked a chord of anger within him. Now more than ever he could do with Ruth here...

No, not here. Not in the middle of nowhere, carrying their child around a potentially violent pathogen–

He forced the thought away.

"Panspermia can't be ruled out." Personally, Scott didn't subscribe to life starting beyond the solar system then hitching a ride on a comet until it found earth. To his mind, it was a convenient passing of the buck: *how did life start elsewhere?* Yet...

"Hubble photographed geysers bursting from Europa, shooting miles into space. If there was life in the ocean under that frozen crust, then it's just possible..."

"So you're saying this could have come from Jupiter's moons?"

Scott raised his hand. "No, I'm just hypothesizing. A remote possibility. It's more likely the plankton came from our oceans. Whipped into the stratosphere by storms. With the radiation up there, it could have mutated..."

It sounded just as doubtful as the Europa theory, but it was the only rational concept he could cling on to at the moment.

"How's the other guy?" He stood and peered through a partition window that split the tent in two. No attempt had been made to free the second taikonaut, who was connected to an identical battery of equipment.

"Stable."

Scott turned back to Patient One. "What possessed you to cut him free?"

"His BP dropped to 62 over 41, BPM was down to 29. We thought it might help, but there was a sharp spike in BP and heart rate the moment we started cutting. As if he was feeling its pain. Other than that, they don't appear to respond to outside stimulus and the EEGs of both of them are consistent with a coma."

"Coma? There must be some consciousness happening here." He looked thoughtfully at Patient One's twitching fingers. "He was calling for help down there. Somehow he was aware we close. When we were surfacing, they deliberately made a noise to attract our attention."

"We don't know it was deliberate."

From her expression, he supposed she was thinking the same thing. How was could they possibly have been aware, cocooned in a dark tin can at the bottom of the ocean? Was the symbiont somehow stretching the man's perception abilities?

"Until we understand what is happening here, no attempted should be made to cut them free."

"Agreed."

Scott turned to watch Raven's expression as he added: "I need Maya and Eric with me too."

He had been unsettled when Maya hadn't been allowed into the room with him. Along with the guard at his lab door, he felt a tingle of authoritarian big-brother about the way they were being treated.

"If you need an assistant—"

Scott held up his hand. "Environmental factors may well be affecting how that thing grows. Eric knows the spacecraft. He knows how pollutants, rare metals and chemicals react."

"And Doctor Johnson?"

"She has a degree in chemistry and engineering and understands marine environmental factors. More importantly, she has first-hand experience of what is happening. And what about the Chinese?"

He saw Raven's face pinch slightly. "What about them?"

"Do they have any specialists we can utilize?"

Her pause was brief, but telling as she decided how much to tell him. "Our Chinese friends are not entirely happy with us at the moment."

"Because you stole the Tiangong?"

She raised her eyebrows questioningly.

"Hardly stole. The facilities here are superior."

"But that wasn't what was agreed, was it? And I've seen no Chinese crew around."

Raven sighed and sadly shook her head. "It's political bickering, Scott. Not something we should be concerning ourselves with."

From her tone, he believed she was frustrated with the situation. However, surrounded by bristling warships, submarines and god-only-knew what else, he questioned her choice of 'bickering'.

It was hardly bickering when an armed skirmish could break out at any moment because of the simplest misunderstanding.

EIGHTEEN

ENDLESS OCEAN. A plane so flat and calm it was possible to perceive the curvature of the earth in all directions. On one side, the cerulean sky blended with the water, whilst the opposite horizon was a strip of vivid orange as the sun kissed the earth.

Scott clutched his coffee with both hands for warmth. What breeze there was carried a chill, but the sunlight blanched the cloudless sky, warming his face. He savored the feeling, not daring to close his eyes. He had been below decks for close to two days without a hint of the outside world, and only when he snapped at Raven, refusing to do any more work, were the three of them allowed to go outside.

Even then, they were contained to the fly tower deck, although it offered the best view for a thousand miles around.

Below, the Tiangong was now covered by a tent, a practical move to house and prevent potential contamination. Eric muttered it was merely to keep the Chinese blind. The Liaoning and two Chinese frigates lay to port, with no sign of activity on their decks. Circling the USS Gerald R. Ford was a sleek destroyer, USS Paul Ignatius. Its menacing phalanx CIWS (or sea-whiz as the crew call it) Gatling gun was pointed slightly away from the Chinese carrier, but the threat was hardly subtle. The Ventura sat between the two superpowers, and crew could be spotted walking the decks, exercising or smoking as they gazed into the endless expanse. The atmosphere of busy purposefulness that had welcomed Scott and his team had now evaporated into stillness. The constant buzz of aircraft flitting between ships had ceased.

All sense of time, place, and civilization was slowly eroding.

"We are nothing more than prisoners. You both realize that?" Erik spoke quietly. Below deck he had kept conversation purely focused on work, his eyes constantly straying to the security cameras that seemed to be everywhere. Now outside, savoring the pure air, his thoughts had become vocal. "No communication to the outside world. Kept from the rest of the crew."

The latter hadn't been strictly true. While a majority of the crew were still kept off the flight deck and out of the hangars, the team could once again eat with them since Raven had declared there was no risk of contamination.

"Security protocols..." Scott began, but stopped when Eric gave a dismissive huff. He glanced inside the tower where Maya was animatedly talking to Alanis. From their smiles, it could be just another ordinary day, but he knew Maya was equally concerned with their increasing isolation. She was just good at faking it.

Erik spoke up again and nodded towards the Chinese aircraft carrier. "I asked to speak to the Captain. They refused. What do you think will happen if they keep this up?"

"As far as we know, they're sharing everything we know."

"We are at the Great Wall of Silence. My country won't allow anybody to sail off with their property and kidnap their citizens."

"Eric, I know we're all feeling cabin fever, but talk of stealing and kidnapping isn't constructive. If there were any hostile intentions, don't you think you'd have military jets screaming overhead just to prove a point? Besides, what do we have to tell them?"

He knocked back the rest of his coffee, enjoying the last dregs warming his throat. His studies of the growth had failed to identify the phytoplankton. The larger spar samples tested positive for chitin, a long-chain polymer that formed the cell walls of fungi. Except this one was combined with some unidentifiable elements, which made it incredibly strong. Eric had begun referring to it as the building material of the future.

It was all new territory for them.

Scott had been quick to squash sudden claims that it was of extra-terrestrial origin, pointing out there were numerous extremophiles on earth that hadn't been studied or classified.

However, the growth was ideally suited for the vacuum of space, hanging in some form of suspended animation before apparently being triggered by the warmth of the sun to profligate across the Tiangong's solar panels.

Eric and Maya had used a majority of their time to piece together the mission data to create a timeline of events.

From first detection, the growth had taken over the solar panels within two weeks, resulting in a catastrophic power failure nine days later as the station's batteries dwindled. The crew had conducted five spacewalks in an attempt to clean the panels and during that time the infection had entered the module. Exactly how was still unknown.

It took four days for the growth to seal the airlocks both inside and out. A second computer controlled Tainzhou cargo craft had been sent up to pave the way for a Shenzhou module to rescue the crew, but the craft had been unable to dock. They were able to study the Tainzhou's external cameras that had relayed images back to mission control showing the extent of the problem. Fungal-type growths the size of automobiles clung to the Tiangong. Almost every inch was covered, those in direct sunlight forming the larger masses.

Assuming the growth had entered the module during the first spacewalk, it lay dormant for a further nine days before emerging like an angry cancer, spreading inside the hull at an alarming rate. Ticking over on emergency power, the life support systems all but failed. Remarkably, the growth could alter the internal atmosphere so quickly; it became the only thing keeping the crew alive.

Fearing the possibility of the infection spreading the earth, Mission Control made the grave decision to de-orbit the Tiangong and allow it to burn up in the atmosphere. Communication with the crew had already been lost; they would have been obvious to their intended fate.

Once the command had been given for deorbit and the last of the power used by the thrusters to maneuver into position, all comms died. The Tiangong's internal monitoring devices ceased, so what happened between that moment and it reaching the bottom of the ocean, went unrecorded.

The hiss of the pneumatic hinged door made him turn to the bridge as Maya stepped out, gleefully inhaling a deep breath. Alanis stepped half out, keeping the door open.

"Break time is over, gentlemen."

Despite, or perhaps because of, her constant upbeat demeanor, Scott was beginning to develop dark thoughts about Alanis. Her friendly brown eyes, and dark skin would otherwise be considered pretty, but he was beginning to feel it was a mask.

Stop it, he berated himself. Isolation had a way of twisting the mind, so even the friendliest of people turned on one another. Not that they had been away for long. Perhaps it was a sign Eric's paranoia was rubbing off on him.

"Back in the dungeon?" Eric quipped.

Alanis's smile didn't falter. "Professor Raven is adamant you keep to the schedule."

"Are you going to force us down there?"

Alanis's smile didn't budge, but her eyes hardened and her knuckles gripped the door handle just that little bit tighter. Despite her slight frame, Scott had little doubt she was more than capable of handling herself. A young woman in the Navy wouldn't be an easy target for anybody. Maya must have seen the same change in attitude as she quickly intervened and gently touched Eric's shoulder.

"It's getting dark, anyway. Colder too."

Eric spat over the side of the rail, then gave a terse nod. He took a step past Scott – then stopped, causing Scott to walk into him.

"Sorry..." his sentence faded as he followed Eric's gaze to the water.

"What is that?"

Scott moved back to the rail, gripping it tightly to quell a slight sense of vertigo as he craned over the edge to get a clear look at the water below.

The ocean was glowing around the ship, milky strands of

phosphoresce formed in the lee of the ship's dark side. Alanis and Maya joined him, both taken by the sight.

"Wow..." cooed Maya. "Looks neat."

Alanis pointed to the Ignatius. "It's there too."

The water around the destroyer emitted a soft glow, brighter in the ship's wake as it patrolled around the aircraft carrier.

"Chemiluminescence," said Scott. "Probably bioluminescence."

"Is that normal?" asked Eric with a trace of alarm.

Scott hesitated. "It's natural, if that's what you mean. Usually caused by dinoflagellates." He noticed Maya glance at him as she recalled the name. "It happens when they're agitated, like if you swam through it. But I have never seen it like that before." He pointed back to the darker water.

As their eyes adjusted, they could all see fine glowing filaments in the water stretching out to the Ventura. Maybe fatigue was getting to him, but Scott couldn't shake the image that they were probing claws poised to snatch its prey from the water.

NINETEEN

"AS FAR AS YOU CAN ASCERTAIN?"

Captain Peers' fingers drummed the rim of his coffee cup as he re-read the report on the iPad. "They're words that wholeheartedly fail to summon any confidence."

Seated across the table, Scott's expression didn't flicker. The Captain carried an attitude of absolute authority and control, but in the realms of science he was completely out of his depth and his bluster drew that into focus.

Maya sat next to Scott, slouched back in the chair, exhausted. They had all been desperately working around the clock on seeking answers to what the growth was, and how they could save the lives of the taikonauts. Eric sat a few seats away, glaring defiantly at the captain. Raven was the only other person in the briefing room, slowly pacing back and forth.

"We're not here to build confidence, Captain," she spat back with an edge to her tone. Over the last day, her corporate façade had slowly crumbled, revealing cracks of a real person beyond. One, she even hinted, that had a family was keen to return to. "We're dealing with hard data, not how it makes you feel."

Peers' eyes narrowed, but he didn't take the bait. He glanced out of the window at the Chinese aircraft carrier still parked a couple of miles off their bow, his attention drawn by the scream of a Shenyang J-15 patrolling between them. The Chinese fighter had been circling for the past thirty minutes on a seemingly pointless exercise.

Scott tapped the table to draw the captain's attention. "The bioluminescence definitely comes from the Tiangong. It's a strain of dinoflagellates almost identical to the ones I swabbed from the spacecraft's hull."

As soon as they had seen it, orders were relayed, and a Zodiac deployed to take samples from the water. Scott had spent the night analyzing the samples before forcing himself to sleep. His watch told him he had managed a solid nine hours, but he still felt groggy as he resumed his analysis.

"The water pouring from the hull onto the deck went overboard. Our containment procedures were... well, non-existent."

Peers forced a smile as he turned to Raven. "So you fucked up, Professor?"

"We took the exact quarantine procedures we all agreed on–"

The Captain raised his hand, accepting the comment with a nod. "Fine. Question is, what do we do? Can we kill it?"

Scott frowned. "Kill it? We don't even know what it is yet. And why should we want to do that?"

"Having a biohazard in the water–"

"It's not necessarily a biohazard. It was growing at the bottom of the ocean before we pulled it up. Most dinoflagellates are harmless. As for killing them, they've been around since the Triassic period. They're pretty stubborn."

Raven stopped pacing. "You said they were almost identical. What do you mean, 'almost'?"

"There are about 4500 species, most of them in the fossil record. There's maybe 16 or 17 hundred still alive in the oceans. At least, the ones we know about. Now I keep sending data out to USAMRIID and I keep requesting information, but it's very much a one-way street."

"You know our work here is classified."

Maya gave a dry laugh, speaking for the first time since they had entered the room. "If it's so classified, why are we sending everything we know out to the world, but not hearing answers? Shouldn't it be the other way around? It's beginning to feel like a prison here. But without the social fun."

The captain put both elbows on the desk and steepled his fingers over his mouth as he looked intently at her.

"I'm sorry you feel that way, but we are not, by any means, operating under normal conditions here."

Eric sat upright, raising his chin defiantly. "That is correct. We are not. I wish to visit the Liaoning and discuss the situation with my superiors."

Peers shrugged and leaned back in his chair, flashing a friendly smile. "I assure you, your superiors are quite happy that you are here."

The statement was punctuated by another roar as the fighter jet circled again at high-speed.

"Never the less, I wish to discuss the matter with them personally."

"You want to go to them?" Peers waved his hand towards the distant aircraft carrier. "Go ahead. All you have to do is walk straight off the edge and swim. I'm sure they'll welcome you with a towel and hot tea."

Eric thumped the desk with a balled fist. "You are keeping me here against my will!" he shouted.

The calm measure in Peers' voice finally snapped. "God-damned it! You're here because *they* want you to be here! Not potentially infecting their ship!" He flicked a looked at Raven, who hadn't moved a muscle, then his voiced dropped to something more reasonable. "And we need you."

Eric flinched when Raven placed a hand on his shoulder, but she didn't remove it. "Professor, you're as much a prisoner here as any of us. Myself and the Captain included. But right now, we have two of your countrymen in critical condition, and we must get to the bottom of just what this thing is before they die. We have people back in the States, the UK and China all working on the information we're providing." She looked at Maya. "Please don't confuse our pressing desire to save the Taikonauts' lives with being inhospitable. We're just being practical."

It wasn't much of an excuse, but Eric seemed a little mollified.

Raven continued. "And I believe you made a discovery last night when the others were asleep."

That was news to Scott. Both Maya and Eric had excused themselves early as he pressed his analysis.

"I ran strain tests on a sample taken from inside the Tian-gong. The results were..." he shook his head. "They must have been incorrect."

"Why?"

Eric held up his hands. "I accept that ship out there is the one I helped build, which means that growth must have saved it on re-entry." He gave a sidelong look at Scott, a silent acknowledgement of this theory. "The sample I studied showed great rigidity. The closest comparison I could draw on is graphene."

Scott looked puzzled. "What is that?"

Maya answered for him. "It's a type of carbon, but incredibly strong. Like, a hundred times stronger than steel, but amazingly light. It was only discovered back in 2004, right under our noses."

"The growth has a similar two-dimension hexagonal lattice structure within it. I'm not entirely sure that has ever been seen in a living thing before."

Raven sat down at the end of the table as she processed the information. "So it's tougher than we thought?"

"Beyond any manmade material I have encountered. It appears a coating of the growth, reinforced by the internal spars, was enough to hold the Tiangong together during re-entry. From the tests I've conducted, it's resistant enough to absorb the heat of re-entry too. Then, as the craft sank, it also absorbed the water pressures, maintaining hull integrity."

"Sounds like a miracle find," Peers said, scratching his cheek thoughtfully.

Eric nodded. "If that is true, yes. Perhaps we have discovered the ultimate construction material. Imagine buildings you could grow!"

Raven nodded. "Indestructible aircraft."

Something was puzzling Scott. "If it's so tough, then how could be just cut it with a handsaw?"

"He's not saying it's tough," Maya pointed out. "Just that it can take the strain longitudinally." She moved her hands horizontally to demonstrate. "Think of the way an egg can withstand weight one way, but if you hit it in the side – just like you sawing those spars – then it can't hold its integrity and it breaks."

Raven gave a little laugh that was close to relief. "That's astounding. If you're right."

If Eric was about to defend his injured pride, he was drowned out by a sudden warning klaxon that screamed across the ship. Captain Peers stood so quickly that his chair slammed into the bulkhead. A voice then an icy calm voice punctuated the alarm:

"General quarters, general quarters - all hands man your battle stations!"

TWENTY

MAYA'S EYES were wide with alarm as the patter of dull thuds once more reverberated through the overhead piping conduits running through the lab. Scott thought about offering some words of comfort, but didn't trust his voice, as he was feeling more frightened than she looked.

Yeowoman Alanis had been shepherded down the internal stairwell as general quarters sounded. They passed a handful of crew dashing to their stations, but other than the grating siren, there was an abandoned air about the ship. Scott would have liked to have seen a few more people panicking, but it felt more like a Sunday tour of museum. They had been taken directly to the lab and told not to leave. The door had been shut and locked behind them as muffled dull thumps echoed through the steel superstructure.

"Are the Chinese shooting at us?" Maya had asked.

Eric scowled. "Why would you think that?"

"Because they're clearly pissed off with the Yanks stealing their property."

"And you think force is the only solution." Eric shook his

head sadly, then lapsed into one of his trademark silent sulks. The siren stopped, but the occasional staccato thumps continued off and on for another half hour.

Then silence.

They waited anxiously for a further twenty minutes before Scott tried the door.

"Still locked."

Maya slouched in a chair, put her feet up on table and closed her eyes.

"You're just going to sleep?" snapped Eric.

She didn't bother opening her eyes. "Unless you have a better idea?"

Nobody did. Scott examined the large specimen tank in which he had left the black coral sample. It now had twice as many tendrils spiraling off in all directions. A quick check of the environmental data revealed a peculiarity.

"Salinity is down," he muttered. The other two didn't respond, but it was an astonishing result. "It's halved."

Maya didn't move from her comfortable position. "So?"

"So the water in the tank is becoming fresher. The coral is acting like a desalination plant. They need salt to live, but this..."

"That's useful, right?"

It was. The implications about a natural coral being able to turn saltwater into drinking water could solve droughts... but at what cost to the ocean? The discovery was setting off an alarm in him, nothing he could put his finger on, but something...

To distract himself, Scott set about cutting a sliver from a sample of the cocoon Raven's team had taken from Patient One and placed it in the Life Technologies Ion Torrent Next-Generation sequencer, one of the many thoughtful machines the lab had been kitted out with. Hoping to get some identifiable information from the sample, he set the machine in motion just as the hatchway opened and Raven entered.

Eric was the first to jump to his feet to challenge her. "What is going on?"

Raven held up a hand to calm him. "There was a technical problem in the engine room. Nothing to worry about."

Maya rose to her feet, casting a disbelieving eye at Raven. "I thought the Chinese had opened fire."

Raven frowned. "Why would you think that?"

Maya glanced at Eric but didn't answer.

"It was an equipment failure. It has dealt with."

"You locked us in here," Eric pointed out

"Because of the possibility of fire. Sooner you'd be safe in here than burnt to a crisp outside – not that there was a fire," she quickly reassured them, "but we can't be too careful. And right now you are the most important assets onboard."

Scott folded his arms, studying her carefully. Her hand was trembling, whether from fatigue or something else, he didn't know nor did he think he'd get a straight answer if he pointed it out.

She gestured to the door. "I guess you're all hungry. Lunch is being served in the briefing room."

Something felt off, but Scott couldn't quite pinpoint it. He realized he was scratching his arm. Beneath his shirt sleeve, his eczema was burning worse than ever. He hadn't brought his medication with him and was too stubborn to ask the ship's doctor for any antihistamines. In the heightened climate he feared it would lead to a round of pointless medical scrutiny.

Maya and Eric were both on their feet in silent acceptance of Raven's offer. Scott cast one last look around the lab before following.

The hiss of the closing door blotted out the sudden bleeping as the DNA sequencer begged for attention.

THE VIEW from the briefing room's panoramic windows looked the same. If there had been any altercation with the Chinese, there was no evidence of it now, so Scott put that theory to bed.

While the spread of food on the table was more varied than the canteen, it looked hurriedly presented in foil trays, but the scientists' hunger wouldn't be sated by presentation and, along with Captain Peers and Professor Raven, they helped themselves to heaped plates.

The Captain regarded Eric and gestured his fork across to the Liaoning. "I have notified Admiral Liu that you are feeling homesick." A flash of irritation crossed Eric's face. The suggestion of weakness was not a characteristic he wished the share. Peers continued, "and they assured me you can go over with your fellow taikonauts. Just as soon as we can get them back on their feet."

For some reason, that rang as a hollow promise to Scott, but it seemed to satisfy Eric who gave a curt nod with a mumbled "thank you."

"I don't see why we can't talk to our families," Maya said.

Raven replied with a sudden clipped coolness. "I'm afraid secrecy is part and parcel of the operation. And your contract."

Maya's scowled response reflected her tone. "Do you have family, *Jan*?"

"A son. An architect in Boston."

"I'm sure you appreciate talking to him?"

"I can get by. As I am sure your husband can, too. And I'm sure the payday you're receiving for your services here should certainly help."

The thunderous look on Maya's face forced the Captain to intervene. "We can allow external communications the moment we set sail. I give you my personal guarantee that the three of you will be the very first to call your families. Hell, I know my wife will be thankful for a few extra days radio silence from me."

His easy smile finally broke the ice, and both Scott and Maya chuckled. Even Eric broke a smile.

Did Scott catch a flash of relief across Raven's face? "Good. Now, Eric, your report on the structural make of the foreign material was extraordinary. This could be a truly revolutionary. The question is... where did it come from?"

Eric shrugged, and all eyes turned to Scott who shifted in his seat, uncomfortable with being the center of attention.

"I am waiting for the results on various tests, but at the risk of repeating myself, having some feedback from external agencies would have sped this along. The samples taken from the water next to the ship indicate it is the same material in a different state. It's as though..." he hesitated from finishing that thought, just under everybody's scrutiny he looked at the floor and continued. "As though we are either seeing the life-cycle of the phytoplankton as it matures through various environments. Or it is rapidly evolving, adapting..."

He gathered his thoughts. "It's fast growing, virulent almost. It appears both photosynthesis and the salt in the water are catalysts for its growth, which is how corals grow. But this isn't coral in any form I know of. The black coral we recovered from the crash site appears to have been mutated."

Raven cocked her head. "Mutated?"

Scott nodded. "The growth absorbed the natural black coral down there, then sped up its growth. The geothermal vents are pumping rare elements to the surface. Perhaps that is affecting it."

"You used the word virulent. So..."

"So we have a plankton, that in all aspects is acting like a virus."

Peers swapped a confused look between Raven and Scott. "Forgive me, but when you say plankton, I think of whale food."

"That's right," Scott said, "but it comes in a huge variety. They're *eukaryotes*, similar to bacteria. They move, hunt, reproduce. They're simple organisms, but much more complex than an ordinary virus."

Peers put down his fork and looked thoughtful. "That material we extracted from the shipside is proving to be an issue." He studied them for a moment, filtering his thoughts. "We sent divers down, and they... well you should see for yourself."

He tapped through a few options on a touchscreen, and the monitors on the desk came to life with handheld footage as a diver sat on the edge of a Zodiac, floating between the Gerald R. Ford and the Ventura. White streaks ran just beneath the surface, like pale pipelines. The diver splashed overboard, and the image became a torrent of bubbles. When they cleared, a gasp escaped the lips of the team.

The water was crystal clear. A network of white spindles running horizontally ten feet below the surface like the silken strands of a spider's web. Some spars the diameter of an arm, others had coiled and fused together like mighty tree trunks.

The camera turned, bringing the solid dark wall of the aircraft carrier into view. Below the water, the growth covered the hull.

Peers spoke as they watched the diver swim parallel to the ship. Spars branched out towards the direction of the rest of the fleet. "What started as that bioluminescent plankton rapidly assembled and solidified. We're completely encased in the growth. The engines are choked. All of this happened within twelve hours of taking the initial sample."

Maya leaned closer to the monitor as the diver edged towards the hull. "We were told there was a problem in the engine room."

"Because of this. The Paul Ignatius has the same problem. They're now encased too, joined to us by the hip, so to speak. That's billions of dollars of military hardware snagged by *plankton*. They suffered terrible critical failure. The growth is circling the Ventura." He glanced at Eric. "So far the Chinese haven't been reached. They have been shelling the water to destroy the growth." That explained the fighter plane's low level runs, Scott thought. "But It has a limited effect. After half a day, it regrows and we are back where we started."

Raven peered at the monitor over Scott's shoulder. "So when the Captain asked how we kill it, now you know why."

The footage ended, leaving everybody stunned. Finally, Maya spoke up.

"Critical engine damage? What's your definition of critical?"

It took a long moment for Captain Peers to respond.

"At this moment, the entire American fleet is dead in the water. And until we can get this under control, nobody else is coming within a thousand miles the rescue us."

TWENTY-ONE

ONCE AGAIN, they were escorted back to the lab by Alanis, this time in silence. Maya checked the Yeowoman wasn't too close and whispered to Scott.

"Have you noticed anything odd about our chaperone?"

"No." He always dreaded the conversations that inevitably veered towards discussing other people's feeling or behavior. His alexithymia made sure he'd missed every nuance.

"Something's been on her mind for a while now. At first I thought it was, y'know, being stuck out here. Just I've been seeing the looks she's been giving us."

"Not good?"

"Not good. Like you'd peed in her barbecue."

"Me?"

"Not literally. And not you. All of us. I don't think she trusts us. As if all this is somehow our fault."

Peers had made it clear they were dead in the water with no possibility of an airlift out – the seaplane that brought them here wouldn't risk the landing. The Liaoning was monitoring the growth and keeping a healthy distance, so it didn't become ensnared.

Re-entering that lab, they were immediately taken by the soft, alert tone from the DNA sequencer. Alanis paused in the doorway, watching as Scott studied the screen with growing interest.

"This can't be right..." be mumbled, typing commands to decipher the reams of data on-screen. "Something's buggered up."

"What's happened?" Alanis asked, still standing outside the room.

Eric looked over Scott's shoulder, but the data was unfamiliar. Bioscience was a gulf away from his realm of engineering. "What does it mean?"

Scott tapped a sequence of letters on the screen. "It's not defining the genetic structure." He saw the blank look on Eric's face. "It is calibrated to sequence for DNA, which we all have, or RNA, which is what viruses have."

He noticed both Alanis and Maya were paying more attention, although clearly not following.

"Life followed two basic paths, DNA and RNA." He used the index fingers on both hands to mime a divergent path. "All complex life on earth evolved from DNA. RNA is a polymer with a ribose and phosphate backbone. DNA is longer with a deoxyribose and phosphate backbone."

Maya rolled her eyes. "That's as clear as mud, doc."

"You're familiar with the spiral staircase image of DNA?" He spiraled his two index fingers around, bringing to mind the ladder like chain the others were familiar with from textbooks. "RNA only has one of those staircases." He left one hand fall away. "It's an older form of life, DNA succeeded it. All complex life is based on DNA. But this has detected *both* markers."

Eric shrugged. "So it has detected both in the sample? Surely that happens?"

"Not both. A hybrid. Three strands..." he shook his head. "Triplex DNA was a theory, wildly discarded... it was considered unstable. I need to run another batch. Something is corrupted here."

With Eric and Maya assisting, Scott prepared another sample for the sequencer. While the matching hummed to life, they noticed Alanis had silently left them. Minutes later the sequencer again beeped for attention. This time Scott instructed the computer to visualize the data for the benefit of the others.

Rather than the usual pair of spiraling sugar-phosphate backbones that formed the traditional sides of the 'ladder', there were three, with the 'rung' base pairs linking them together in a seemingly random pattern.

"Another error?" Maya asked.

"Highly improbable." Scott looked at the sample growth from which they had taken the sample. "That came from the crewman. If I had to guess, it is absorbing his DNA."

"Which means...?"

"It's adapting like a virus, integrating his DNA." A shiver ran through him. The consequences were alarming. He turned away, glancing at the security camera peering at them. "I need a fresh sample."

Maya was already heading to the intercom. "I'll ask Raven to come down."

Scott raised his hand to stop her. "No. I want to take it myself. Don't you think it's about time we took the initiative?"

They followed his glance towards the security camera.

IN THE END, it was Eric's engineering knowhow that had disable the security camera. He simply pulled the cable from the back. Alanis had left the hatch unlocked, and unguarded so they had no problem leaving.

Maya's acute sense of direction soon had them heading in the right direction, past several signs written in baffling military acronyms. They moved with purpose, aware that it probably wouldn't take long before their vandalism was spotted.

The first hatch they came to was sealed, blocking the corridor. Certain they were moving in the right direction, Maya spun the wheel lock. It turned with the minimal of effort and the hatch smoothly swung open, revealing a deserted passageway beyond. They stepped through.

This passageway was identical to the one they left behind, lit with the same intensity of fluorescent lighting. Nothing was out of place, yet there was something uncomfortable about it. The lack of sound, the lack of personnel.

"It's like a ghost ship," Maya's voice had dropped to a whisper.

"The air conditioning is off," Eric pointed out. "Listen."

The usual resonances from the air con were hugely noticeable once pointed out. The silence was absolute. Nobody was moving in passageways above. The crippled engines remained silent.

"Like the Mary Celeste..." Maya whispered.

They continued along, footsteps echoing as they strained to listen for the inevitable patter of Alanis's furious steps behind them.

They paused at another closed hatchway blocking their path.

"Are you sure this is the way?" Eric asked as he put his hand on the wheel to open it.

Maya huffed. "This is the way we entered to the hangar. On the same deck, straight aft. If you don't believe me go back and ask el Captain for directions."

Eric heaved on the wheel and the door fluidly opened.

"It feels wrong," he snapped.

There was a gentle rush of air as the hatch opened. Air rushing *in*, Scott noted. Beyond, the passageway was dark. Every light extinguished.

"Now *that's* wrong," Maya whispered, her hair moving in a sudden gentle breeze.

"Maybe a complete power outage in this section," Eric mused.

Scott wondered how that was possible. He was torn between going back, but goaded by curiosity to step into the darkness.

A darkness that was suddenly punctured by the flashlight on Maya's mobile phone. Her light scanned the corridor.

"Looks fine to me." She stepped through, taking the lead with her light. "I don't think the hangar is far off now."

The darkness amplified the stillness. Scott's palms became clammy, perhaps from nerves, but also from the increase in temperature. With no air con, the corridor was getting increasingly humid the further they progressed. Maya's light glinted off condensation forming on the deckhead.

The atmospheric comparisons with the Tiangong were unavoidable. An unspoken look between Eric and Maya indi-

cated they were thinking the same. Any doubts ground to a
halt when they reached the next sealed hatchway, and the
flashlight cast aside the darkness to reveal ten hazmat suits
hastily crumbled on the floor.

Eric swore in Mandarin, then added in English, "This is
a bad omen."

Scott felt his heart hammer his chest and automatically
froze at the sight of them. If they had been in a hazardous
environment, simply dumping potentially infected suits was
a disaster. Then he noticed the seals around the various
openings were still intact. The small markers would have
been damaged if the suits had been worn.

"Spares." He took a pent-up breath as he stepped closer,
crouching and to inspect them.

"Why leave them here?" Eric asked, looking around for
anything else out of place.

"They were in a hurry," said Maya in a low voice.

Scott handed him a suit. "I guess we shall find out when
we open that door."

The next several minutes were spent carefully putting
the suits on. Scott ensured they emptied their pockets of any
sharps that could puncture the suit. He had a pen in his
pocket. Eric took a USB stick from his, which he kept
pointing out had no sharp edges.

Internal radios hissed to life before their hoods went on.
A small bottle of oxygen, providing about fifteen minutes,
inflated the suits. Scott diligently checked his companions'
the pressure and calibrated the oxygen levels before checking
his own.Only when they checked the time elapsed time on
Maya's phone did they openly wonder why Raven hadn't yet
sent anybody to stop them. They should surely have been
missed from the lab by now.

Eric once again gripped the hatch wheel and braced himself to turn it. There was an unmistakable flash of fear in his eyes that even Scott recognized.

"Ready?"

When he received two thumbs-up, Eric spun the hatch open...

TWENTY-TWO

"HOLY SHIT..." the words choked in Maya's throat.

Scott was the last through the hatch, and he quickly closed it behind him, locking it. The dull thud made the other two jump.

"What the hell are you doing, locking us in here?" said Maya with alarm.

"It's not locked. Sealed, but it's only watertight. For a microbe, that's still a motorway to the rest of the ship."

"What do you think happened here?" Eric asked, nudging Maya's phone light towards the roof.

The walls and deckhead were black and charred. The standard grey paint had either burnt away or had peeled and blistered through the primer underneath, revealing scorched steel. Overhead pipework was buckled and damaged. Light fittings melted.

"Looks like a major engine malfunction to me," Maya moved closer to inspect the wall. She reached out to tug at a curled paint fragment.

"Don't!" Scott warned. "It could damage your glove."

Maya quickly retracted her hand. "I've been on many a wreck after a fire. The temperature must've been pretty severe to do this kinda damage."

"I would have thought the engine room was lower."

Maya's shrug was barely visible through her suit. "On old battleships I've been on, it sometimes runs the length of the ship. On a monster like this, I can't say. Thank god they got it under control."

She led the way forward. Eric kept close as they inspected the damage. Scott hung a few paces back. He was beginning to feel uncomfortably warm in the suit and beads of sweat were popping on his forehead.

"It explains the sealed bulkheads and air con," Eric pointed out. "A fire would have unleashed a lot of potentially dangerous pollutants, carcinogenics, maybe even some rare toxic elements."

They passed a stairwell which was sealed from decks both above and below, both hatches displaying significant fire damage. Scott wondered if the damage had reached the hangar itself. Would they have risked moving the quarantined taikonauts?

The locking wheel on the next hatch was buckled slightly, the product of intense heat.

"I reckon the hangar is through here," said Maya confidently.

Eric tried to turn the wheel, but it wouldn't budge. "The heat may have buckled the mechanism."

Maya handed Scott her phone and joined Eric, putting her strength in wresting the wheel around. There wasn't enough room for Scott to help, so he stood back and looked around.

The grunts of effort from the other two came over his

internal speaker, but his own breathing almost drowned them out. He was panting, almost as if he'd been running. The skin on his arms felt irritated, and he longed to scratch it, but didn't dare risk rupturing the suit.

He focused on calming down.

"It's budging," Maya said through grit teeth.

Scott looked around, swaying the flashlight to highlight the dark conduits overhead.

"Keep the light on us, mate!" Maya snapped.

Scott was about to – but something caught his eye overhead and he swung his light directly on it.

"Hey! The light!" Maya howled.

"Don't open the door!" Scott barked.

But it was too late. As the words spilled out, he heard the sudden clunk as the hatch's internal mechanism gave way.

"Scott, what're you..." Maya stopped when she saw the focus of his attention. "Are those...?"

"Yes."

Bullet holes pocked the conduits and the surrounding deckhead, leaving ugly fist size notches that indicated automatic weaponry.

Maya ran a finger along the rim of one. "What the hell were they shooting at?"

With a long hiss, the hatchway to the hangar swung open.

TWENTY-THREE

A TAUT PLASTIC sheet dripping with condensation blocked the hatchway. Scott pushed through, brandishing the light from Maya's phone. He stepped into the large plastic decontamination chamber they had entered the last time they were here. Beyond, the transparent wet walls was utter darkness. The others joined him, the sound of their respirators and constant dripping the only sounds.

Scott wiped his glove across the transparent plastic sheeting, displacing a curtain of water. He pushed the light against it to illuminate the void beyond. The sheets hung limply; the chambers weren't pressurized and therefore was now useless. Peering through the wall he couldn't make sense of what he was seeing. The others joined him, clearing their own condensation patches.

At first glance, it looked like a forest of spindly trees. A slight shift of the light added perspective, and they could now see the infectious growth filled the hangar beyond, vanishing in to the darkness of the roof.

Scott shifted the light over seven huge masses bulging

from the wall with, more stretching into the blackness. "What are those?"

"They're F-35s," whispered Maya, afraid her voice would disturb something unnatural. "Damn, I bet the whole fleet's been swamped."

They could just see rough shapes poking through: stubby wings or the occasional engine air intake, filled with vicious fibers burrowing into the mechanics. Two huge propellers snarled in gunk and a large saucer-shape poised above it - the enormous radar dish of an E-2 Hawkeye – showed nothing was beyond destruction.

"Remember that *fire*?" Eric's tone was bitter. "Raven lied to us. They all did." He pointed to the alien environment beyond the sheet. "This is what was happening."

Scott tried to recall when the alarm sounded. A day? Two days? "The growth rate is unprecedented."

"The stuff in the water is changing just as fast," Maya pointed out.

"True. But that was using the sodium chloride in the water. This is feeding off something else."

"We should go back. Surely they won't have left the taikonauts here," said Maya.

Eric huffed. "Do you trust them to care that much?"

Ahead, the airlock door, which should have been sealed, was wide open. Decontamination protocols had been ignored in a hurry. Scott took a tentative step half-though.

The sides of the plastic tunnel beyond had been torn apart and the rest of it was non-existent, just tattered plastic fragments hanging limply in the stale air.

Scott gently stubbed his toe against something stuck on the floor. He angled the light for a better look. It was a mass of melted plastic bonded to the floor. The surrounding metal was charred and black.

"Looks like there was an explosion." He circled the light around the remnants of the tunnel and back to the plastic globule. "Melted all of this."

He extended the light in one direction, towards the entangled forest.

Larger aircraft further down the line were completely choked by the growth, leaving only vague shapes like some nightmarishly wrapped presents.

The opposite wall, the light revealed a similar snarl of foreign growth around another line of aircraft. The last six in the row were nothing more than charred skeletons. The growth around them had thinned in the blaze, but remained intact.

Eric could resist a moment of pride. "It appears my heat calculations were correct."

Maya pointed to another hatch in the wall around which the fire damage appeared the worse. "I reckon the fire broke out there. Spread into a parallel corridor to the one we came down." She indicated to the entombed aircraft. "It's a miracle it didn't spread to the rest of these."

Scott frowned. "A miracle?"

She nudged his light and indicated to a series of cylindrical tanks on the wall. "They're full of avgas. I bet the fuel dump is towards the aft. If that caught, it could've blown a hole in the hull and we would have sunk pretty quick."

"Question is, what caused the fire?"

Scott swung the light back towards the aft section of the hangar and the partition wall that separated it from the second hangar. He wondered if the outbreak had spread in there. The aircraft elevator was raised flush to the deck above. The surrounding seams, and the hydraulic scissor-lift snarled thick with growth, giving the appearance of a warped tree at the center of a subterranean kingdom.

Beyond that, at the very far end, Scott was surprised to see the ragged torn flaps of the taikonauts' isolation tent were still intact. The fungus had formed around the tent, leaving only the entrance clear. Still, tendrils ran into the darkness inside.

Scott took a step – and felt Maya squeeze his arm.

"Do we really need to do this?" she asked.

"I need that sample if we are going to get a clearer picture of what is going on." He indicated to the lift. "Let's assume the spillage from above seeped down here, as it did in the water. That shows how vigilant the phytoplankton is. In a vacuum, in the ship, in the water. Wherever it goes, it finds fuel to speed up its growth."

"So they shot at it." Eric smiled at their quizzical glances. "They're American. That's what we heard. Sustained gunfire." He shrugged. "My countrymen tried to bomb it out of the water." He shrugged. "Human nature. Attack what we don't understand. When that failed, I wager they tried to incinerate it."

Scott stepped towards the remains of the tent, displaying more confidence than he felt. Closer, he could see the plastic had melted the fringes of the access corridor, and moisture-soaked melted ribbons hung limply. The flash-light illuminated the interior, which, to his surprise, looked intact.

He was glad of Maya's comforting presence closely behind him as he stepped into the tent. Gently parting a hanging sheet, he could see the Patient One still sunk into the block of growth on the table. A network of fungal filaments had spread out, smothering the monitoring equipment.

Even as Scott drew closer, it was impossible to tell if the man was still alive. His gaze swept the gnarled roots of the growth encroaching from outside. Probing tendrils had twisted together, connecting him to the larger mass outside.

"It's all fused together," he said in a low voice. "It's forming a single colony..."

The partition to the second crewman had been torn down by connecting coils, and if anything, the growth had doubled in size around him.

Eric and Maya kept to the entrance, refusing to touch anything.

"How are you going to get a sample?" Eric asked, uneasily glancing around, flinching at the sound of every droplet.

Scott had expected the lab would have been as they'd left it, complete with equipment. If there were any tools here, they were completely inaccessible.

He drew closer to the taikonaut's head. Here the growth remained thinner, and the contours of the man's face could just be discerned. His lips parted slightly with straw-like tendrils running into the edges of his mouth and down into his throat. It was impossible to tell if he was still alive.

Scott leaned closer, squinting for any sign of life.

The fibrous mass across the man's face was damp, droplets of water trickling into his open mouth. It was quite conceivable that he may have drowned, pinned to the table, if his swallow reflex was paralyzed. Then he recalled how the crewman had enough motor skills to tap for help.

Perhaps he was still conscious? Mummified in a living hell.

Scott reached for a growth around the man's jaw, which was just protruding enough for his fingers to dig underneath. A quick tug did nothing. It was as hard as concrete.

"I need a little help with the light," he called over his shoulder.

At first nobody moved, then Maya reluctantly joined him. She took her phone and positioning it as best she could so as not to cast grisly long shadows over the gnarled face. Then she gasped and flinched backward.

"What?"

She hesitated. "I thought... I thought I saw his eyelid move..."

"It's just the shadows."

Maya took a breath and positioned the light again.

This time Scott used both hands to pull at the growth. It was difficult to detect movement through the thick gloves, but he swore he heard a tiny crack.

"It has set like glue." He moved, using his knee as an anchor point. "I only need a small sample." How he was going to securely transport it back to the lab was another problem that suddenly crossed his mind.

He dug his fingers around the lip of the growth and put his weight into it as, with both hands, he heaved.

The noise was loud, like an iceberg lettuce being cleft in two.

The growth came away in his hands – and Maya screamed.

Scott watched his own movements in horror as the man's jaw tore away, still encased in the growth. The skin beneath was placid and frail, easily tearing with nothing more than a perfunctory splatter of blood, revealing bone and teeth.

His gaze was inexorably drawn from the gore in his

hand to the man's face. The missing jaw revealed a damp pale red hole straight into his throat. Most of the detail was blessedly obscured by fungal tendrils wrapped both in and out of his trachea, but the now-free tongue writhed like a dying snake.

Worse, the man's eyes were now open.

Pain registered in them, but not a sound was raised. They snapped shut, the flailing tongue flopping still.

Scott dropped the obscene jaw fragment and took a step back, his stomach heaving. He desperately swallowed the rising vomit. Puking in the suit would not be the ideal thing to do right now. Maya steadied him as he stumbled.

"Is he still alive?"

"I don't..." Scott fought for breath. "I don't know." He composed himself, averting his eyes from the man. A pointless act as the scene replayed in his mind. "Maybe he was dead already. That could've been his nervous system reacting."

"I don't think corpses do that."

"They do. They move after death as nerves trigger. There was hardly any blood." he forced himself to look at the body. There was almost no bleeding, like the last dregs in a pipe. A body couldn't function with such blood loss... could it?

Then Scott noticed a clear puss was dribbling from the wound. "I don't think it's merely keeping him alive. I think..." he didn't want to voice his thoughts. It was too hideous.

"You think *what*?" Maya's tone was sharp. Like him, she was barely keeping it together.

"It's feeding on him. Keeping him life just enough."

"Enough for what?"

Fertilizer was too casual a word, but that's all he could

think. His gaze followed the growth merging with Patient Two.

"A colony..." he muttered again.

And it was moving.

At first he thought it had been an illusion as Maya shifted the light source, but the tendrils across Patient Two were coiling, subtly shifting position, and now they could both hear it.

"We need to go!" Maya snapped.

She rushed to the door. Scott followed – then back-tracked to retrieve the jaw sample.

"Leave it!" she snapped, stopping at the doorway to see the mass rippling from one taikonaut to the other.

Scott seized the jaw. It repulsed him, but he'd be damned if he was leaving empty-handed. He looked up to see the movement was slowly spreading like a slow wave through the entire mass.

That's when he felt the easily identifiable stab of fear. Apparently, there were some limits to his *alexithymia* – and the ingrained *fight-or-flight* response was one.

They sprinted into the hangar where the noise became amplified as the wave pulsed in every direction.

"Eric! Run!" Maya bellowed. She stumbled as the floor undulated. Catching her balance, she swept the light around. "Eric?"

There was no sign of him.

TWENTY-FOUR

"ERIC? ERIC – WHERE ARE YOU?"

The words were swallowed by the wall of growth, stretching two stories high and slowly coiling around itself like a perverse optical illusion that gave the impression the room was spinning.

The whole effect was disconcerting. Scott lost track of which way they had entered – in every direction he turned, the mass was moving. Maya gripped his arm as she swayed and pulled him around, for they were face-to-face, their helmet's glass plates scraping together.

"We have to get out of here," she breathed.

Another pulse heaved the floor, yanking their footing from them. They held onto one-another to stay upright. It was accompanied by a loud, dry snapping sound that increased intensity. Their attention was drawn to movement on the wall.

Bodies were pressing out of the growth.

"Christ... the crew," Maya was overcome with horror. "This is what happened to the crew!"

Distinct human forms were pinned at random angles all the way up the wall – some upside down - limbs twitched like marionettes to escape their cocoons. Hundreds of them. The growth creaked as it became taut over their profiles.

"It's feeding on them." Scott staggered backward, trying not to step on the growth as it slid around their feet. He tried to recall the statistics the pilot had spewed when they came into to land. Over two and a half thousand crew members... God knows how many of them had been caught up in this massacre.

"Go!" Maya pulled his arm and turned to run towards the door through which they'd entered - only to stop sharply as the growth knotted together, blocking their path.

"There!" Scott nudged her towards a doorway in the wall. A plastic containment sheet hung across it, protecting the large dark observation window of the elevator control booth. Several dull red lights still blinked from within.

The mass spiraled around the protective sheets, expelling the bodies of more crew. Limbs jerked erratically as they pressed out of the mass like stop-motion puppets. Tendrils began to extend from the floor like rearing snakes. One whipped Scott's hood. Only a quick jerk of the head stopped the probing tentacle from reversing course and wrapping around it.

A violent blast of heat and a lolling orange flame suddenly shot past them, splashing over the mass on the wall. The tendrils immediately retracted. The growth didn't ignite, but black smoke rose as it charred – the human bodies beneath silently thrashed in pain.

Eric ran to their side, a liquid tank strapped to his back and the nozzle of a flamethrower gripped in both hands. He unleashed another torrent of flame as more limbs flailed towards them – before they rapidly retracted.

"Inside!" he instructed.

They ran through a slit in the plastic screen, up a short flight of steps, and into a small dark control room. Any hope of another exit was quickly dashed.

In the darkness beyond the window, they could hear the rhythmic cracking of the moving mass.

"Great!" Maya kicked the control panel in front of them. "Now we're trapped!"

Eric slid the flamethrower off his back and handed it to her.

"Least we know how the fires started."

Scott helped Maya put the liquid tank on her back. "Where did you find this?"

"There are weapons strewn everywhere. They must have emptied the armory here." Eric cast his eyes over the controls. Only a few square buttons were illuminated. "There's still emergency power... but which one..." Frustrated with the acronyms on each button, he swore in Mandarin and randomly hit them all.

A few lights flicked to life in the hangar, but most obscured by the growth. Those still functioning lit up the constantly moving mass outside.

Scott cast his eyes over the control desk – then stabbed a button.

Thunder boomed in the hangar, accompanied by a mighty cracking noise. Detritus fell from the hangar's deckhead as the central tree shook, dislodging huge chunks of phytoplankton growth as the lift descended. The fibrous growths may have been enough to battle the pressures of the ocean, but with a load capacity of over two hundred tons, it shattered it like dry wood as it rapidly descended.

"We make a run for," said Eric determinedly.

Scott hesitated. "How do we send it back up? The control is here."

The walls rippled with renewed energy, a rolling wave flowing along the walls in both directions. It was just a matter of time before it would center on them. Eric shoved Maya towards the door.

"Clear a path!"

She sprinted out, unleashing a tongue of flame across the floor ahead of her as tendrils reached for her. Scott didn't hesitate to follow, still aware of the grim human jaw clenched so hard in his glove that he could feel the teeth.

Maya ran onto the elevator and blasted another flame at the wave blistering the wall, pushing more skeletal bodies outward as if the people themselves were struggling to escape.

As soon as Scott's foot was on the platform, Eric stabbed the ascent button and ran full pelt. He was fast.

There was a two second delay as the pneumatics kicked in. Then the elevator jerked to life, a little sluggishly as it fought against the debris gumming the mechanism... but rise it did.

"Eric!" Scott screamed, dropping to his knees and extending his hand.

The two opposing waves perfectly struck together above the control room, sending out a flurry of creepers towards Eric. Scott was stunned by the speed, but forced himself to focus on Eric. They were already six feet up, moving at a pace, when Eric leapt for him.

Eric's fingers sank into Scott's forearm – but the slick

sleeve and gloves had him sliding back down with the sound of tearing fabric.

Ten feet and Eric was yanked from the floor as his additional weight yanked Scott fall flat on the elevator deck. He increased his pressure, feeling Eric's hand firmly grip his.

"Got you!" Scott wheezed triumphantly.

Any satisfaction was lost as he rolled onto his side in an attempt to haul Eric up. The deck was rapidly approaching, the square of daylight perfectly aligned to fit the elevator. If he couldn't get Eric the platform, he would either lose his arm or Eric would be severed in two.

With a grunt of effort, Scott heaved with everything he had. He felt Maya step over him. She bent for Eric, hooking him under his armpit. Together they pulled.

Eric cocked one leg onto the elevator... then the other. Just as the elevator slammed into position flush with the deck.

For a moment, the three of them lay there panting. Yards away sat the Tiangong, and a gentle breeze ruffled their suits.

"That..." Maya managed between deep breaths, "was too close."

Eric grinned from pure relief rather than any trace of humor.

Then the elevator trembled.

And descended once again.

Sheer panic powered the mad scramble to the deck as the elevator sank from view. The four F-35C Lightnings were parked to the side, untouched by any infection and beyond the Gerald R. Ford's bridge towered over the deck. They ran for it and were glad to see figures running towards them. It was Alanis leading five Navy boys – each armed with black M4-carbines aimed at them.

"Stop, or we're authorized to use deadly force!" Alanis warned them.

The trio stopped.

"It's us!" yelled Maya, ripping her hood off.

"Don't!" Scott held out his hand to stop her – but his warning was too late. Maya looked at him, her eyes widening as she realized she'd violated the rules of decontamination he'd drilled into her.

Scott didn't respond. He was looking at his own arm. The suit was torn along the forearm where Eric had held on to him.

Shit.

It had ruptured for sure as he could now smell a pungent sulphureous odor that made him gag. He noticed the fabric across the back of Eric's hood had numerous tiny tears across it. He slid a finger on one to highlight it. Eric pulled off his hood.

Professor Raven ran from the control tower, stopping a few yards behind the guns. She looked despondent when she saw the state of the team.

"For God's sake! Why did you do this?"

Scott was in no mood to shoulder the blame. "Why didn't you tell us what had happened? How many of the crew are infected?"

Raven massaged her forehead, and he saw the stubborn wall she had constructed around her, crumble. She could barely keep her composure.

"As far as we can tell, about 2,200. The rest... some got evacuated to the Paul Ignatius." She shook her head, giving the impression that it hadn't been the best idea. "Now that is infected too. Our fleet *is* the hot zone. The Chinese are keeping *us* isolated. And you just violated what little quarantine we had here."

Scott couldn't believe his stupidity. His own stubbornness had put them all in danger. Just as the image of Ruth popped into his mind's eye, he felt the deck tremble beneath his feet. He slowly turned towards the aircraft elevator.

Something was emerging.

TWENTY-FIVE

IT BLOSSOMED into the air like a tree captured on time-lapse photography. Nothing more than blindly groping fibrous tendrils that thrashed the air before flapping down onto the deck and anchoring it in place.

More branches filled the lip of the hole in the deck, hauling a larger mass from below.

Vaguely humanoid in shape, in fact they could see it was three crewmen fused together in the growth that hid all but the broadest features. Multiple arms flailed out, broken bones meant the limbs coiled like tentacles and provided locomotion. It was an odd movement, reminiscent of octopuses propelled across the seabed on its limbs. And aside from the jarring creak of flexing matter, it was utterly silent – even as the simulacrum of a head split in two, mimicking a victorious howl.

Scott instinctively backed away – but was stopped by Alanis, firing two shots close to his feet.

"Halt!" Her terrified gaze was drawn back to the thing over his shoulder as her crew opened fire.

The fully automatic rounds pounded the creature. It lashed out as the men focused the shots at the crew cocooned within. Chunks of oozing matter flew in every direction – the bullets were having the desired effect and shredding the monster apart.

Moments later, the bulk crashed onto the deck, then slid through the elevator hole, smattering across the hangar floor with a sickening, wet sound. Somewhere, presumably from the bridge, the elevator was remotely activated, and it slammed back in position, covered in pulped inanimate growth.

Scott looked back at Raven and the others... then noticed fragments of the creature had fallen in their direction and lay at their feet. As he watched, Raven pulled a small chunk of matter from her hair... then shot him a vitriolic look.

Now they were all infected.

DECONTAMINATING everybody who had been on deck was a logistical problem they lacked resources to solve. It was dark by the time the remaining crew, safely sealed in the bridge, could start making preparations.

Captain Peers had announced over the PA system that sections of C-deck had been isolated that led directly to the lab. Scott, Maya, Eric, Raven, Alanis and the five frightened Naval men were now restricted to the lab until some guarantees could be made that they were not infected.

It took a huge amount of will power for the crew not to lay accusations at Scott and his team, but the looks they exchanged said it all. Even Alanis didn't speak to them. In the lab, the Navy contingent sat as far as possible, three smoking cigarettes.

Food and drinks had been hastily stacked in the lab before they had been sealed within, but nobody had any appetite. Raven darkly reminded them it might be the only food they see.

Scott didn't care. Hunger was not on his agenda. He ran through the bizarre sights he'd just witnessed. The mutated phytoplankton were feeding on humans. But the inflection then somehow used their nervous systems, not just for loco-motion, but sensory data too.

Raven picked up a USB hard drive that had been placed on his workbench.

"Since it's to hell with the Navy's desire for secrecy, this contains every byte of data we have. After all, all their lives were now in your hands, Scott."

Maya glared at her. "So you're finally going to stop screwing with us?"

Raven's defiance crumbled. Her shoulders sagged and for a moment it looked as if she might collapse. She leaned on the bench for support and hung her head.

"I'd like to live through this, if it's all the same to you."

The answer hit home for them all, but it didn't stop Maya hating her any less.

Scott's first step was to analyze a sliver of the jaw he retrieved. The sequencer confirmed it was the same DNA/RNA combination as before, now identifying the human elements inside. Under the microscope, the story showed ultrafine filaments bonding with bone, enamel, flesh, muscle and nerves.

Its growth was all-invasive.

"I don't understand what I'm looking at," Raven said after comparing the various sequences they had run. After three hours, several of the crew were asleep, and they all felt the weight of fatigue on their shoulders.

Scott rubbed his eyes and sat on a bench, letting his legs swing freely. He'd been on his feet all day.

"RNA can rewrite DNA. That is a signature virtually all viruses follow. Ebola genetically edits material during an infection. That's what we are seeing here, except at an incredible rate and the result forms Triplex-DNA. Three strands." He waved a hand around the lab. "We're limited with our facilities here, but it seems to me this phytoplankton, for whatever reason, specifically affects the human genome. The data sent from the Tiangong was incomplete."

"We lost communication."

"But the crew would have continued recording events, right? Even the station's environmental readings would help me understand this better. We have far too many holes to even guess what a vaccination against this thing would look like."

"The Chinese claim we have all the records. If it's any consolation, your early analysis still stands." Raven tapped the hard drive that had been connected to a laptop. She had transmitted his results and an hour later had actually received replies from USAMRIID. "They confirmed it's similar to *Karenia brevis*."

"A dinoflagellate, like I said."

Raven nodded. "This like the ones that form red tides near Florida. That particular one releases a *brevetoxin* which attacks the nervous systems of fish. If ingested, it can poison people. Only, our organism is much more complex. It's not single celled for one. The USAMRIID's current best hypothesis is that it either mutated, or is from extraterrestrial origin."

It didn't feel right to Scott. Ordinarily, he would have been filled with adrenaline from the thrill of discovery. Now he just wanted to close his eyes and sleep, although he was fearful of whether he would ever be able to wake again, or slowly die like the crew consumed by the invader.

"Again, they concur with your theory about the water geysers on Europa. What has everybody baffled is this RNA hybrid. That's what appears to make us particularly susceptible to infection."

She yawned and cast a look over at the others. They were all now asleep.

Scott watched Maya's slow breathing. It was almost hypnotic. Minutes passed before he spoke again.

"I've thought about a test to see if we're infected. A simple blood test should show an anomaly... although if the infection is localized to a particular part of the body, we could accidentally overlook it."

"What do you mean?"

"I was thinking about the crew back there." The mere thought of it made his mouth run dry. He popped open a Coke can and took a long gulp. "They were still alive, to some degree."

"The Tiangong crew were sentient enough to call for help."

Scott's lack of response got a curious look from Raven. "What if we misconstrued that? The crew in the hangar appeared to move, but what if that was merely motor functions being activated in a semblance of locomotion?"

"The infection was controlling them? Making them walk? Making them call for help?" Raven gave a dry laugh. "Scott... you didn't see how they first attacked the crew." Her expression became haunted as she thought back. "They had the growth embedded in their skulls, under their skin... but they still looked like people. The walked, they deliberately *targeted* others. That demonstrates human, or at least, animalistic intelligence."

Scott's legs felt weak, so he sat on the floor, upright against the bulkhead. Raven joined him there.

"*Ophiocordyceps unilateralis,* otherwise known as the zombie-ant fungus. It's a spore that attacks carpenter ants. It's able to penetrate inside the ant's body, feeding from it – just like we saw back there. And it's able to control the ant's mind. A stalk grows from the host's head, then it is made to climb as far as it can, before the capsule growing at the end of the stalk erupts, casting new spores far and wide. The fungus controls an ant for a very specific purpose."

"Reproduction."

"Exactly. Then there's that question of what intelligence actually is."

Raven waved at him dismissively. "I get it."

They lapsed into silent contemplation of that horror. Only breaking from it when they both yawned.

"So, this test of yours?"

"A simple blood test to see if we're infected. I suggest taking a sample from the base of the skull..."

"The skull?"

"If the infection targets motor functions, then the brain would be ground zero. Of course, I could be completely wrong. We don't even know how it spreads."

"No time like the present."

With great reluctance they took a sample of blood from each other, opting to take it from the scalp. With tired shaking hands, it was an unpleasant experience. The samples were soon in the sequencer and the machine set to begin its analysis.

With everybody asleep and nowhere else to sit, Scott and Raven sat back down against the wall and closed their eyes as the machine rumbled to life.

"What do you miss about home?"

The question caught Scott by surprise. It had been, what, a week or a little less. He'd been on expeditions for far longer than that without missing a single home comfort. Then again, they hadn't been enforced isolation and the stakes of studying a bacterial colony in some remote cave were far less than now. Pressure had a way of warping time.

"I don't know." Evasiveness was the best course of action.

Raven gave a small chuckle. "Sunday walks. That's what I miss. There's a forest close to where Derek and I lived. In the fall, the whole thing burned with orange and brown. An epic farewell to the summer carpeting the floor with path you could almost believe led to someplace magical…"

She wore a sad smile. Scott thought it easier to leave her to the memories and settled silently back. Despite his fatigue, his mind was restless and sleep refused to come.

Every time he approached the sleep event horizon, his mind gently reminded him his life would be forever changed when he returned home. Tasks he had previously considered mundane when colleagues eagerly spoke about attending football games with their kids, now carried a weight of responsibility and something else… was it pleasant anticipation?

The usual sense of dislocation, of observing his feeling from afar, began to assert itself. However, the enforced isolation made that voice ever more distant…

He became aware he was gently scratching his arm. He

opened his eye to check Raven was still trying to sleep, then inched up his sleeve. The skin beneath was rosy red, broken by dry flaking cracks which were the preferred entry point for an infection.

"Discovering if we're infected or not is a million miles from finding a cure," he said quietly. Luckily worry that burned him internally came from his lips as a reasonable statement.

"USAMRIID are on the case, too." Raven's tone betrayed her agitation. "The problem is there are far too many unknowns."

"And far too many convenient ways it's adapting."

Raven said nothing, but the sound of her shifting position made Scott open his eyes. She was leaning forward, looking at him quizzically. "Meaning?"

"This is some strain of phytoplankton what is mutating rapidly. Not one single individual, but an entire colony. As if it was rewriting its own genetic code with every passing moment to adapt, to survive whatever if thrown at it."

He sat forward too, unexpectedly relieved he could give voice to concerns he didn't dare admit to himself. "This one just so happens to land on the Tiangong's solar panels and then infiltrate a sealed capsule. Adapt. Then survive re-entry and then every hostile environment the earth has to throw at it. As ridiculous as it sounds, it feels more like a pre-targeted attack."

"An alien invasion?" Raven was deadpan. Even Scott could tell that.

He shook his head. "All I mean is extremophiles evolve to live in one specific habitat. Acid lakes, nuclear reactors, thermal vents. Not all of them. The confined environment is what stops them from spreading." He idly scratched his arm to soothe the irritation. "If only the Tiangong had precise records of the moment it had first touched the solar panels. We could build a precise timeline of factors from first contact."

Raven's eyes were on Eric. He seemed to be deeply asleep. Still, she lowered her voice further.

"The Chinese claim they gave us everything they had. Between you and me, I think they are still holding back."

Scott leaned back against the wall. He couldn't understand why they would hold vital information back, nor why there was such a sense of paranoia amongst everybody. He'd always assumed when people had their backs to the wall, that was when they best worked together. Now he suspected it was to stop being stabbed in the back.

He closed his eyes, but no longer wanted to sleep, partly fearful he would die locked up in the bowls of an infected ship at the remotest corner on the planet. There were too many unanswered questions blocking his path and every time he fought against them, his thinking became fuzzy, concepts and thoughts evaporating like clouds.

Raven couldn't sleep either. "Do you think they're still conscious? The crew back there?"

From her tone, he could tell she wanted the answer to be 'no', but he had been wondering the same thing. Were the infected aware their movements were being hijacked. As the body withered and died, was there just enough for the mind to stay active. Patient One's EEG scans seemed to indicate so. A helpless passenger as his body was eaten from within. The silent screams on the faces he saw would permanently inhabit his nightmares – but were they muscle spasms or rictuses of untold agony?

"My husband, Derek... he died of cancer." Scott opened

his eyes to see she still had hers closed, but a tear edged its way down her cheek. "Bone cancer. Very aggressive. It ate him from within. Towards the end he was on so much medication it was pointless being alive. The doctors were just delaying the inevitable. I always wanted to know what was going through his mind..."

She gave a sharp sniff. Scott awkwardly put a hand on her shoulder, but couldn't think of anything to say.

Blessedly, sleep took her moments later.

TWENTY-SIX

SCOTT AWOKE with a start and immediately felt a flush of panic at what had roused him.

Raven was still asleep next to him, curled in a ball against the bulkhead and gently snoring. Everybody else slept too. Maya had folded herself across two chairs, Eric on another, both sound asleep. Alanis and the crewmen hadn't moved from the far corner.

A warning box flashed on the sequencer, occasionally emitting a soft notice alarm. It had finished, meaning he had slept for at least four hours. He stretched, scratched his itchy arm, and read the screen. The sequencer had found a family history of rheumatism in him and a potential hereditary liver problem for Raven. Probably the least of her concerns right now. There were no signs of any other foreign bodies and proved they were not infected.

Or that the test didn't work.

He took a stool and scrolled through the laptop data that had come back from USAMRIID. It provided more in-depth analysis on the samples, but nothing that provided any immediate help, but a new thought was demanding of his mind.

"Flocculation..." he muttered aloud.

He scrolled through the data again, focusing on the sample comparisons to the Karenia brevis blooms. They were close, but not identical.

He looked around at the equipment. The lab had been fitted to the highest specifications available at the last moment, however that was for sampling and analysis. Nobody had expected the need to manufacture any form of defense to fight an infection. They were woefully ill prepared to make any form of vaccination. The nearest chemicals they would need lay on opposing continents. Nobody was going to bring them in.

Once more, the isolation felt like a physical punch. They were at the mercy of fate.

The thought filled him with dread. Their only current hope was that the test worked. He needed to run more samples and, at only two at a time, it would be a drawn out processes.

He gently woke Eric and explained the situation. Then he took a blood sample from his scalp and placed it in the sequencer. Maya was next. She woke with a start, apparently in the middle of a nightmare. As he took blood, she dryly commented that the reality was still more ominous than anything her subconscious could throw at her.

The crew remained asleep as the sampling was set in motion. Raven was on edge, keeping her distance from the others. He crossed to her side and talked quietly while pretending to look through the laptop data.

"What's on your mind?"

Her eyes darted between the rest of the team. She

chewed her lip and rubbed her fingers together in clear signs of anxiety. "You and I are fine. What if they're infected?"

"Let's hope they're not."

"But if they are, they could still infect us!" she hissed.

There was a flash of anger in her eyes. Perhaps a sign of cabin fever? Scott wasn't sure, but he couldn't afford anybody freaking out in such a tight containment space.

"Not necessarily. There is a lot we don't know. The incubation period of the infection for one. Or *how* it infects. Is it inhaled? Through body fluids? Through the skin..."

She gripped his arm, fingers digging hard. "We shouldn't be left in here with them."

Scott tried to gently shuck her off, but her grip was firm. "We're following *your* quarantine procedures, Professor."

Her voice rose to a sharp hiss. "And I wouldn't be in here if you hadn't broken them and gone into the hangar!"

Eric and Maya were looking over now. With a sharp jerk, Scott pulled her hand away, but kept his voice as calm as possible.

"The blame game can go further back than me, but that won't help us. If I'm not affected after being exposed in the hangar, then it's likely we're all fine." He looked at the others, unsure if they were looking at him with hope or doubt. "It means we have to stay in here a little longer, but the odds are in our favor. And right now, this may also be the safest place on the ship."

That seemed to placate Raven a little. She sent the data to the bridge and spent the remaining time on the laptop and keeping her distance from the others.

Scott spent another two hours reading through the laptop reports and was rather dismayed to discover it was mostly confirmation of their own theories. He had been hoping for further insights or some piece of revelatory data.

Alanis was the first of the crew to stir away, her stiff shoulders cracking as she stood and yawned. Professor Raven gave her the latest update and assured her she would be examined next, after Eric and Maya's results came in.

Alanis nodded, but couldn't conceal her nervousness. With little appetite, she opened a can of Coke and watched numerical data slowly appear on the sequencer's screen as it ripped through the samples' genomes.

With the rest of the crew awake and sharing suspicious looks at the scientists, the rest of the time was spent with a growing sense of mistrust.

Eventually Maya and Eric's results came through as clear and Alanis and a crewman named Johnston were next. Realizing they faced another twelve hours to clear the rest of the crew, Eric became snappy before announcing that those who were in the clear should leave.

"To hell with quarantine procedures!" he snapped at Scott. He crossed to the intercom and buzzed the bridge. A Warrant Officer put him through the XO who was in command while the Captain slept.

"These procedures were put in place by Professor Raven," Keller pointed out.

"And I am updating them," Raven snapped back. "Circumstances change."

"I'm not sure–"

"Well I am," Raven said. "At least four of us are in the clear and there has been no provision to isolate us." She cast a glance at the crew in the room. "I'm sure we are *all* fine," she added for their sake, "but we shouldn't be together."

She indicated to an email on her laptop. "The last from

USAMRIID. They confirmed this."

More arguments batted back and forth resulting in Keller reluctantly agreeing to wake the Captain. It was a further six minutes before Peers came on the line, sounding deeply disgruntled, especially when Raven made her demand again.

"How confident are you with your test results?"

Raven cast a defiant look at Scott, daring him to contradict her.

"I'm staking my own life on this, sir. I'm *absolutely* confident."

"And Doctor Bowers?"

Raven cast him a glance, demanding an answer.

Scott had no desire to be locked in the room if one of the others turned out to be infected, but his conscience gnawed at him. Raven was making a sham of her own quarantine procedures. How could he go along with this?

Ruth. She needed him. Or more specifically, their unborn child needed him. He had never felt he had been truly needed, yet now he did. Self-preservation reared its head.

He bowed his head. "As Professor Raven confirmed. The test results are clear."

"USAMRIID also recommended this," Raven said smugly.

There was a pause before Captain Peers spoke again. "When did you hear from USAMRIID?"

"The email came in an hour ago."

The next pause was so long they wondered if communications had been cut. "Then we will arrange to segregate the others and decontaminate the lab."

Despite his reticence, Scott felt a surge of relief. It took another hour for a staged quarantine area to be set up outside the lab, during which Raven assured the rest of the crew that it was unlikely any of them had been infected and they would soon be out. At the very least, it stoked their morale.

Knowing it would take at least another two hours to deep clean the lab and the sequencer would still have to run an analysis on the final crewmen, Scott synced the sequencer's output results to his phone, thankful that the ship's wireless network was still functional.

Scott was relieved when the door opened, revealing a network of airtight tunnels hastily erected outside. Even that enclosed space felt like an expanse compared to the lab. The crew were to be remain behind before being segregated to a separate billet kitted out with cots to make the rest of their incarceration tolerable.

Eric then Maya stepped into a separate tended area where they were told to strip naked as the decontamination sprays cleansed their bodies. They did this without complaint. Modesty had long since been abandoned. Their clothes would be incinerated, and they were given medical scrubs until they returned to their quarters to be reunited with their own possessions.

"You go next," Scott said to Raven. He was still examining the data coming through from the sequencer. He was so preoccupied he didn't hear her reply. Something in the data had caught his attention; something that didn't quite make sense.

He wasn't sure what it was, but some forgotten knowledge was teetering on the edge of his mind, desperate to draw attention to itself.

He was certain that the answer lay within the stream of numbers... all he had to do was figure out how to see it. But at the moment unholy hell broke loose.

TWENTY-SEVEN

A DULL TOLL vibrated through the ship. A heavy reverberation that showed no signs of ceasing. A tremor rippled under Scott's feet and there was the vaguest sense of motion. Almost instantly a repetitive beep sounded as the lights flickered. His immediate reaction was that they were under attack.

"That's the collision alarm," Yeowoman Alanis said, jumping to her feet. "Something must have struck us–"

She cut off with a choked howl as crewman Johnston next to her convulsed with such savagery he slammed his head repeatedly against the steel bulkhead, blood splattering from his scalp like a torn balloon. It did not stop him.

With a crunch of flesh – and the sudden release of a sulphureous smell - hair-like tendrils wriggled from his tear ducts and spreading across his eyeballs, soaking in the moisture. His desiccated eyes cracked and crumpled like paper. Thicker strands burst from his ears and nostrils, questing for exposed skin to bind too. Even finer filaments punctures from his pores, writhing like fine silken worms as they knitted together to form a waxy mycelium layer over him.

Scott was rooted to the spot as the fibrous growth rapidly stretched across the man's skin. Exploratory tendrils punctured through his uniform, writhing as they sampled the air.

The man lunged forward with a creak of fibers and the unmistakable sound of now fragile bones snapping. He crawled between Scott and the exit, each movement sharp and uncoordinated, as if not his own.

The two other crewmen were cornered behind their mate, unable to avoid the fast moving tendrils probing towards them. The moment they contacted flesh, the growth stuck fast. No amount of shaking would dislodge it. When the men used their hands to pull the mass free, they became helplessly entangled as the growth anchored itself into their pores.

Their screams pitched higher as they were rapidly consumed.

Scott pulled Alanis towards him as a growth spiraled for her head. It narrowly missed and fixed onto the bulkhead.

He looked around. Trapped.

He had never regarded himself a physical man, but now facing death some deep animal instinct took over his actions. Where he planned and stressed over details, this inner fight-or-flight reflex was powered by spontaneity.

He jumped up for the pipe above his head, grasping it with both hands. Heat from the hot water pipe bit his palm as he heaved himself up, feet dangling off the ground.

It was just enough.

Under his weight, a joint bolting it to the overhead beam gave way, and the pipe sheered in two. A blast of red hot water sprayed over the entrapped men. Their screams rose as they were scalded, a veil of steam rising. With a grunt Scott heaved the pipe towards the unfortunate beast blocking his exit. The spray hit with enough force to send it reeling against the bulkhead. While the growth itself appeared resistant to heat, its host wasn't.

The smell of burning flesh made him gag. Through the steam he caught sight of the writhing figure, red raw patches of flesh exposed through the alien mass. With no solid flesh to cling to, the growth slithered to the floor, writhing like maggots.

Alanis had enough presence of mind to haul him towards the door. They hopped through, Alanis swinging the watertight door closed behind them and sealing it.

Scott dropped to his knees, blowing on his scalded hands and catching his breath. Alanis was staring back at him with shock, tears rolling down her cheek as she tried to process what had just happened.

The vibration through the ship suddenly abated, leaving only the trilling collision alarm. Behind the plastic quarantine panels Raven, Eric and Maya watched, uncomprehending. Scott knew one thing for sure. The speed of infection was accelerating.

After a painful decontamination, stripped nude and scrubbed by rough brushes and an array of stinging chemicals, Alanis and the scientists had been given fresh clothing taken from the billets before being escorted to the bridge.

THE VIEW from the bridge was grim.

Heavy black smoke poured from the stern, obscuring the end of the runway, the parked fighter jets and the Tiangong. Gusts of wind occasionally parted the murk, revealing a tangle of metal that Scott found difficult to identify.

"That's the Paul Ignatius." Captain Peers was monotone as he gazed through field binoculars.

Another parting in the smoke revealed the battleship had crashed into their side. The center of its keel must have snapped as the entire vessel was bent in a shallow V, the prow fully poking from the water and slowly rotating as the entire ship twisted, gradually sinking. For hundreds of yards beyond it, the sea was on fire as spilt oil and fuel furiously burned.

"The crew...?" Maya could barely speak above a whisper.

"No survivors." After a long pause, Peers corrected himself. "There were none even before she was fired upon."

"Fired upon?" Raven gasped. "By whom?"

Peers lowered the binoculars and cast him a look. "Well, it wasn't us."

Eric suddenly found himself the center of attention. "Why would we do that?"

Peers stared at him with barely contained hostility. "That's the question, isn't it?"

Maya looked between Peers and his XO. "What do you mean, no survivors?"

The commanding officers swapped a jaded look. Keller took up the story.

"The outbreak reached them. We lost contact as the crew was attacked. The ship was dead in the water. Then, it was torpedoed. It drifted towards us. Hit us hard." He looked at the captain, unsure if he should say any more.

Peers lowered his binoculars and rubbed his tired eyes. "We now have a reactor leak and multiple fires we're barely containing with what little crew we have."

A drawn out silence followed this admission. Everybody tensed at the implications. Along with the commanding officers, scientists, and Alanis, there were only twelve others stationed at their posts on the bridge.

The panoramic windows offered a complete three-hundred sixty degree view of nothing but a horizon on which the sunset on one side, and a curtain of impenetrable night rolled towards them on the other. Finally, Scott found his voice.

"What have the Chinese said?"

"They denied doing it, of course. They even offered rescue assistance, which we refused. But let's face it," he pointed at the wreck, "that is an act of war in anybody's playbook."

"I don't believe it," Eric said, shaking his head sadly. "It makes no sense."

Peers glared at him. "We have lost contact with our sub out there. Maybe comms are down, or maybe your people sank that too?"

"Perhaps your people think they have supremacy out here. They certainly think we have stolen their property, so that wouldn't surprise me."

You did, Scott though but didn't see how saying that aloud would help anybody.

"Keeping me here is against my wishes. Captain."

Peers broke into a genuine laugh. "Hell, son, I'm happy for you to go. But they don't want you either. They grumble we took the Tiangong, but in retrospect they dodged a bullet."

Peers gave his XO a meaningful look. Keller sighed and positioned himself in front of Eric. "Professor Dong, we respect your skill set, but I must ask you not to go anywhere unaccompanied." His eyes darted to a muscular security man standing at the elevator. A pistol was strapped to his thigh, a machine gun over his shoulder. He watched Eric, unblinking.

"Am I a prisoner?"

"As much as we all are. And under the circumstances I wouldn't question my generosity in not locking you in the brig."

Eric folded his arms and leaned against a bank of equipment, wisely deciding not to argue.

"How secure is this ship?" asked Raven, her fists were clenched, knuckles white.

"The hull was breeched below the waterline. The flooding and fires have been contained. As for the outbreak – well, that's your department."

"And the radioactivity?" Maya asked.

"We think contained. For now," he added ominously.

Scott watched the Chinese aircraft carrier, still about a mile away. Several fighters were on its deck, poised to launch at a moment's notice.

The only other vessel was the Ventura. In the dying light, the white growth stretched between them, like a submerged coral reef. Lights still burned onboard and he could see figures move. Apparently the infection hadn't yet reached them, but they were stranded, surrounded by it.

Scott finally spoke up. "We have another problem. The growth rate of the infection is increasing." He felt everybody waiting for him to continue. Uncomfortable at being the center of attention, he paced. "We are dealing with so many unknowns. We don't know how the infection is passed. By touch, aerosol, we don't know. My hunch, although I'm not willing to stake anybody's life on it, is that it requires physical contact."

Raven frowned. "Based on what assumptions?"

"It spread underwater. Affected the coral growth around the Tiangong. That doesn't rule out it could spread by air, but then we would probably have already been infected in the hangar."

Raven nodded in agreement.

"Crunching the numbers from how many of the crew have been infected, and then seeing the transformation just now..." He faltered as the terrible images of the crewman came unprompted. "I assume it is adapting to our DNA, and each iteration is spreading quicker and quicker."

He suddenly recalled what had got his attention on the sequencer moments before the horrific incident. Captain Peers' voice rode through his stream of consciousness.

"I need a weapon to fight this thing." He looked meaningfully at Scott, but it was clear he didn't expect any miracles.

"I was thinking about the base of the outbreak."

"Plankton blooms," said Raven.

"Specifically, the type closely related to red tides, which are poisonous algae blooms–"

"I know what they are," Peers sighed. "What's your point?"

"The Japanese use clay flocculation to disperse and kill the blooms." He looked around at the sea of blank faces. "They mix clay that has been left over from phosphate mining and spray it into the water. It's a technique known to purify water. The clay particles act like sediment and rips the plankton apart, while other plankton consumes it and are literally too heavy so are pulled down, where they can no longer photosynthesize and die."

Peers looked thoughtful. "How does that help us? Especially if this thing can live outside of water."

Scott ran a hand through his hair. He could feel an idea forming, but it was just beyond his mental reach. "I'm not sure. Maybe some form of aerosol that breaks it apart before it can spread?" He shook his head, searching for clarity. "Like I said, there are still too many things we don't know. Perhaps USAMRIID could—"

"We've lost all satellite communications." The Captain heaved a deep breath. "We're out on our own right now."

From the look on Raven's face, that was news to her, too.

"What about them?" Eric pointed across to the Chinese carrier. "They may have the facilities we need."

Peers gave a dry laugh. "And there's the rub, isn't it?"

Scott suddenly went for his mobile phone – then remembered it had been taken from him during the decontamination.

"I need to access the computers in the lab."

Peers nodded to one of the crewman, a woman with short blonde hair, stationed on the far bulkhead. Scott hurried across to her as she accessed the system, each keystroke deepening her frown.

"It's not responding," she said. A few more keystrokes and she shook her head. "Nothing there is responding. The lab is offline."

"The water," Said Alanis. She couldn't keep the tremor from her voice as she recalled her companions' gruesome fate. "Nobody stopped the flow from the heating pipe, did they?"

"We couldn't." Keller stepped forward. The bags under

his eyes indicated he hadn't slept since the nightmare had started. "The valves to do that manually were located aft, in the infected area. The room would have filled with water."

With the ventilation system closed and the watertight hatch sealed, the men would have drowned. If they were still alive, that is. Scott felt a pang of guilt.

"What about the sequencer data?"

"We have it backed up," Raven assured him.

"How far back?"

"Just after our results."

The screen he had been looking at was during Alanis and the infected crewman's scan. That data was lost... but it suddenly hit him. He had seen something familiar; and he knew what it was.

"Crispr..." he breathed. He saw Raven shoot him a questioning look.

"What is that?" Maya asked.

Tumbling thoughts rendered Scott silent as fragments slipped into place, forming a picture he wasn't entirely sure could be true. The sequencer indicated a genetic editing sequence he'd seen before with Crispr, a genetic splicing system used to edit DNA.

That meant the growth on the Tiangong wasn't natural.

It wasn't extraterrestrial.

It was genetically modified by somebody on *earth*.

He looked at Eric, remembering the USB drive that had fallen from his pocket. Then he met Captain Peers' steely gaze.

The question was now *who* had unleashed a manmade plague.

TWENTY-EIGHT

"DOCTOR BOWERS?"

Scott had walked up to the starboard panoramic bridge window overlooking the long white fingers under the ocean as they searched for the Ventura and the Chinese carrier beyond. Captain Peers spoke to him again, but his voice sounded far off, as if from another room. It took a moment for Scott to realize his eczema on his arm, which had calmed since decontamination, was now bothering him again.

The Americans had purposefully taken the Tiangong. Was it because they feared being exposed as the originator of a terrible experiment that went wrong? Or had an experiment onboard the space station gone terribly wrong, and the Chinese had hoped the evidence would burn up in the atmosphere?

Scott suddenly wanted to be as far from either superpower as possible. Yet here he was, on a knife edge, uncertain which way the enemy lay or what they would do to keep their deadly unauthorized experiment a secret.

And where better than out here. Trapped. With no contact with the outside world.

He was jarred back to the moment by a gentle pressure on his shoulder. Maya was gently touching him.

"Are you alright?"

He saw a flash of concern in her eyes. Out of everybody around him, she was probably the only one he could trust with his hunch. He managed a tired smile.

"I'm just trying to piece everything together." He looked at Raven. "Without a functional lab, there's nothing we can do." Then a thought occurred to him. "Although it would be useful to look through some sort of events log on the Tiangong."

"You saw the video feed," Peers said with a hint of irritation. Or was Scott just projecting that on him?

"I meant that it must have had some operational monitoring system. You know, like an aircraft black box recorder."

Eric nodded. "Yes. It does."

Peers quickly interjected. "If it did, then we didn't find it. And any data streamed from the station hasn't been shared by our Chinese pals." This time the sarcasm wasn't disguised.

All eyes were now on Scott, making him feel exceptionally uncomfortably. He looked back at the Chinese ship.

"Then there's nothing more we can do here. We must leave."

Peers snorted. "And how do you suggest we do that?"

"Abandon ship." The Captain made no attempt to hide his revulsion at the thought, but Scott swore he saw a glimmer of hope cross the XO's face. Scott pointed to the mass bonding the smoking USS Paul Ignatius to the carrier.

"The infection is out of control and we have no facilities to cook something up to stop it."

Peers scowled, his voice rising. "This vessel is still afloat, Doctor. Still functional–"

"Functional? Barely! Most of your crew are dead. We're trapped in here with no other offer of help except from the Chinese! How long do you think it will take that infection to reach us?" Peers opened his mouth to answer, but Scott ploughed on. "Two hours judging by the current rate it's spreading. Now isn't the time to go down with your ship, Captain!"

Peers scanned his crew, searching for any brave opinions. None came. He finally settled on Raven. She cleared her throat, taking a little longer than necessary before answering.

"I concur with Doctor Bower's estimation of how long we have left." That obviously wasn't the answer the Captain had hoped for. She quickly added, "Although I see no reason for *temporarily* evacuating the ship. Once we have figured out how to combat the growth, the ship can be decontaminated and repaired."

It was clear to all that was a bitter pill for the Captain to swallow. He shook his head.

"You said help is not coming, Captain." She indicated to the Chinese carrier. "Like Scott said, it's right over there."

He barked humorlessly. "You want us to be prisoners of the Chinese?"

"Why would you be prisoners?" Eric asked. "We're not at war. And as you graciously pointed out to me, I am not a prisoner here." He flashed a thin smile back at the Captain.

A tense silence gripped the room as Peers navigated through his narrow band of options. He paced the bridge.

"This bridge, this tower, is completely self-contained. That's why they call it an island. We have rations, separate power and a contained air filtration system designed to withstand a nuclear attack. Nothing is getting in here."

Scott felt his blood boil at the man's arrogance.

"So we slowly starve to death? That infection doesn't appear to have any time constraints, Captain. If this is a waiting game, we will lose."

"We're safe," Peers snapped. "Which means we have options!"

"Not unless the infection was already in here," Maya said flatly, her gaze firmly on the Captain. Then Scott saw it too.

What he had first took to be signs of fatigue etching the Captain's face had already shifted as veins beneath his cheeks swelled up. With a strangled cry, he held up his right hand, twisting it as he watched the skin undulate. Fine yellow hair-like fibers poked from his pores, rapidly stretching over his skin. He gave a gasp before the infection spread from his tear ducts, across his eyes, blinding him in an instant as the soft tissue of his eyeballs ruptured.

Everybody retreated as Peers convulsed – arms extended Christ-like as, with the sound of rendered flesh and cloth, his back erupted in a swirl of fungus-like growth that extended several feet from his body and slammed into the window, fusing with the glass.

Peers' body began to twitch and vibrate as if he was receiving a surge of electricity. Scott was fixed to the spot, but a part of his mind observed with scientific detachment as he assumed the growth was seizing the man's nervous system. Then, with herculean force, Peers was pulled back against the window as the tendrils retracted. The bomb-proof glass, now weakened as it was riddled at a microscopic level by fibrous growths, cracked under the impact. The sound of shattered bone and glass was excruciating. Thick cracks scorched across the glass, expanding with an inevitable screech... until the pungent scent of salt air seeped in.

Their only protection had been destroyed.

The sharp sounds of a gun report jolted Scott. Crimson punctures sprouted across Captain Peer's chest before a fourth bullet cleaved his forehead in two. His body spasmed from each impact, his mouth a rictus of a scream that was choked as more tendrils extended from his throat like a blossoming tree.

Gerald Keller stood in a shaking weaver stance, smoke drifting from the barrel of his pistol. Tears stung his eye as he watched his friend and commanding officer destroyed before his very eyes.

"He's dead already!" screamed Raven, pushing the barrel towards the floor. "But a bullet won't kill it. Back off!"

It was an unnecessary warning. Everybody had already moved to the far end of the bridge, watching the Captain's corpse sway and spasm as growths probed from his body, anchoring him to the floor and deckhead as its mass increased in volume. Already its fingers were stretching towards the door.

"It's trying to trap us inside."

"Are you trying to tell me that it can *think?*" Raven exclaimed.

Alanis was closest to the door – but still hesitated as she swapped a terrified look with the XO. Despite his training, her commanding officer was completely out of his depth.

"If we stay," said Scott as he watched with revulsion as the Captain was consumed, "we die."

The XO gave a short nod to Alanis, who put all her weight into unsealing the hatch.

Keller's voice was low and dry. Even before the order came, everybody hurried towards the door. "Abandon ship."

TWENTY-NINE

ERIC STOOD at the edge of the deck, waving his arms. "*Hei!*" he repeatedly yelled until his voice was hoarse.

Scott and Maya stood beside him, wary of the sheer drop to the ocean at their toes.

"They won't notice you," Maya said as she eyed the Chinese carrier a mile away.

Eric stopped to catch his breath. "Are you joking? Every eye on that ship will be watching us."

Scott nodded. "Even if they could send help, they will be debating whether or not they should." Eric was about to disagree, but Scott cut him off. "That's exactly the decision I'd make, too." He glanced back at the rest of the crew on the open deck, eighteen of them around the XO. All in shock.

At one end of the ship, the growth covered the Tiangong and the quartet of F-35s lined on the side. Above, a boubous growth was already swelling from the bridge's broken windows.

They were trapped. It was only a matter of time.

"Over two thousand people dead..." said Maya, emotion causing her voice to tremolo.

"There could be some alive, trapped below." The words were out before Scott could stop himself. Any poor unfortunates were undoubtable living on borrowed time.

He didn't have the bandwidth to focus on social niceties. While he had restrained his own external panic, inside his fight-or-flight reflex had kicked in – and fight was not a current option.

Jumping off the deck, into the choppy waters would break dozens of bones, if he was lucky. Should anybody survive such a plunge, thick white fungal streamers were clearly visible feet beneath the surface, some as wide as a road, and striking those would be like impacting with rock.

There were no ropes, ladders, or any simple way to leave their steel prison. His mental schematic reminded him that a platform on the port side allowed small crafts to be launched. However, accessing several infected decks in the dark, and with no form of defense, was nothing more than a suicide run.

A thousand miles from everywhere.

Trapped with an unstoppable killer moving in and the Chinese as their only hope.

It was a stark conclusion Scott reached the very moment the USS Gerald R. Ford shuddered as if an earthquake had struck. The vibrating metal underfoot made Scott's knees jar, and he stumbled onto all fours as his balance was swiped from him.

An enormous wall of water suddenly rose from the stern. Amongst it, huge chunks of steel that fell onto the deck with colossal clangs. They were hull fragments from the Paul

Ignatius; some the size of trucks that effortlessly crushed the F-35s.

A second detonation shook the vessel and almost instantly the deck tilted. Scott and Maya fell to all fours, while Eric fell flat on his back and slid.

"The bastards have torpedoed us!" Keller screamed.

A thick column of black smoke rose from the stern and the deck vibrated with the increasing sound of wrenching metal. The ship continued to incline to port as it sank.

Scott's fingers scraped the smooth deck, but there was nothing to latch on to as the angle rapidly increased. The rest of the crew howled as they slid and rolled to the far side of the deck. The Tiangong and fighters were adhered firmly to the deck by the growth, but loose debris bounced across the runway, splashing into the cold water.

Scott's stomach churned as his speed increased as the deck reached a sixty-degree incline. He flipped onto his back and watched in horror as the rest of the crew shot over the side, enveloped by a displaced column of water that erupted over the deck as the side of the carrier struck the water.

Scott knew that the current from the sinking vessel could drag him down too far for him to kick back to the surface. Despite this, he instinctively sucked in a deep breath a second before he was catapulted over the side.

He spun head-over-heels, dropping like a cannon ball into the frigid waters. His shock from impacting the water was overwhelmed by the cold, which felt like pins stabbing through his exposed skin. His eyes were tightly closed as he was jostled by powerful swells and currents. All sense of direction was obliterated.

Something slammed into his back, and he stopped descending. He opened his eyes to see he was lying on his back as a watery storm of projectiles speared into the water above him, spewing bubble contrails in their wake.

His lungs were burning as he sat motionless, caught on the enormous growth spread around him. To his left, the lifeless gaze of a crewman stared at him – a wide shard of metal had cleaved his chest almost in two and pinned him to the mass. Blood and entrails still clouded from the gaping wound.

The gruesome sight almost choked the last of Scott's air from his lungs. He pushed himself from the spar and kicked to the surface. He was only five meters down, the towering superstructure of the aircraft carrier looming above him like a skyscraper. Detritus continued to slide into the water, including heavy chunks of steel from the Ignatius' hull.

He broke the surface, gasping for breath. It took him a moment to take it all in.

The Gerald R. Ford lay on its side in the middle of the ocean, the five acre deck now a sheer eighty-degree wall of steel above him. Ducking his head below the water, he saw the ship was grounded on colossal tendrils of the growth. He marveled how the organism could cradle over one-hundred twenty-two metric tons without effort. But it had, preventing the ship from sinking to the depths of Point Nemo... and it had no doubt saved his life too. The stern was a mass of black smoke with occasional orange flames spouting amongst the dark folds. He tried not to think what would happen if the nuclear reactor had been breached.

"Scott!"

He kicked water and turned to see Alanis swimming towards him. Eric and Maya were further behind, treading water.

"I'm okay". More of the crew surfaced behind her. He

made out Keller, but couldn't see Raven. There were notice-
ably fewer people than had been on the deck.

Alanis indicated towards the prow. "That way. Keep
away from the stern. Go around!" With powerful strokes, she
led the way.

THE SURFACE of the ocean was like a millpond. Smoke
from the sunken ships rose vertically, staining the clear blue
sky in a black mushroom cloud. With numb limbs, Scott
battled exhaustion as the survivors rounded the stern and
swam several hundred meters towards the rest of the fleet
before being forced to stop to rest.

To his surprise, they had found a section of growth so
close to the surface they could stand. Not having to treading
water was a small mercy, enough to put the concern of
touching the growth out of Scott's mind.

There were now eighteen of them left. Only half were
faces he recognized from the bridge and one red-haired man
he recognized from the mess hall. Scott was relieved to see
Raven was amongst the survivors. The XO attempted to
maintain some leadership, although every sentence was
threaded with hesitation.

His strategy was simple: head for the Chinese carrier
and pray they would grant clemency. There had been no
sign of activity from the Liaoning. Not a single aircraft or
patrol boat had been sent out to inspect the wreckage. It
remained half a mile away from the disaster area, stoically
silent.

He wondered if the crew had faced the same fate. But if
so, why had they torpedoed the Americans?

"We won't make it before nightfall," Raven said between

violent shivers. "An hour? Hour and a half this exhausted? It'll take longer."

"We don't have a choice," Keller stated, rubbing his arms for warmth. "In this water we'll hit hypothermia pretty quickly if we stop. Overnight, not a one of us will make it."

"What about over there?" Scott pointed to the Ventura which lay equidistance away. Even from here they could see the white tendrils reaching from the ocean as far as the plimsoll line, anchoring the ship in place.

Keller shook his head. "Looks like a deathtrap to me. It reached them way before it would have hit the Liaoning. And the Chinese will have better medical facilities." The XO was reluctant to decided.

Scott felt everybody's gaze on them both. He noticed Alanis and the red-head were clutching each other for warmth, and a tiny part of him decided it was for more than just body heat. Social cues may be unintelligible most of the time, but there was no mistaking the hope on Alanis's face.

He didn't know why they valued his opinion over the XO's. It was likely both men were right. Death lay at either door.

THIRTY

VIOLENT SHIVERS WRACKED SCOTT. He could no longer feel his limbs. With every stroke, his strength was sapped, and he battled to keep his eyes open as he fought a creeping slumber that he knew he couldn't wake from. Conversely, his skin felt afire.

Hypothermia.

Scott sensed his life expectancy was down to mere minutes. As he struggled to keep his eyes open, the lure of the Maldivian beach tempted his imagination. The warm sun against his cheeks. Ruth's hand gently squeezing his own as he felt her breath tickle his ear:

"You're going to be a father..."

The words sent an unexpected tremor of joy through him. He stroked her cheek, feeling a closeness to her that had been lacking in the last year. His hand reached down and stroked her stomach, plump and round beneath the fine linen dress.

"It's a girl," she said, flashing a smile. She took his hand, squeezing it tightly as her voice dropped earnestly. "Promise us you'll never leave."

"Of course I won't." The doubt in her eyes troubled him. Why didn't she believe him? "I promise."

That got a smile. Then a sudden twitch of pain as she batted away his hand and splayed her fingers over her bump. With a grunt, she staggered backwards, just beyond Scott's reach.

"What's...?"

"My waters have broken!" she hissed, spasming as more pain shot through her.

He looked down to see a wet stain darken the linen, but even as he watched, the black mark turned an ugly red. Something was very wrong.

"Ruth!"

She cried out and suddenly threw herself onto her back with a sickening thud. Scott was paralyzed, able only to watch as she spasmed. With a crack of tearing flesh, the white fungal growth suddenly tore out of her swollen stomach like a claw reaching for the air.

"Scott! Scott!"

A sharp pain in his throat focused him back to focus on Maya's face. He spat out cold salt water, his face an inch from submerging. She increased the pain, forcing him to open his eyes wider.

"Stay with me!" she urged.

The world around him became a sharp amalgamation of a stark blue sky tainted by a smoky black scar. The USS Paul Ignatius half-emerged from the ocean rolled on its starboard side, water pouring from the huge, exposed propellers, which were clogged with the white invasive growth. Behind him a sheer wall of grey steel; the Liaoning.

"It's too late." The words slurred on his lips. He had been in the water for eternity with no knowledge of how he had reached the Chinese ship. He was vaguely aware that others floated around him, some treading water.

He had no way of knowing whether this was reality or a hallucination.

A scream to his left begged his wary attention.

A crewman was flailing in the water. Scott's first reaction was a shark attack, but as the man began tearing off swatches of clothing, a vague memory of hypothermia symptoms came to him: paradoxical undressing. The poor man was convinced he was burning to death and everybody around him was too tired to stop him.

Scott could only watch as the man sank beneath the water. There was no thrashing; no clawing to the surface, just waters calmly folding over his head like quicksilver.

Scott's brain felt foggy as thoughts danced beyond the edge of comprehension. Sleep would solve it.

It would solve everything.

A tiny rational part of his mind warned him that he should succumb to it, but he couldn't stop it. He was even hallucinating now. He could see figures standing far above him. Judging him as they watched him die...

THIRTY-ONE

BRIGHT LIGHTS BURNED Scott's retinas the moment he opened his eyes. He blinked tears away and squinted until his eyes adjusted to the harsh light.

He was on his back. Flexed his fingers and toes revealed sensations had returned to his limbs; amongst which was a throb in his right hand. He lifted it, revealing clear tubes from an IV piercing the top of his hand. A rhythmic beep from behind his head told him his heart rate was relatively normal.

He raised his head, noting that he was naked under a silver thermal blanket, lying on a gurney. As his eyes adjusted beyond the powerful halogen light overhead, he could make out the plastic walls and roof of an isolation tent.

His memory seeped back. The long swim to the Chinese aircraft carrier. The fight against the soporific lull of hypothermia. The figures on the deck above...

His mouth was dry, but he managed to speak. "This... Liaoning?"

Movement from the end of his bed garnered his attention. A figure in a bright yellow hazmat suit stepped through a gap in the plastic. Before he could ascertain any details, a bright light shone in his eyes from a pencil torch in the figure's hand.

"Pupils are normal." A woman's voice, with a subtle Chinese accent. The flashlight turned off, forcing Scott to blink several times to regain his vision. Beyond the hazmat's faceplate a young Chinese woman beamed a mischievous smile. "We'll soon have you playing cricket again, Dr Bowers." Her smile was so infectious, Scott couldn't help but laugh.

And that made his chest hurt like hell.

"TIME CONSTRAINTS PUT us as somewhat of a disadvantage, Professor Bowers." Professor Huang Yi possessed a youthful appearance symptomatic with the Chinese, but since escorting Scott through decontamination he had realized her mind was as sharp as a trap. More than worthy of her role as Chief Science officer onboard the Liaoning.

"I'm not one to sit around and rely on hope," Scott said, sipping hot green tea. A cocktail of drugs had fought the onset of hypothermia, but he was far from back to normal. Even a month of convalesce wouldn't be enough. Yet three hours after waking, he was now in a bare mess hall in the bowels of the aircraft carrier.

Eric sat to his left, dressed in an identical flight suit all the survivors had been attired in after their own clothes were destroyed. He still shivered violently and kept a silver blanket wrapped tightly around his shoulders. Maya was opposite, looking remarkably fit and rapidly plucking whatever food was in reach of her chopsticks. Despite her tiredness, there was little to indicate the trauma she had experienced over the last few days.

Raven sat opposite in a wheelchair. She was weak, but as stubborn as ever. An IV drip kept her pumped with fluids and whatever drugs the ship's doctors had deemed appropriate to keep her awake.

"Hope is for fools," Raven growled. "And you people have a lot of explaining to do." She glared at Huang, a silent challenge. "And we're not telling you anything until the rest of our crew are released."

Huang's smile didn't waver. "Released? They are being kept under quarantine for safety."

"Whose safety?"

"Everybody's. Please, Professor Raven, suspicion and accusations will get us nowhere."

"You torpedoed our fucking ship!" Raven exclaimed. "I imagine only to cover-up whatever God-dammed experimentation you were doing up there." A shaking finger pointed vertically up. "So don't try to lecture me on morals or trust."

"And opinionated too." Huang's eyebrows rose a little, a motion calculated to raise Raven's ire.

"What you have done is an act of war!"

"Please, the both of you, shut up." Scott wrapped the table to divert attention back to himself. "We're faced with something a little bigger than petty rivalry between nations."

Raven twitched at the notion. He had expected support from Huang, but the amiable smile on her face vanished, replaced by visible tension. The ensuing silence made everybody feel uncomfortable.

Eric shot off rapid sentences in Mandarin. Huang

answered with short replies that sounded to the non-speakers around them, vitriolic and argumentative.

"Guys," Maya gestured to them both. "With all due respect that we're onboard a Chinese vessel, can you keep it to English for those of us who are too lazy to learn another language?"

Eric lapsed into silence, whether or not instructed to, Scott couldn't tell. Huang rubbed her neck, gazing thoughtfully at the deckhead before she spoke again.

"I have been pondering how to say any of this. Understand, I am a scientist like you. Not an orator or politician. Yet the Admiral thought is best I speak with you, rather than you hear it from a Military man whose opinion you probably will not trust."

Scott leaned back in his chair and gestured for her to continue.

Huang hesitated, uncomfortable with the words she had to find. "We are all dying."

Eric and Raven swapped an alarmed look.

"I hope you mean in an existential kinda way," said Maya.

"We are all infected. You, me. Everybody aboard this vessel."

Silence once again consumed the room as her words sank in. Huang leaned forward, fingers idly tracing patterns on the desk as she composed her thoughts.

"The infection is disseminated by airborne spores, and they spread under the water via the growths you have witnessed. What luxury there seems to be is that people react differently to the incubation period."

Scott held up his hand. "No. We ran a blood test—"

"Your tests were inconclusive."

"How would you know that?"

Huang's smile broadened. "Because I saw the data. You had a spy on your ship."

All eyes turned to Eric, who looked ashen. Before acquisitions could fly, Huang spoke louder. "Not one of ours!"

Scott frowned. "I don't understand."

Huang shrugged. "We warned the Captain. We intercepted and eventually decrypted messages. As to who the mole is and who they are working for. Another government..." she circled her hand in the air, then looked pointedly at Raven. "Frisco Dynamics is a private company. There are others who would pay handsomely for information."

"My team was thoroughly vetted," Raven snapped back.

"This is irrelevant," Scott interjected. "It doesn't impact our current situation. You claim we are all infected?" Huang nodded. "The if you can detect that, surely you have identified factors in synthesizing a cure?"

Huang shook her head. "With our limited tests, we have yet to identify any unifying factor that holds the infection at bay."

Eric looked around the room in alarm. "So anyone of us could just..." with both hands he mimed his head exploding.

"Yes. That is why we are operating in small cluster units. To minimize any potential cross-infection. The bridge here has been sealed. As well as the hangar and engine rooms."

Raven sat back in her chair, looking weaker than ever. "Surely you have more answers than that. After all you guys created this thing."

"You saw the footage, the data," Eric said. "It was found outside the Tiangong. This was nothing to do with us!"

"Bullshit!"

"Dong is correct," Huang insisted. "The infection came from outside."

"But it's manmade." Everybody turned to Scott. "The gene splicing technics... I saw them. This Triplex-DNA is not a natural mutation. This was artificially created. Synthetic life created... for what? New biological warfare?"

Huang sighed and nodded. "That is my conclusion, as well."

Raven laughed. "Oh, so you now finally admit your guilt."

Huang's face scrunched into something approaching hatred. "Always the American way, Professor Raven. Look for an enemy where there isn't one; then get stung by the hidden foe who was luring you into their trap."

"What the hell is that supposed to mean?"

Huang turned and looked expectantly at Scott. He felt an unexpected flush to his cheeks, as if being targeted to admit his guilt.

"What?"

"You saw it." Huang said simply.

"Saw what?" He was confused. Wondering why she was victimizing him with such an oblique accusation.

"The one who attacked the Tiangong. The one who sank your ship."

Scott looked at each of the others in turn, baffled. He could read mistrust from each of them. "I haven't got a clue what she's..."

But he did.

A memory stirred at the back of his head. Something neglected because of the onslaught of events. An enemy that had attacked them before. An enemy he now realized had been dogging their heels at every turn...

Point Nemo.

The most remote place on the surface of the earth where two great superpowers had been brought together... only to find out they were not alone.

There was another deadly foe hunting them.

THIRTY-TWO

FROM THE EMPTY flight deck of the Liaoning, the emerald waters of the Pacific Ocean looked calm and inviting. It was, however, an illusion created by light reflecting from the shallow tendrils of phytoplankton growth stretching from the smoking black mass of the stricken US fleet just a mile away.

Huang ran her binoculars over the scene, but the smoke obscured any details. She handed them to Scott, who traced the white growth web beneath the surface. Every now and again he would spy a body in the water, clamped in place. A dead crew member held in a snare. Every time he paused, wondering if he'd detect any signs of life, but secretly hoping not to.

A glance over the Ventura revealed the deck and moon pool was still free of infection, despite the growth cradling the outer hull. There was no longer signs of life onboard.

Fortunately, prevailing winds kept the wrecks' toxic smoke at bay, drifting it south west, but a weather report had indicated rougher weather approaching from the north, which would pivot the smoke over the Chinese vessel. Any hope to escape it was quashed when Huang reported the aircraft carrier was stuck in place by the growth. It had reached the propellers, locking the stern in its death grip.

And there was another deadly threat lurking beneath the water.

"How do you know they are Russian?" Maya asked as Scott handed her the binoculars. She had no desire to see the carnage any closer, so offered them to Eric who shook his head. Raven had been taken to the sick bay, too weak to join them despite her protests.

"The sub I saw at the volcanic vents didn't have any markings on it," Scott added.

Huang looked at him with a hint of amusement. "Submarines seldom do. However, sonar profiling identified it as a Yasen-class. Cruise missile capable. We detected the torpedo launch on the volcanic vent. In the noise that followed, we lost track of it. It only showed up again when it sank the Paul Ignatius and then slammed a pair of torpedoes into the Gerald Ford."

"Trying to stop the recovery of the Tiangong, then trying to hide the evidence." Maya looked thoughtful. "Why?"

Huang glanced at Eric and spoke a few short words to him. Eric looked embarrassed, refusing to meet the others' gaze.

"There were indications the Tiangong received an unscheduled visit prior to the outbreak," he muttered.

Scott felt a spark of anger that any details had been withheld. "And you chose not to say this because...?"

"I was instructed not to." He gave a simple shrug.

"Some trusting partner you turned out to be," Maya snapped.

"It is not Dong's fault." Huang nodded to the wreckage on the water. "Until we detected the submarine, we assumed the Americans were responsible." She cast a meaningful look at Maya and Scott. "And their allies."

Scott signed. "Far be it for me to say sharing your information may have come too late. What else aren't you telling us?"

"We have footage of the... encounter. You should see that."

"Yes. We should," snapped Scott, who was rapidly tiring of the political games. "Maybe if you shared this earlier, we could've found a cure, instead we are all dying because your side withheld what they knew."

Huang was torn. "Yes... but orders—"

"Screw orders!" Maya snapped.

Huang looked pleadingly at her. "We don't know who to trust. There could be Russian spies even here..."

Scott stabbed an accusing finger at her, but his words were drowned by a sudden klaxon and a torrent of Mandarin. Huang swung her binoculars up and scanned the horizon.

"What is it?" Scott asked, following her gaze.

Wordlessly, she pointed to the horizon. Maya swept the binoculars back and forth before she spotted it. A small angular silhouette of another ship on the horizon.

"It's a battleship. A big one."

Huang's voice was close to her ear. "It's Russian. And it's heading this way."

EVEN BEFORE THE scientific team had a chance to clear the deck, a pair of Shenyang J-15 fighters rose on the stern elevator, and high-vis wearing crewmen filtered from various access doors to take up their positions. With a blast of air the Shenyangs were catapulted down the runway and leapt to the air, afterburners blazing.

In less than a minute, Scott and the others had been shepherded from the deck and stood in an elevator heading into the bowls of the ship. Aside from the signs, it looked similar to the Gerald R. Ford. The same drab colors; identical pipework running across the deckheads; the same watertight hatches.

Huang led them into a spacious lab that was kitted out with twice as much technology as the hastily assembled US effort. Scott couldn't help but feel annoyed that the Chinese were far more prepared. Raven was waiting for them here. Once the hatchway was closed, the siren faded to a dull squawk.

"Russians?" snapped Raven. "How the hell are they involved in all of this?"

Huang opened a laptop and logged on to a secure server to access a video file. "We warned your Captain. If he decided not to share that with you..." A tilt of the head indicated there was nothing she could do about that. She double-clicked a video file and turned the screen so everybody could see.

It took a moment for any of them to discern what they were looking at, but then sunlight glinted from a black solar panel. It was fixed camera footage from outside the Tiangong. As they watched, the earth rolled into view beyond, an orb of swirling white and vivid blues.

"This static camera recorded the moment."

As they watched, a black smudge poised against the earth slowly grew in size, resolving into a dart shaped craft. It reminded Scott of the now defunct Space Shuttle, only smaller and completely black.

"The XB-37," Eric gasped.

Huang nodded. "That was our first assumption, which is why we didn't share the footage with the Americans." For the benefit of the others, she added, "it is an American unmanned Space Plane built by Boeing and used only by the Air Force on stealth space missions."

Scott gave a doubtful chuckle. Eric nodded.

"It's true. The XB-37 usually stays in orbit for months. For years. Whatever experiments it performs are completely secret."

As they watched, the new craft slowly maneuvered into position. Small white flashes from the thrusters rolled the craft over so that the opening cargo doors were now directly over the solar panel.

With great precision, a robot arm extended from the darkness of the cargo bay. The details were wreathed in shadows, but there was a hint of something held in the claw. Precision servos moved the arm towards the delicate solar panel... then quickly retracted. There was no light to make out details, but it was clear whatever had been held in the claw was now missing.

With a silent flurry of thrusters, the craft quickly banked away out of shot, even as the claw retracted back into the bay. In seconds it was out of view. Huang stopped the video footage, and they stared at the frozen image of the solar panel against the earth.

"You saw it deposited something onto the panel," she said.

Scott nodded. "The same area the growth started." The

fact this was a manmade crisis was now indisputable, even if the reasons behind it were more mysterious.

Huang tapped the screen. "The unusual thing is that this was the only camera that detected the intruder."

Raven spoke up, "It is a stealth craft."

"Maybe," Huang said. "But what I mean is there are several external cameras on the Tiangong, but with it a number of blind spots. That craft used a very precise trajectory to always remain in those blind spots."

"It was entirely successful," said Maya wryly.

"That is because this camera had been recently placed during a spacewalk to observe the solar panel. The crew had been detecting fluctuations in power consumption, a possible manufacturing defect."

Now Scott understood her comment about moles. It wasn't paranoia. "So the only way of knowing where all the cameras were originally placed..."

"Came from the original blueprints." Huang finished. "We found no signs of hacking our systems. Although that doesn't rule out the possibility..." she let her conclusion hang as she swapped the video for an enhanced still of the intruder. "And closer examination shows this isn't an XB-37. It is a similar design, but not as elegant."

Maya leaned in for a closer view, then nodded. "So not quite a copy." She was thoughtful for a moment. "Reminds me of the Buran."

Now Raven was lost. "What is that?"

"The Soviets built their own Space Shuttle, the Buran. It was bigger than the American's. More of a heavy duty workhorse. They ran test flights, but it never reached space. The USSR ran out of cash, then crumbled. The poor old Buran now lies in some military junkyard somewhere."

Huang nodded. "That is our assessment, too. The Russians are the only other power with such technological capabilities. Until we detected the submarine, it was a theory. Now..."

Scott realized he was scratching his arm with more intensity than usual. From beneath the flight suit sleeves, he was alarmed to feel a trickle of blood. He stopped, self-conscious, but nobody seemed to have noticed.

"Why would the Russians, or anybody, do this?" Eric asked. He was having trouble accepting the situation.

"Pure and simple biological warfare," Raven said in a low voice. "This infection was obviously designed to survive the most extreme environments and penetrate the most isolated facilities we could build. The vacuum of space offers the ultimate test bed. They couldn't test it on the ISS, after all, they have Russian crew there."

Eric shook his head. "I still don't believe it."

"It creates a perfect tension between China and the West." Scott was following his chain of thought with no clear destination ahead. "Russia has always wanted to destabilize that relationship. Then the evidence would burn up in the atmosphere. All traces destroyed."

Raven picked up his line. "Except it worked better than expected and wasn't destroyed."

Scott was warming to the theory. "The sub was their first boat on the scene. By blasting the volcano, they hoped to destroy the evidence, or at least the salvage team. Us. And when that didn't work..."

"The rest of the fleet," Maya finished.

Huang hung her head, every movement laced with uncertainty.

A tremor suddenly shook the room. Scott was instantly

brought back to the torpedo strike. He looked at Huang in alarm. A deep silence fell amongst the company as everybody strained to listen.

Another shimmy trembled the floor and walls. The hatch opened, and a crewman pushed the door half open and snapped a few words to Huang, flashing the others a worried look, before he hurried away leaving the door open. Before Maya could asked about the latest development, Huang snatched the laptop and shoved it into a padded satchel. Her voice cracked with worry.

"We need to prepare to abandon ship. We're under attack."

THIRTY-THREE

THE JOURNEY through the passageways was undertaken in strained silence. Occasionally, a tremor would rattle through the ship and the lights would flicker, but the klaxons remained mute.

Huang led them without hesitation, zigzagging through identical corridors that, save the Chinese signage, could have belonged to any nationality. They used alternate stairwells to rise up the levels and avoid isolated areas. This forced Raven to abandon her chair. On foot she was slow and unsteady and she begrudgingly accepted Scott's offer to support her on his shoulder. The absence of any other crew member was a marked departure from the panic onboard the Gerald Ford. Finally, Maya couldn't remain silent.

"How many of the crew have you lost?"

Huang caught her breath as they ascended five fifth levels and reached another closed bulkhead. "About sixty percent. By then I was able to create something that slowed the infection within a host."

Despite the danger, Scott stopped in surprise. "A cure?"

"No, an inhibitor. I tested it on myself. We must keep moving."

Scott found his feet and hurried after her. "How does it slow the infection?"

Huang unlocked another hatch and pushed it open with her shoulder before stepping through. "I used warfarin as a base. It's a blood thinner. I added microbeads to stop it from rapidly dissolving."

A thought sprang into Scott's head, but just as quickly, it vanished.

Huang patted the satchel at her side and glanced at Scott. "All my data is on this."

"If it's just on your hard drive, then that isn't going to help us very much," Scott snapped back dryly.

Huang shot him a look. "It's a start. And..." she broke off, unsure what to say next.

Eric's eyes narrowed as he guessed. "You've already tested it on us, haven't you?"

Huang nodded. Scott stifled an outburst of indignation. He was used to the West's steep requirements to approve tests on people, at least officially. Huang guessed what was on his mind.

"I had little time for approval."

Maya was outraged. "I control what I put into my body. Me. You have no right–"

"Spare me the moral outrage. Perhaps it has prolonged your survival?"

"And what if it hasn't?"

Huang shrugged pragmatically. "You are going to die, anyway." She caught Scott's look. "And don't tell me how different things are in the West. Your governments do the same whether or not you like it. MK Ultra? The infamous

American experiments using LSD. I am missing some key data and I think we're close to a cure, but I need your help, doctor."

A loud staccato hammering from beyond the door ahead caused her to fall silent. It had sounded like high caliber gunfire.

"We need to make our way to the stern. We have lifeboats should we need to evacuate immediately."

"And go where?" said Eric.

Huang looked at him and automatically snapped back in Mandarin, before switching to English. "You are welcome to die here, or at the hands of the Russians. I suspect their interests lie in burying all the evidence at the bottom of the ocean," She indicated to the laptop. "Especially what is on here. Even if they monitored the Tiangong, they wouldn't have all the data required for a full analysis. That's why they needed a spy. We have some of it. But there is more: full atmospheric data from inside the Tiangong and analysis results conducted by the crew on samples and themselves."

"Where is it?"

Huang hesitated.

Maya frowned. "We were told communication with the Tiangong was lost early during the infection."

"Correct. However, the crew were able to physically drop hard drive data back to earth."

"Mercury..." Eric said suddenly. "I thought it had been abandoned?" For the benefit of the others, he held up his hand to indicate the Tiangong. "Communication loss with the station was always a possibility. We proposed a system of escape pods, small projectiles just large enough to dump data and samples in, that could be sent back to earth pending any severe systems failure." With his other hand he mimed a finger-sized pod ejecting back to earth. "Named after the Greek Winged Messenger."

"And risk spreading the infection," Scott said dryly.

"No," said Huang. "The first prototype of Mercury pods had been installed to judge their viability. They were wireless, capable of receiving short-range data bursts from the space station and backing up the systems. They just latched onto the airlock's docking mechanism."

A memory resurfaced from when they had inspected the Tiangong on deck. Scott angrily grabbed Eric's arm and spun him around.

"You knew about this!"

Eric batted his hand away. "What're you talking about?"

Scott took a menacing step forward, forcing Eric to back against the wall. "When we were inspecting the Tiangong's airlocks you acted a little oddly. You told me it was nothing, but you lied."

"I... I..." Eric looked on the verge of breaking down. "I saw the airlock had been used. There was damage that shouldn't have been there. I assumed a docking had failed and damaged the connectors. I knew about the Mercury, but I was never told it had been installed. That's why I said nothing. I just assumed I was wrong."

More heavy thuds rapped from beyond the door. Scott ignored them, his eyes on the laptop.

"How much data do you have?"

"Until the crew were incapacitated. However, we know more readings were uploaded to another Mercury pod. Right up until the Tiangong began re-entry."

Scott felt a jolt of excitement. "You have the entire incubation process?"

"Yes. However, the Mercury didn't detach. As far as we

know it came down with the Tiangong, but it wasn't recovered."

"So it's still down there?"

"Yes. The final dataset that could help stop this outbreak is at the bottom of the ocean. We can only hope the Russians don't know about it." Huang took a breath to compose herself. "But for now, we must reach the lifeboats and be ready for evacuation. Ready?"

A general collection of nods followed nervous glances.

Huang positioned the satchel across her back and spun the wheel lock open.

Daylight seeped in, accompanied by a chilly blast of air. They powered onto the deck, Scott keeping his head bowed as wind stung his eyes. He bumped into Huang who had suddenly stopped in front of him.

He looked up in time to see a Sukhoi SU-57 fighter roar over the deck like a predatory falcon, the Russian's Red Star roundel prominent on its tail.

The Liaoning's Type-730 Gatling gun mounted over their heads screamed to life like a mythical siren, luring the falcon nearer. 5800 rounds per minute were discharged with devastating efficiency, bisecting the Russian fighter as it passed over.

One flaming hulk smashed down on the fight deck, scoring along the runway before flipping from the angled end of the flight deck and into the ocean. The other half exploded in a savage blossom of fire as it disappeared over the side of the deck.

"Holy shit!" yelled Maya, instinctively ducking for cover as another Sukhoi tore the length of the Liaoning, just dozens of feet over the water to keep below the hull so the Gatling gun couldn't draw a bead.

The Russian battleship had kept to the horizon, but had been joined by another larger one – an aircraft carrier. The whirl of rotors dragged their attention to the massive bulk of a Mi-26 helicopter which rose from the ocean's surface, taking cover behind the aircraft carrier's conning tower in a blind spot between the ship's three Gatlings. Eight Russian Spetsnaz troopers were already abseiling from the tail ramp.

"Run!" Huang yelled, shoving Scott forward.

They sprinted across the deck, led by Huang. Eric and Scott found themselves at the back of the pack, stringing Raven between them. Every step was taking it out of her, her face scrunched in pain. Nobody looked back as the Gatling gun opened fire again with hammering that shook their ribcages.

With a scream, a Sukhoi, which must have been flying inches over the waves, sharply rose from behind the up-slung flight deck and raced down the length of the carrier. Its missile pods flared. A second later, the Gatling gun was silenced as it exploded in a violent mass of flame and shrapnel as the projectiles hit home. Pieces of molten shrapnel cascaded across the door they had exited and they all felt the heat from the blast.

Huang took cover at a building at the edge of the deck. She wrested the door open.

"It's too dangerous out here. Come on!"

Maya followed her in. Scott took a step, but was restrained by Raven's arm around his neck. He turned to see Eric, who was holding her other arm, had hesitated as several crewmen ran onto deck some way further down. Glancing behind he saw three Spetsnaz, clad in jet-black biohazard suits, heads concealed by helmets, emerge from the smoke of the Gatling gun. They carried specially built waterproof

APS rifles, which they turned on the crew in a hail of deadly fire.

Three crewman dropped before they could return fire. Then Eric stumbled and Scott immediately assumed he'd been struck.

"Eric..." he began, but then felt Raven's weight increase as two bloody holes in her chest expanded. She dropped between the men, dead before she hit the floor. Eric whimpered and hopped over her body to take cover through the open hatchway.

Scott stared at Raven's body as blood pooled across the deck. His limbs refused to cooperate, and he found himself dumbly rooted to the spot as more gunfire whipped past in both direction; bullets so close they sounded like kamikaze mosquitos, but the noise of the world fell away as if he were suddenly thrust underwater.

Raven's wounds seemed over saturated, a red beyond red, as nauseous panic swelled in his solar plexus as the distinct metallic scent of blood struck his nostrils, which added to his rising anxiety.

Then a calm voice rose from his mind. A whisper from Ruth urging him to flee. Not a sound as such, more his subconscious rallying him back into action.

Before he knew it, Scott leapt through the hatchway even as bullets slammed into the thick metal with such force, they left dents. He landed hard into the passageway beyond as Huang swung the door closed, muffling the chaos of the outside world.

THIRTY-FOUR

THE SENSE of dizziness and plunging sickness in his stomach reminded Scott of a particularly potent joint that had laid him sick for two days in university. It was as if the bad high was coming back with a vengeance. The aftereffects of the adrenaline surge that had carried him down the corridor, combined with the sickening vision of Raven's bloody corpse was hitting him hard.

Huang had led them down a side passageway, before joining another on the opposite side of the ship that led to the stern. Her zigzagging was an attempt to lose any Spetsnaz pursuing them and to avoid areas that had been quarantined because of the infection.

But enough was enough, and Scott found he wasn't the only one who needed to stop.

They leaned against the bulkhead to catch their collective breaths. Nobody wanted to make eye contact. Nobody wanted to discuss what had just happened. The possibility of the infection growing within them somehow paled against the direct human threat.

"This is insane," said Eric, his eyes affixed to the floor. "Why don't we just surrender?"

"Because they just murdered Raven!" Maya snapped back. "And the crew, your fellow countrymen. Didn't you forget that detail?"

"Soldiers fighting soldiers..." he muttered. "She was caught in the crossfire. For all we know, she may have been the spy!"

"Well, that makes me feel so much better." Maya regarded him with open contempt.

"Out on the water we'll be open targets," Scott pointed out.

Huang gestured around. "And if we stay we have a guaranteed death."

A morose silence gripped them all as they contemplated both black scenarios. Alanis suddenly stepped into the center of the corridor, peering behind them, with her head cocked to the side. Scott started to ask her what was wrong, but she held up a finger to silence him. Her other hand reached for her holster and slowly withdrew the pistol.

Her silent action spooked everybody. But the subtle sound of footsteps could now be heard. She urgently gestured to a door a couple of yards away. Eric reached it first and spun the wheel with such force the lock gave a loud clunk as it hit its stop. Huang nudged him aside and slowly opened it.

Scott held his breath...

Then watched as a Spetsnaz, looking like some alien invader in the all-black hazmat suit, stepped around the corner. Alanis immediately unleashed two shots straight for the helmet. The first shattered the glass visor, and the man crumbled backwards around the corner.

"GO!" she yelled.

Huang and Eric were already through the door, running down the flight of steps beyond. Scott shoved Maya through before him, as Alanis walked backwards, her pistol still raised. Then they both saw the Spetsnaz, flat on the floor, scuttle into a firing position and unleash his automatic's magazine at them.

Alanis pushed Scott through door as the bullets hammered into the steel door that now served as a shield.

In the dim stairwell beyond, Alanis yanked her holster off as Scott slammed the door closed. With a few deft moves, she thread the leather straps around the hatch's wheel and tied it to a vertical pipe on the wall.

"It'll buy us some time."

Metal grating clanked underfoot as they rushed down two flights of stairs to join Huang and the others in a tight service corridor. Pipes and conduits ran the length, lit by the occasional hanging bulb.

"I think his runs to the bow." Huang jogged forward.

Scott was finding it difficult to follow. His nausea had increased and his eczema was flaring like hell. When he rolled up his sleeve to look, his skin looked pale and fragile and he swore he saw traces of white veins which disappeared when he scratched.

Was it the light playing tricks? Or was the infection taking hold? He rolled his sleeve back down – but Alanis had already noticed.

"We're all infected," he cautioned.

"So she told us. But if it takes hold of you, I'll shoot." She tapped his forehead.

Scott gave a curt nod. "I'd want you to."

A gunshot rang out, punctuating a pipe above their

head. A jet of pressurized steam spat into the corridor, veiling their attacker. Everybody pushed themselves flat against the bulkhead, the irregular conduits providing some form of cover.

A voice shouted out in Mandarin, but the Russian accent was clear even if the words were not.

"He wants us to surrender," said Eric with more than a hint of relief.

Huang sneered. "If he wanted us dead, he would've missed. They don't know the scientists from the crew. I bet that's the only thing keeping us alive."

"They could help find a cure," said Eric, peering through the veil as the soldier shouted again.

"They've showed that clearly enough," Maya scoffed. "Friendly bunch."

"You're awfully keen on giving up," Alanis snapped.

Pinned against the wall opposite her, Eric scowled. "I'm keen on staying alive!"

"Then we run," Huang said, nodding to a corridor to the left, branching further into the vessel.

Alanis nodded. "After three, I'll cover you." She silently counted down – and everybody ran for the side passage. Veiled by steam, their attacker couldn't see them, but to deter a random shot, Alanis fired a volley of shots behind her to force the Spetsnaz back into cover.

The branching corridor was short, ending in another door which Huang had already opened by the time Scott and Alanis caught up. Behind, the Spetsnaz fired two blind shots.

Stepping into the new room, Scott was hit by a wave of humidity and the stench of infection.

"Smells like hell in here," Maya said, coughing. "Literally."

"It's dimethyl sulfide," said Scott as he looked around. "From the phytoplankton."

Only a few lights worked, most flickering, close to extinguishing, but what they illuminated forced them all to a sudden halt.

They were on a catwalk, midway up a cavernous room that was tall – rising at least three decks, and long, running maybe a quarter of the ship's length. The growth had seeped in through ventilation conduits that were now warped and twisted.

Close by, a pair of open doors were almost blocked by broad white trunks that glistened with moisture. The growth rose from floor to deckhead, coiling around broad cylindrical pillars that stood three abreast, reoccurring further into the gloom. Water dripped steadily off everything, giving the air the scent of a damp forest floor. The entire room had been adapted to the outbreak's perfect microclimate. And amongst the growth...

"The crew..." hissed Maya, eyes affixed to occasional outstretched arms poking from the mass, or face pressed out in a frozen rictus.

Movement from the corridor behind forced them to take refuge behind a biomass of gunk that cut diagonally across the room. Bathed in shadows, Scott craned to watch the Spetsnaz enter the chamber. His rifle swept the room, seeking targets.

Scott dragged his gaze from the soldier to Alanis who was hastily gesturing that they should move deeper into the room. Scott shook his head and indicated to the growth around them, which only irritated Alanis further.

"We're infected already," Huang whispered.

"That doesn't mean it can't get worse," Scott hissed back.

"Worse than a bullet in the head?"

"That's made my mind up." Crouching, Maya moved further down the catwalk, gingerly stepping over growth roots.

Eric hesitated before following. Reluctantly Scott followed, Huang right behind him. They crossed a walkway, slipping past the central pillar so that their escape wouldn't be seen. And it almost worked.

Maya's foot caught a jagged fungal spar, and she tripped with a noise that echoed through the room. She reached out, grabbing the first thing she could–

Another hand projecting from the wall, covered in a sheen of mycelium growth. The cocoon victim's fingers closed around hers.

She yelped, trying to pull free.

Scott reached for a fire extinguisher on the wall, covered by only a thin layer of gunk. He tore it off and bludgeoned the arm holding Maya. She stifled another scream as the face buried further into the wall, turned its eye towards her.

"He's alive!" she hissed.

Bones cracked under the onslaught and Maya was released, the arm hanging awkwardly.

"Not necessarily–" Scott began, reaching to help her up.

"Stop!" The snapped order came from behind them.

Scott froze as the Spetsnaz turned the corner, rifle aimed squarely at Alanis. With his visor shattered, they could see the pale, sweating face of a young man who's training had beaten every ounce of emotion from him.

"Gun down or I shoot," he said with a heavy accent.

Alanis's aim didn't waver as she took a slow step to the left. "I don't think so, Comrade."

He inched the gun higher, eyes narrowing a fraction. There was zero doubt he had no issue killing her. "I mean it."

"That 5.45 round will pass right through me," Alanis said calmly. The Russian nodded menacingly. "And blow a hole in the plating behind me."

The Russian didn't seem to care, but his gaze flickered slightly. Then Scott saw the first traces of emotion: doubt. Scott slowly turned his head. What he had first assumed were several vertical pipes now took in a more menacing presence.

Through a few areas where the mycelium coating thinned, he could make out a red star with a yellow outline painted on the side of the black hull. A chilling yellow and black decal sat just underneath.

"You've got to be kidding me," he gasped. "Are these nuclear bombs?"

"Cruise missiles," Huang acknowledge.

"You have them on an aircraft carrier?" gasped Maya, aware of the basics of military etiquette.

Huang tilted her head. "Not officially..."

The Russian shifted nervously as he heard the conversation.

Alanis's didn't show any hint of worry. "I'm probably as uncertain as you are about what would happen if you shot it. But I don't think any of us want to take that chance. So drop the rifle."

The Russian shifted his balance from one foot to the other as he assessed the situation.

"I will take the chance," he said, although his body language remained unsure. "And you are not a scientist. You are expendable."

Emboldened, Scott aimed the fire extinguisher upwards

and unleashed a CO_2 stream straight up at the wall behind the Russian.

"What're you doing? I'll shoot her!" snarled the Russian, inching the barrel forward.

Scott back away, dropping the extinguisher just as the flow ran dry. He raised his hands in surrender.

"Don't shoot!" He dropped to his knees to emphasize his point.

The Russian was too focused to see the effects of the CO_2 spray. Like a grotesque origami sculpture the fungal wall behind him unfolded. Multiple bodies stacked vertically, even against the deckhead, moved as one. A colossal multi-limbed semblance of a human bonded together and moving in unison. With the speed of a striking cobra, it plucked the Spetsnaz off the catwalk. He screamed, automatic fire spraying across the room before a pair of groping limbs wrapped around his arm with such force they heard bone snap and the rifle dropped.

Eric and Maya were already running from the abomination, but Scott watched with revulsion and astonishment as tendrils of growth poured into the Russian's every orifice, strangling his agonized pleas.

Alanis retrieved the rifle then shoved Huang and Scott forward.

"Move!"

The commotion behind brought the hangar alive. The walls, floor and deckhead undulated in a sine wave rolling straight at them, awakening the animated corpses buried within.

Arms stretched and faces pressed against the layers of growth in silent screams.

Scott's heart pounded and his legs ached as they ran in

single file across the catwalk towards a sealed door. Eric reached it first, but his weight wasn't enough to turn the wheel. Scott didn't slow as Maya lent her weight to it. He glanced behind – and immediately regretted it.

A wave of figures crunched from the wall, spiraled towards them. The mass folded in on itself to form a gaping maw of flailing limbs instead of teeth. Fear convulsed through him and his legs threatened to give way. He turned back to see Eric and Maya, feet pressed against the bulkhead for purchase, use their weight to heave the door open.

Almost as one, they tumbled through the opening and into the passage beyond. Scott was the last one through - tripping over Huang and falling face first against the deck. He rolled over in time to see the viscous mass rise like an enormous serpent in the chamber beyond and strike forward.

Maya reached out to slam the doorway closed – in time for a massive thud to reverberate it from behind.

THIRTY-FIVE

THE DEEP BASSO peel of thunder rolled across the ocean. The once calm waters were now turgid and choppy, breaking into whitecaps because of the shallows created by the malevolent growth.

Alanis leaned on the rail, looking out across the stranded fleet and the still burning US ships. The wind had changed, blowing the toxic smoke more in their direction, but fortunately it was still some degrees away from consuming them. Beyond, the sky was sullen with a heavy storm. Lightning flickered across the panorama; a celestial omen.

The Russian fleet was almost consumed by the storm and there was no sign of their aircraft buzzing around. The lack of foreign aircraft on the flight deck indicated they had been repelled, but how many Spetsnaz remained onboard was impossible to tell.

Alanis pushed against her stomach as another stabbing pain jolted through it. A consequence of infection? She couldn't tell, but she was more than aware she wasn't feeling as strong as usual. Something was wrong; and it was getting worse.

"How long do you think we should wait?" It took a moment for Alanis to realize Maya was addressing her.

Alanis adjusted the Spetsnaz rifle over her shoulder, more to buy herself a few more seconds to think. She had counted on meeting the rest of her crew here. That had been the arrangement made with the Chinese Petty Officer who had fled from the medical bay with them. In the chaos, she had lost Jordan when he doubled back to check on the XO. Alanis had found herself with just two of her crew and three Chinese officers pinned down by three Spetsnaz. They had taken radios from the crew, but no matter how often she called, she couldn't raise Jordan or any of his team.

She had just escaped with two of the Chinese crewmen, one of whom they had to leave behind as he'd caught a bullet in the gut. Her remaining companion had succumbed to the undulating growth ambushing them on a stairwell.

"Alanis?" Maya gently nudged her. "We need you."

Alanis crossed to one of the three the olive hulled ridged zodiac speedboats hanging from davits. A pneumatic arm was poised to swing then out of the enclosed bay.

"We should evacuate now."

"We don't know if they have taken over the ship," said Eric.

"If the Russians haven't, the infection will. Don't you see? It's out of control."

Scott looked out at the glowering storm. "Why not wait until night fall? At least we won't be seen."

Alanis indicated to the sky. "That storm is thirty, forty minutes out. We've run out of time." She patted a zodiac.

"Climb on." Four steps gave easy access for Scott, Huang, Eric and Maya to climb aboard.

Alanis remained on the top step and indicated to the stern. "Survival packs are back there. Anyone driven a boat before?" Scott and Maya nodded. She gestured to the controls. "Everything's straightforward. The starter, throttle, wheel. Just don't sink."

Eric looked around uncertainly. "It doesn't look very stable."

"It's a good wave runner. Get ready to deploy."

Scott looked sharply between the boat and Alanis as she unfastened the straps anchoring the zodiac to the deck. She jumped down from the steps, back onto the carrier.

"What're you doing?"

She moved to a waterproof control panel bolted to the rail and pressed a rubberized button. The panel lit up. "Somebody's got to stay here to lower you down."

"But you're coming with us?"

Alanis's courage was rapidly dissolving, and she found it difficult to look at Scott. She hoped he couldn't see her hand shaking. "My orders were to keep you safe."

She watched the smoke rising from the Gerald Ford. The faces of her friends were vague in her mind's eye. Details blurred and undefined. Perhaps it was grief, but the drive to go back to find Jordan outweighed those losses. She knew the odds for survival were low, but she refused to admit he was dead until she saw it with her own eyes. And then...

"Somebody has to stay behind to operate the davit." To underline her point, she pushed the crane control. Everybody in the zodiac swayed and caught their balance as the mechanism pushed the boat out over the edge.

"You can jump down. Rappel, or–" Scott began.

"I have to know what happened to the others." She tossed her radio to him. "I'll find another. Keep it on channel thirty-three."

While the others rushed to their seats as the breeze swung the boat back and forth, Scott remained standing, holding the strap for support. He shook his head.

"Don't go back in there."

Alanis managed a melancholic smile. "You heard her," she indicated to Huang. "We're dead already. The chances of finding a cure..." she shrugged. "I hope you do. I hope you get to see your kid, doc."

Scott searched for words as the davits locked in place, the boat now ten feet away from the hull.

Alanis gave him a firm nod. "Remember, as soon as you're released, hit the gas. The Russians will be watching. Good luck."

She didn't wait for a response as he thumbed another button. The cable reels spooled, lowering the boat into the choppy water.

AS SOON AS Alanis was out of sight, Scott hooked the radio to his belt and took his place. Maya had left the pilot seat empty. She looked ashen and gently shook her head.

"I'm in no state to drive."

Scott pulled the lap belt tightly around his waist. "All strapped in?" Bouncing from a single wave could easily pitch them overboard. There were a series of confirmations, followed by clinks as buckles were double-checked.

They hit the water with a bone-jarring thud and the davit cables suddenly snapped away, freeing them. Almost immediately a two-foot wave struck the boat along its length, drifting it towards the bulk of the Liaoning.

Scott stabbed the starter button and the duel seventy horse-power engines growled to life. His hand rested on the throttle, edging it up just enough to keep from colliding with the aircraft carrier. Ahead was open water, beyond the reach of the growth. A fast ride away from the collision of three superpowers.

But even if they could slip away unnoticed, then what?

They had fuel for two hours before the hungry engines left them stranded. It would hardly be enough to distance themselves from the human threat, and next to nothing to draw them closer to civilization.

"What are you waiting for?" snapped Eric using the flat of his hand to thump the side of the boat. "Get us out of here!"

Even drifting, they wouldn't have enough food. Thousands of miles from land – and most of that was nothing but uninhabited rocks, and just as far from any semblance of a shipping lane or a flight corridor.

They could drift for eternity...

... Spreading the plague to whoever found them.

Ruth. Her name burnt into his conscience like a branding iron.

He slammed the throttle forward, and the zodiac responded instantly, the prow rising high into the air as they crest another swell. The open ocean was head.

He twisted the wheel hard to starboard, a curtain of water rising as the boat inscribed a tight U-turn.

"What're you doing?" screamed Eric.

Scott ignored him as he aligned the boat towards his target. Now was not the time to flee. It was time to fight.

THIRTY-SIX

ERIC LEANED FORWARD to reach Scott, but was held back by his belt. It was just as well. The zodiac hit a swell with such speed it lurched out of the water, thrusting him back in his seat with bone jarring force.

"Turn around!" Eric snapped.

"We're only going to die out there," Scott shouted back. "At least this way we have a fighting chance."

The others remained silent, guessing at his intentions as they sped towards the Ventura. He didn't dare keep his eyes off the water. Growths had sprouted from the water, acting as jagged rocks that could split the zodiac in two like a cantaloupe.

He swerved hard left to avoid one just beneath the surface, then brought the boat back on track. A protracted isolated death had not been the deciding driver in his decision, the desire for life was.

It was the single most driver in ever organism. From bacteria through to flora and complex primates. Stay alive at all costs. An indelible torch that every life form wielded. And to do that, all life had the same strategy:

"It's evolving!" he shouted over the roar of the engines, swaying the zodiac around another set of spurs reaching from the water. "In the hangar onboard the Gerald Ford it attacked us with individual components. It moved slowly. But back there, it showed mass coordination at speed. The ability to use all of its parts as a single entity. It's adapting, evolving, learning."

"Learning?" Huang shouted back. "It's mutated plankton. It can't think!"

Extremophiles tested the limits of scientists' understanding of what life could do, even the basics of what life actually was. He long ago relied on thinking what was once unthinkable.

He arced the boat around another mass, looming like a white ice berg, some four feet from the water.

"Perhaps they're using the hosts' minds."

Maya was aghast. "I thought the infected were dead?"

"No. Remember the Taikonauts' EEG readouts? They showed heightened activity, their bodies may not be alive in the traditional sense, but their minds–" The breath was forced out of them as they ramped over a particularly nasty wave, hitting the water hard on the other side. "It might be keeping their brains alive, a semblance of consciousness. What if the infection was using them all together?"

"Like a network computer," Eric chimed in, fascinated, despite his anger.

"Exactly. A hive mind capable of out-thinking any one of us and acting in unison. The problem it'll have is transference of information. Cells communicate quickly because of the microscopic distances, nanometers, involved. Over the course of several meters, the collective reaction time is sluggish."

"Which is how we outrun it," Huang finished.

"Exactly. Once communication speed has increased..." he left the threat hanging.

"Scott! Look!" Maya pointed to something in the sky.

First impressions that it was a lone bird, an albatross perhaps, but when their isolation was factored in, it was obvious no bird could stray so far. It was a drone, too far to distinguish details, but its purpose was clear.

"If they wanted to blow us from the water they've had plenty of time." He heard the doubt in his own words, but the irrational part of his brain clinging to survival cherished the lie.

With no further discussion, they wend their way through the shallows, towards the Ventura. The growth gripped the vessel around the plimsole line, but hadn't spread beyond. As far as they could see, the deck appeared to be infection free even if there were no signs of life.

Eric had become more subdued, keeping an eye on the ever-vigilant drone. In the lee of the Ventura and in shallow waters over the growth, the zodiac gently bobbed even as the wind increased around them.

As they stared up at the deck Eric unfastened his belt and stood up, arms stretched to catch his balance. "I still don't understand why we are here." He cupped his mouth with both hands and yelled. "HELLO! VENTURA! HELP!" His voice was absorbed by the expanse.

Scott followed his gaze to the deck. "Evolution depends on mutations. You know, the old survival of the fittest?"

"Yes. So?"

Scott looked at Huang. "You've slowed the infection rate

within us." She nodded. He looked at the others, as if lecturing his university students. "Which means there are flaws in the infection's genetic makeup that we can exploit. Remember, this is a forced combination of DNA and RNA. That's unstable, it will have weaknesses." He indicated to Huang. "Her research has bought us time. The only way we'll find that weakness is have all the data."

Eric looked at him incredulously. "You want to retrieve the Mercury pod?"

"We must. Or we'll be out-evolved."

Movement suddenly caught his eye from the bow. As the wind picked up, it happened again – a pair of ropes trailing from the deck. Scott eased the throttle and drifted closer for a better view. The roped were tied to the gunwale, about two meters apart, their tips drifting in the water.

"Somebody was sure in a hurry to leave," said Maya.

Now at the rear of the Ventura, the increased wind drove fat raindrops at them. Scott edged towards the ropes.

"That's our way on." He inched forward, the zodiac riding against the energetic waves that wanted to slam them against the heavy Ventura. "Fish the ropes out. Be careful."

Eric held on to Maya as she reached into the water and pulled a rope out. It was the diameter of her wrist and heavily waterlogged. She dropped it onto the deck and reached for the second rope.

"I need another meter." Scott obliged and, after a third attempt, she scooped that onboard too. She reeled in the slack of the second rope. It was a sheer ten meter climb in buffeting wind and rain. Difficult at the best of times, but after the turmoil of the last few days she was afraid she lacked the strength.

The zodiac rolled in a wave, suddenly crunching against

a submerged growth with a prolonged screech. Scott could see the inner starboard deck buckling.

"We need to board now. The wind's picking up."

Maya offered the rope to Eric. He looked at her in horror.

"I can't do that!"

"Then you're going to spend the rest of your life on this boat."

Scott jostled the rudder to ride a wave. It was bigger than he expected, and the small boat was broadsided into the Ventura's stern. The impact jarred everybody. Eric flailed as he teetered overboard–

Scott stumbled over his seat and snagged Eric's arm – disrupting his fall just enough that he bounced off the edge of the zodiac and back inside.

"I can't keep this up! We need to start climbing!" Scott barked as he scrambled back on all-fours back to the wheel. A touch on the throttle moved them feet away from the Ventura.

Huang secured her satchel around her back and took the second rope from Maya. Wrapping it half around her forearm she took in the slack and then swung out.

She struggled to keep her feet from the water as they skimmed the surface. Both feet hit the vertical steel wall at the same time, the rubber soles squeaking as she fought for grip. With every muscle straining, Huang moved upwards, hand-over hand. She adjusted her feet, gripping the rope between them. A move that gave her a swifter ascent.

Maya followed, swinging against the stern. She powered quickly upwards, surprised that she overtook Huang. The wind blew harder and with it the rain increased intensity to the point it stung as it struck their faces.

Scott struggled to keep the boat in position, shielding his

eyes as he craned up to watch their progress. It was an impossible task. The zodiac corkscrewed in a sudden current; the prow striking a white limb that held the Ventura in place. The growth's serrated edge sawed into the metal hull, wedging the boat in place. Water trickled through the gash.

Scott stared at it in disbelief. "Great. Just... great."

It was already ankle deep; the craft floundering to the side by the time Maya flipped over the gunwale. She reached down to help Huang onboard. Then they disappeared from view.

"Throw the ropes!" Scott shouted up. The lines dangled into the water, some three meters away. He shouted again, but perhaps they couldn't hear because of the storm.

The zodiac suddenly shook as it grounded on the submerged growth. It was only a few centimeters under water, but now useless. Scott judged they could wade over the growth to reach the ropes. Eric's reluctance was tempered by the fear of drowning and he kept close to Scott as they clambered over the side and dropped into the ocean.

Water came over their boots and Scott had expected the submerged growth to feel solid underfoot, instead it felt like rubber. Reaching a rope, he took hold with both hands and gave the submerged growth a kick. To his surprise fragments flaked off. He kicked at the part above the water that held the Ventura in place. That was as tough as coral, yet under the water if appeared to weaken.

Eric pulled the rope tight. "I don't know if I can make it all the way up there."

"You can stay here."

"I don't have the strength. I never have."

The surrounding water surged as the rain picked up.

Some broke at thigh height. As the storm increased, it would take them both.

"MAYA! HUANG!" Scott yanked the rope. Still no response. What had happened? He suddenly doubted the wisdom of climbing up into the unknown... but if they didn't, they'd soon be swept away. "I'll go up. Tie the end under your arms and I'll pull you up."

Eric nodded and began looping the rope around his back. "Are you sure this is a good idea?"

Scott gripped the damp role and took up the slack. "I've been out of good ideas since I arrived here. Just make sure you're tied on tight."

With a grunt, Scott pulled himself up, locking his knees and feet against the rope. It was too slick, and he slipped a hand's length before stopping. He stretched again, the muscles in his arms and legs trembling as he increased the pressure to hold him in place.

Cold wind buffeted him almost in circles. Rain stung his eyes. Yet he powered doggedly upwards. Forced to angle his head, he couldn't quite see how far the gunwale was, but each heave on the rope drew him closer.

A fall onto the jagged growth would kill him and twice the slick rope slipped through his hands and feet as it threatened the possibility. Each time he arrested his fall and pushed himself harder up the rope. He found himself pressed against the flat stern; the wind slamming him against it like a tolling bell. Every muscle screamed, reminding him how years of academia had robbed him of any core strength.

"A couple more feet," he snarled to himself. "Just a few more feet..."

Hand-over-hand, he edged upwards – his head suddenly clipping the gunwale. The relief at reaching his destination gave him renewed strength. With rain still stinging his eyes, he almost blindly heaved himself over the rail. He landed hard on the deck and lay there, catching his breath. The rain hammered at him, chilling him to the skin. Shivering, he pulled himself up the rail. Eric's voice drifted from below.

"Scott?"

Scott peered down and saw Eric was on his knees as the waves threw him repeatedly against the hull.

"I'll pull you up," Scott eventually shouted after his voice caught twice.

He doubted he possessed the energy, but if he didn't do something, Eric would drown on the end of the rope. Reaching over the rail, he gripped the coarse wet cord in his hand, braced both feet apart and heaved, lifting Eric a meter. Something rolled underfoot. Thinking it was a bolt on the deck, he stepped to the side.

That's when he saw it wasn't a bolt, but two bloody severed fingers. He let go of the rope with start.

THIRTY-SEVEN

THE BREATH WAS CHOKED from Eric as he dropped back into the water.

Up on the deck, Scott pushed himself away from the severed fingers around looked wildly around. The vacant helicopter pad covered the stern, with access to the bridge tower through a single door. Walkways cut either side of the deck, leading to the huge moon pool behind the tower. There was no sign of life, or to whom the fingers belonged.

Including Maya and Huang.

Eric shouted from below. Leaning closer to the fingers told him two things: they belonged to a man, and the dried blood indicated they had been lost some hours earlier.

Not wishing to draw attention to himself, he leaned over the rail and indicated Eric should remain silent. Then he took the rope, braced one foot against the rail, and heaved with every ounce of strength. The wind and rain increased as if a switch had been pushed up a notch, complete with a loud crack of thunder. He gave the Gerald R. Ford a wary glance, noticing the smoke had moved further in their direction, although the wind was thankfully dispersing the thick cloud.

Scott's arms and legs trembled with each strain on the rope. He found that by anchoring the rope around his body like a capstan he could spread Eric's weight more evenly.

Little by little, he heaved the scientist into sight.

Eric extended a frozen hand and Scott hauled him onto the deck. Eric lay curled up and shivering as he blew into his cupped hands.

"We can't stay here," he whispered.

"I need a few minutes," Eric said through chattering teeth.

"No. If hypothermia doesn't get you, we're going to inhale the carrier's reactor fumes." He saw Eric's eyes widen when he noticed the smoke coiling in the wind. "And if that's not bad enough... I think there's something out here."

Scott scanned the deck as he helped Eric up. Their nearest path inside the ship was straight across the helipad and into the tower. They hurried across. Despite the lack of fungal growth onboard the ship, there was an atmosphere of abandonment that hinted something wasn't right. Midway across the pad, Scott suddenly veered ninety degrees away, pulling Eric by the elbow.

"What're you doing?"

"This feels all wrong," Scott said, now heading towards a metal stairwell that zigzagged down the side of the helipad, the one they had taken every time he'd been onboard.

No sooner had they taken several steps when the door to the bridge tower was savagely pushed open from inside. Aided by the wind, it slammed against the metal bulkhead – and something charged towards them.

At first sight it was one of the Ventura crew. A hulking

man almost six and a half feet tall. His arms hung in an odd swaying motion and he ran with a pronounced limp. Only a second look showed that his head had cleaved in two, his thick beard torn asunder as if tectonic plates in his head had moved north/south to warp his skull. The halves barely held together by laces of white growth.

Scott stared in disbelief for a moment too long. The battered excuse of a man rapidly closed the gap.

A sharp gunshot from behind him made Scott crouch. A chunk of the man's chest blew apart in a bloodless mess of dried flesh and fungal growth. A second loud report blew the man's head clean off his shoulders. That didn't stop his charge.

Scott yanked Eric out of the way as the corpse, seemingly on auto-pilot, sprinted across the helipad and clean over the side – bouncing off the gunwale and into the waters below.

Scott tore his gaze from the beast to their savior: Vasilis. He lowered the shotgun. Looking as if he'd aged a decade but still managed to flash a smile.

"You took your time getting here."

STEAM from the boiling kettle warmed Scott and Eric's hands. The incongruous nook Vasilis had led them to was somewhere deep within the engine room and still had electricity; at least enough for a single naked bulb and a kettle. The Greek poured the water over tea bags in a pair of cups, then generously added heaped spoonfuls of sugar and a slug of brandy.

"There, that'll keep ya going for a while longer." He handed them over.

Scott wrapped his fingers around the warm ceramic, thankful for finally stopping shivering.

"That man... he was different from the others we've seen."

Vasilis swigged directly from the bottle. "The infection never reached the deck here. But some folks still got it. From the, moon pool we think. It spread... but we controlled it a little. From what we could see on the other ships, we got lucky."

"That stretches my definition of 'luck'." Eric rubbed his temples. Scott noticed he looked paler than usual. Fatigue was affecting them all, but Eric couldn't conceal the smallest of reactions such as clenching his fist as he winced in pain.

Vasilis gave a haunted look. "I saw how the infection takes hold. One moment they're normal, the next," he snapped his fingers, "they just go. As if a switch had been thrown. Drop like a sack of olives. Dead before they fall." He wagged a thoughtful finger. "But inside, the disease takes control. Like a puppet." He closed his eyes, painfully relieving the moment. "I have seen it swell the head. Cracking open the skull like a walnut and then they come alive."

"Not quite alive," Scott said in an effort to assure him, although, as usual, his tone was a little too clinical. "Animated like you said. Their neural control has been hijacked..." He lapsed into thoughtful silence which was broken when he heard voices from the two crewmen who had been guarding at the end of the corridor. Vasilis reckoned there were eleven of his crew left, all guarding key areas such as the bridge, engine room and stores.

Moments later Markus appeared with a harpoon gun over his shoulder. Huang and Maya followed.

Scott felt a flood of relief. "Thank God you're okay. When you disappeared—"

Maya flashed a smile and patted Markus's shoulder. "Saved by Markus here. One of those crazies ambushed up on deck. He took care of it." Her jocular tone was at odds with Markus' stern expression; he had been forced to kill a fellow crewmate. "They're mostly on deck. They don't seem to have grasped the basics, such as opening doors."

Huang indicated to a plastic tray holding six glass vials. "I wanted water samples from the moon pool. They have a small lab setup here for monitoring pollution and I want to know why this ship is not infected like the others."

"Because my father made a good ship," Vasilis said with a weak smile.

"That he did. I just need to know how. And the infection here, why is it so different? If the growth has been creating an inter-linked network, how are they able to walk on their own?"

Scott had been thinking about that, and one word had struck in mind. "Drones. Like I said before, it's evolving, adapting. For whatever reason it couldn't spread the infection directly here. It reached the limits of its infection capabilities."

Maya was confused. "How does that explain it?"

"I told you life's primary drive is to stay alive. Its secondary driver is to reproduce. And here it hit a problem, then a solution. What if it could infect a host, and then detach it from the network with the sole purpose of spreading infection?"

"That's why they're so aggressive," Maya frowned as the implications set in. "And if it adapted that quickly... we're not talking about a plague that destroys a few ships."

"No. We're looking at a worldwide infection within weeks if it ever reached civilization," said Eric softly.

"No wonder the Russians wanted to put a lid on this," Maya said.

Vasilis and Markus exchanged a grim look. The Greek sipped his tea, silently reaching a conclusion of his own.

Huang set the samples on a bench. "I may extract some extra information from these." She looked at Scott. "If you can retrieve the Tiangong's data dump from the seabed, we may have enough to synthesize a cure."

"The chances of finding it in the dark, at those depths..."

"It emits a signal, like a black box recorder. It's weak, but I have the frequencies. You just need to be in the general area to pick it up."

Vasilis gave a curt snort. "What if there is no cure?"

Huang looked defiantly at him. "Maybe there's not. But I want to find that out for myself. And if there is no cure..."

"Then we cannot leave." Vasilis finished for her. He eyed each of them. "We will have to destroy every trace of it. Everything!" Then he added in a low voice. "Including ourselves."

THIRTY-EIGHT

THE RAPID PATTER of dripping moisture reminded Alanis of the rainforest. The last vacation with Jordan in fact, clambering up the flanks of the Arenal volcano in Costa Rica. That's where they announced their engagement, knowing it would put their careers in the sights of the Navy's mercurial fraternization policy. They hadn't had time to decide what they would do. They had assumed they'd have plenty of time...

Alanis froze at an intersecting passageway. Glistening white growth seeped from the ceiling, oozing down the bulkhead with the sickening stench of sulfur. The air was cloying and unbearably humid. A noise from the branching corridor made her slowly and silently slip the Spetsnaz rifle from her shoulder. Her thumb automatically checked the safety was off.

The lights flickered offering glimpses of a mass of mycelium spiderwebbing across the corridor. She tried to envisage where she was on the ship. The layout was not too dissimilar to Gerald R. Ford, and she was confident that she was heading to the aircraft hangar close to where she had last seen Jordan.

Then another sound, not the familiar mechanical beat she was used to on a ship. Perhaps a flutter, or subtle crunching. Indefinable, but most definitely organic.

Unfortunately, it came from was the way her internal map was telling her to go.

Steeling herself, Alanis stepped into the new passage. Darkness lasted for a few seconds before a strobing light gave a precious moment of illumination - then plunged her back into the dark.

The precipitation increased. The floor became increasingly slick underfoot. She tried not to think about what lethal spores she was inhaling from the cloying air.

She had been heading for'ard, but this new passage took her starboard. The growth sprouted across the floor like wild tree roots and stepping between them was becoming increasingly difficult.

The occasional flash of Chinese symbols beneath the growth were of no help to navigate through the vessel. She had learnt basic Mandarin, but it was verbal training with little regard given for written text.

There was a person ahead. Impossible to make out details in the strobing light, but certainly human.

Alanis stopped dead and raised her rifle.

"Freeze!"

No response. She shifted her balance, almost slipping on the tendrils underfoot. One of the Americans would have surely responded. She tried her fleeting Mandarin. Still no response. A Russian would have shot her by now.

She edged closer.

"Hands where I can see them or I will shoot." The words were more for her own comfort.

Now she saw the figure was pressed against the wall, and the definition of a black Russian hazmat suit came into sharp focus, the face hidden behind the visor.

Alanis raised the gun for emphasis. "Do you understand?"

Even as she spoke, she noticed the edge of the Hazmat suit was fused against the growth, putting her in mind of a carnivorous plant trapping its prey. How a fast moving soldier was caught troubled her. All she had to go was walk past, and she would be closer to finding Jordan.

She edged closer. Only a couple of feet separating them in the narrow corridor. From the angle of the body, it seemed as if he had been heading towards her. Was she walking into greater danger?

Feeling foolish for brandishing the rifle she lowered it to her hip, although never moving the barrel away from the man. She tensed, ready to sprint past.

A horrendous cracking noise caused the man's body to shudder. Alanis stopped, but skidded on the wet floor. She fell hard on her ass.

An accident that saved her life.

The Spetsnaz's visor exploded into splinters. She caught a brief glimpse of a mangled face as an appendage punched out. It slammed into the opposite wall with the force of a jackhammer – where Alanis's head had been seconds before.

As she fell, her finger squeezed the trigger. The arcing barrel threaded bullets across the man's chest. Bloodless chunks of flesh were torn away – but he didn't stop lashing for her. Alanis turned and ran.

She would have to find another route to the hangar.

THIRTY-NINE

"I SEE FOUR OF THEM."

Pressed against the catwalk in the lee of bridge, Scott lifted his head for a better view across the Ventura's foredeck. Elevated two decks above the moon pool, the vantage offered a partial view across the length of the ship. The driving rain splashed in the pool with such fury that it obscured the control booth window at the end of the pool.

The two submersibles were suspended feet over the water, secured between the cranes and straps securing them to the edge of the pool. Three jet skis bobbed erratically in the water, tied to the side of the pool which they kept crashing against. He spotted movement behind them. Four shambling crew who had moved out of his line of sight.

"I can't see much of the starboard side of the deck," Scott said raising his head – which Vasilis unceremoniously pushed back down.

"We take no risks," the Greek snapped quietly. The bridge offered the best view, but he warned them away.

Wind screeched as it cut through the communications

masts and hurled spume over the side. Vasilis had supplied all-weather gear for the new arrivals, but it did little to stop Scott shivering.

Vasilis and Maya lay by his side. Eric, Huang and Markus kept further back keeping an eye out for danger.

"Can we take them out from here?" Maya regretted asking when she noticed Vasilis' pained expression. They were his companions, friends, now twisted and tortured beyond comprehension.

"With what?" Vasilis growled. "This?" He indicated to the harpoon gun flat on the catwalk in front of him. "Markus has the only gun. We are a research vessel, not a warship. Sailors and scientists, not soldiers. None of us expected to murder friends."

Scott didn't have the capacity to engage with Vasilis's personal trauma. A part of him, a small part, felt selfish for focusing on his own future, but the desire to make it back to Ruth, to move into fatherhood, was driving now.

Vasilis continued, "You can harpoon them through the heart and still they come. It is like trying to injure a tree."

"They were just ambling," Scott pointed out.

"They respond when you get close, but that doesn't make them any less dangerous. I saw one pull a man's arm off. We might make it to the subs, but we still need time to launch. And that's not our main problem." He pointed to the small control booth at the far end of the moon pool. "Somebody must be in there to open the pool doors, otherwise we're going nowhere."

"What if we wait for nightfall?" Maya suggested.

Vasilis shook his head. "Light doesn't affect their hunting ability. They're just as lethal in the dark. And then we can't see them coming." He indicated to the burning aircraft carrier, now nothing more than a dark smudge in the driving rain. "The wind is still keeping the smoke away from us. But it is liable to change."

A mass of toxic and radioactive fumes blowing across the Ventura would surely result in a swift death. Time was against them on multiple fronts; hesitation or contemplation were luxuries that could only lead to death.

Survival was now a matter of instinct, and Scott was deeply troubled by the notion. Nature was merciless on those who acted on impulse alone.

"If you insist we do this," Vasilis said, "we must do so now."

Common sense was screaming at Scott, demanding he return below decks and wait for help to come. An irrational hope, of course. The only route to rescue lay with the Russians and life with them would be temporary.

Scott met Maya's gaze. Her liquid blue eyes were bloodshot, but kept the defiant sparkle that had been there from the beginning. She gave a sharp nod.

"Then let's go," Scott said firmly.

Vasilis flashed a hand gesture to Markus who rose and crouch-ran ahead of them, his shotgun pressed firmly against his shoulder, the barrel leading the way he had seem in countless special forces movies. At the top of the stairwell, he gestured for Huang and Eric to join him.

Vasilis stood and followed, Scott and Maya in tow. They stopped at the top of the steps and looked over the empty deck.

Vasilis patted Scott firmly on the shoulder.

"I will head straight for Mowgli and pilot the sub with you. Markus knows how to operate the launch mechanism." He looked at Maya. "You'll go with him and watch his back."

Maya gave a curt nod. Vasilis turned to Huang and Eric. "You two will need to cover is across the deck. Once Mowgli is underway, Markus will take you to the lab until we return."

Eric nervously licked his lips. "What if you don't return?"

Vasilis treated him to a thin smile. "Then you will no longer be my problem." On autopilot, Vasilis crossed himself.

Markus slinked down the stairwell to the deck – the suddenly froze.

From the blindside of the bridge an infected woman shambled into view, one leg dragging as if she hadn't quite understood the basics of locomotion. Some twenty feet away, she seemed oblivious to their presence.

As Markus trained his shotgun on her his face darkened in recognition and a tear streamed down his cheek. With a motion of his head indicating the others should follow, he crouch-ran to a line of fuel barrels lashed to a metal rail. The storm masked any noise or scent from them.

They sat on the floor behind the barrels and composed themselves. Purple lightning forked overhead, accompanied by a mighty boom that made the infected twitch nervously, turning to-and-fro to detect the source of the noise.

Scott watched curiously. "When ants are infected by a fungal spore, it takes control of their motor functions. There is no real consciousness involved, just a series of chemical triggers. That's what we have here." He gripped Markus's arm. "That's what you must understand. They are not your friends now. They're just empty husks acting on base impulses to attack and infect."

From Maya's grimace and Markus's scowl, he guessed his pep talk lacked any subtlety.

Vasilis indicated to the suspended Mowgli. "Gaining access will be the problem. Do you see the maintenance rungs on the spine of the crane?" Scott shielded his eyes from the rain and saw the 'n-shaped' rungs rising up the side of the cab, then flat along the top of the jib. "We scale up the crane, then slide down harness, onto the Mowgli's hatch." Scott didn't relish the task, but without the time to lower the submersible into the water and board it in a more civilized manner, he didn't have a choice.

The infected didn't respond to another flash of lightning, but jerked as the thunder peeled around them.

"It's blind," noted Scott. "It's using sound, possibly smell and vibrations, but visually we have the upper hand."

"That doesn't make me feel any safer," said Eric. "This whole plan is foolish."

Huang snapped at him in Mandarin. Whatever she said was enough for Eric to look away in shame, his cheeks burning.

"There's another," Huang pointed beyond the woman, whose head was still scanning the sky, to another halfway around the moon pool. It had emerged from behind the raised control room. "Where have the others gone?"

Two missing.

Vasilis brought the harpoon gun around to his chest, cradling the useless weapon. "Let's go."

Scott gave a curt nod – then they both crouch-ran towards the crane. Scott was sure the infected vision was shot, but he still didn't want to take the chance. Fortune steered the two infected away from their path as Markus led others counter-clockwise around the pool.

Halfway to the crane and they still had gone unnoticed. Scott couldn't believe their luck.

Nor should he.

The woman's head snapped around and stared in their direction. Scott froze, but Vasilis continued silently padding across the deck. Scott's heart was in his mouth – but the woman didn't take a step. Her head moved slightly as if listening. He could see how her skull had grotesquely split half an inch from her left jaw to above her top-right ear.

Vasilis reached the crane before he noticed the woman looking their way. He too froze, one foot on the ladder rung, coiled and ready to spring.

The woman took a step – then looked sharply up as another volley of purple lightning stabbed the sky. Masked by the pounding thunder, Scott sprinted for the ladder. Vasilis took his cue and rapidly climbed the rungs.

By the time Scott reached the crane, the others were yards away, turning the corner of the moon pool – and straight into the path of one of the missing infected who had wandered from a hatchway in the deck. Wearing torn engineering coveralls, the man rushed them at incredible speed. Scott stopped himself from crying out a warning, saving himself unwelcome attention.

Maya caught the sudden movement and gave a startled cry. Just a few steps away a pair of long-handled catch poles were clipped to the rail around the moon pool. She snagged one both hands and spun around like a discus thrower - using her full weight slash it sideways.

The dual hooks ripped through the man's throat. Parched alabaster skin crumbled as the infected's momentum drew the hooks in deeper. He didn't stop as half his neck tore away. With a sustained crack the head lolled sideways, hanging from his chest by only a sliver of skin and muscle. It didn't stop the creature's attack as it zeroed in on Maya.

As the hook sunk further in, the wooden handle was torn from her hand. The end clattered to the deck – scraping as it was pushed forward. Maya gasped as she backed against the rail, the beast clawing at her. There was no escape.

Then the pole's leading edge slammed against the bottom of the rail, drawing the man up short and acting as a catch pole that was lodged in his torn neck. It prevented him from getting closer. His gnarled fingers inches from Maya's face.

Just meters away, Markus rounded his shotgun – but hesitated from shooting the infected's back as it would hit Maya too. He jinked his aim to the deck and pulled the trigger.

The violent retort blew the man's leg off, unsettling his balance. He toppled sideway. Maya snatched the catchpole and levered it around, using the infected man's own weight to crash him against the rail. She followed through by thrusting all her wright forward, flipping the creature over the rail.

The pole was plucked from her hands as the man splashed into the choppy moon pool, arms and legs kicking wildly as the semi-dismembered head began dragging it down.

Scott reached the top of the crane's cab in time to see the water around the man pop and fizzle like Alka-Seltzer as he sank.

Vasilis was half-way up the thin spine of the crane, holding on with both hands as the wind attempted to unsettle him. "Bowers!"

The third Infected had scaled up the front of the bridge tower using the thin portholes rims for purchase. This one was distorted to define the gender; all traces of humanity had been mutated beyond reason. Alerted to its quarry, it powerfully launched himself off the wall of the bridge - arcing straight for Scott.

Instinct forced him to roll to the side. One hand still gripped the horizontal rung at the base of the crane's jib as he tumbled off the edge. His body swung down hard, slamming against the side of the cab and crushing the wind out of him.

The Infected's limbs windmilled without coordination. It rammed into the side of the cab with such force the rear Perspex window shield fractured as his legs struck almost perpendicular. It's dehydrated midriff sliced against the crane roof's extended metal lip. It cut through his stomach like a blade.

Soft desiccated flesh was torn asunder with a hideous crack. Its kicking legs dropped to the deck and continued thrashing while the severed torso skidded across the roof.

With a grunt, Scott swung himself back up onto the cab, rolling onto his back – only to come face-to-face with torso, its mouth extended in a silent hiss. It reached out a hand, fingers elongating and twisting as the growth had expanded to reach him.

Scott swiveled around and used both feet to boot the Infected's head. Its weakened jaw snapped off as the half-body fell – bouncing off the top of the Mowgli submersible, before splashing into the moon pool and quickly submerging.

Vasilis exchanged a wide-eyed look with Scott before hurrying his trek along the jib.

On the edge of the pool, Markus was shouting in Greek, clearly urging the others forward as the two other Infected shambled across the deck. But speed was with the living. They reached the far control booth well ahead of their pursuers.

Vasilis slid down the retraining strap holding the sub in

the water and had the hatch open by the time Scott joined him. They swung into the sub and sealed the above them. They put their headsets on as Vasilis took the pilot's seat and powered up the system. Eric's voice came through from the control booth.

"–Read me?"

"Copy," Vasilis said. "Everybody safe?"

They could hear a muffled banging underlying Eric's words. "We're all in one piece. Just not so sure how we plan to get out of here alive."

"One thing at a time," Vasilis said dryly. "Tell Markus we are ready for launch."

The submersible shuddered as it descended to the water. Scott peered through the Perspex canopy between his feet as they splashed down with a jolt. The once clear water was clouded with white fungal filaments and he could no longer see the bottom of the pool.

"I wonder what's breaking up like that?"

Vasilis was mildly annoyed about being distracted from his pre-launch checklist. "Mmm?"

"The phytoplankton's bonds isn't maintaining integrity."

A metallic reverberation sung through the water as the doors beneath them opened. A sudden swirl of water cleared visibility just enough for him to see the dark shadows of the doors opening.

Vasilis keyed the mic. "Visibility is shit. Release the line."

Scott wiped the sweat from his brow and Vasilis took it as a cue to increase the air conditioning. They both looked up expectantly, waiting for the strap to release.

"We're still tethered."

"Hold on." They could hear muffled voices over the radio

before Eric came back. "It reads this side that the crane has disengaged."

Scott stood and peered through the hatch's circular portal. "There's some growth entangled around the mechanism."

Vasilis nodded. "Lift us up again."

After an overly-long pause it was Maya's voice that came over the radio. "We can't. Looks like the crane's drive motor has burned out. If there was any crap in the mechanism..."

"We need to release it manually," Vasilis glanced across at the control booth, just visible over the water's surface. "There's no way they could make it out of there just to do that."

"Do you have a knife?" Vasilis handed him a penknife from his pocket. Scott gripped the hatch's lever.

"Watch the waterline." Vasilis eyed the water level that was now at head height. He didn't need to warn Scott that if it lapped inside, there would be no stopping it, and the sub would be dragged into the depths.

With a hiss of air pressure that sent Scott almost deaf, he popped the hatch and clambered on his seat to help hoist himself out. Sitting on the lip of the hatch, he could just reach the cradle's hook. Jabbing the knife into the fungal growth around the mechanism he was surprised to see it come easily away. Once again, Scott wondered what had changed in its makeup. Aware the water was only inches away from spilling into Mowgli, he checked his balance with each stabbing motion and soon had most of fungus cleared out.

A plume of water erupted at the sub's stern.

Scott jerked aside, almost toppling into the water. The vehicle's position shifted in the water, pivoting the open hatchway towards the water's surface, as something heavy clambered up the rear thrusters.

It was the severed torso of the crewman which now looked more horrific than ever. The face had melted like candle wax in the pool. Fine chunks glistened as it continued to slop down its cheeks. It hauled itself up the thrusters with difficulty as some fingers had bonded together making the hands resemble clubs. Ragged sodden clothing hampered its progress as it dragged behind.

A swollen fist narrowly missed Scott as he reeled backwards. He wildly sunk the penknife. The short blade embedded into the thing's forehead but doing nothing to slow it.

Scott dropped through the hatch, buttock-first. He bounced from the arm rests of both passenger seats before crumpling on the floor.

"Release! Release!" he yelled into his headset.

"NO! THE HATCH!" Vasilis screamed, half-rising from his seat as the sub keeled sideways as the thing shifted position.

Water poured through the portal – splashing Scott squarely in the face as he stood and reached out for the open hatch. He pulled, but the weight of the creature kept it pinned open.

"I can't–" he began as more water poured over him.

Vasilis saw the problem and threw his weight against the throttle, sending the thrusters in reverse.

The infected's tangled clothing yanked it backwards with such force parts of the waterlogged cloth acted like cheese wires - dicing chunks of skin. The creature was hurled off the sub, instantly freeing the hatch. Scott brought it down with a dull thud, stemming the water flow.

"UNTEATHER!" he yelled as he dropped into the foot of water that had accumulated at the base of the sub.

They heard the whip of the harness straps scrape against the acrylic hull as the lock was released. They sank into the cloudy water, both men silently praying the attack hadn't damaged the thrusters or Mowgli's integrity... or they will soon be crushed to oblivion.

FORTY

STAGNANT GREY MIST hung in the air. It only moved when Alanis pushed through, forming a cookie-cutter hole through it.

The bulkhead and deckhead were obscured by the mist. After just a few steps, she was completely disorientated. Every step was muffled. The temperature was rising like a sauna. Only when she stumbled across four Shenyang-15 fighters choked in thick growth, could she confirm that she had made it to the hangar. Like the Gerald R. Ford, crew had been entombed up the wall, their faces too obscured for her to distinguish whether it was any of her team. Her fear and frustration was building, and with it a slight regret that she didn't flee with the scientists.

If she had done so, would she be able to live with herself, no matter how short that life span threatened to be? No. The faintest hope that Jordan was still alive was all she had to live for now; and even that was merely for the chance to die together.

She kept the Spetsnaz rifle slung from her hip and

strained to listen for any signs of life. Only the steady patter of rain stirred. Finally she could take no more of it.

"Jordan?" Her voice fell flat, swallowed by the nothingness around her.

Almost immediately she regretted giving away her position. She clutched the rifle barrel even harder. If Jordan had found his way here, he would have the sense to quickly backtrack, but to where?

The bridge.

It was the obvious safe room onboard the vessel. She wondered how many of the high-ranking Chinese crew had found their way there and whether they would permit foreigners to seek refuge amongst them. That's where she would have to go next. She touched the radio on her belt. Since heading deeper inside the carrier it had been useless. She wondered if Bowers and the others were still alive.

A dreaded cracking sound rippled around her; an ominous wave of shifting growth she now associated with imminent attack. She slowly turned, trying to work out from which direction it was coming.

It was coming from everywhere.

Black shapes stirred in the mist. Barely humanoid shadows manipulated like marionettes at the end of fibrous growths. Alanis knew they were zeroing in on the noise. Unleashing a barrage of automatic fire would confirm her presence and the single magazine of bullets would do zero to protect her.

This is how it would end for her.

But she was not a quitter. She had never been. It wasn't in her nature to silently cave in. Pressing the rifle butt firmly against her shoulder, she toggled it to single-shot and took aim. Headshots might count for something.

Before she could squeeze the trigger a suddenly tongue of flame spat from the mist, enveloping three deformed figures immediately in front of her. Lessons onboard the Gerald R. Ford had shown the growth was fire resistant, but unprotected human flesh wasn't. It was enough of a distraction for the encroaching figures to swivel away from her as a Spetsnaz trooper sprinted towards her.

His hazmat suit was ripped, his helmet had been torn clean off revealing the firm handsome features of a man a year or so younger than Alanis. A flame thrower was slung over his back, the nozzle gushing more liquid fire at the looming shapes. He shouted something in Russian. The words were unfamiliar, but the meaning was clear: run.

He torched a wall, revealing a doorway and singeing the fungal growth around it. Alanis tossed her rifle over one shoulder and bolted for the exit as the Spetsnaz blew another torrent at twisted shapes emerging from the wall. The fire provoked the colony and sounds of tearing and ripping increased with renewed fury in the surrounding mist.

She had also seen that he wasn't wildly laying suppressing fire – he was aiming with purpose. A pair of five-thousand gallon fuel tanks were bolted to the wall just meters away beyond the aircraft.

Alanis was through the door, the young man just behind her as he unleashed another stream of fire. He was just through the door when the fuel tanks exploded with a deafening dull thump.

The pressure wave hammered both of them off their feet and spent them sprawling down the corridor as the hangar lit up behind them in a volcanic fireball.

FORTY-ONE

"THEY'RE AWAY," Maya confirmed as the Mowgli sank beneath the water.

Eric's hand reached for the moon pool door controls – Maya's shot out and gripped his wrist to stop him.

He shook her loose and rubbed his wrist. "If we don't close the doors, we'll sink."

"They need to get back. And I for one don't wanna wait for them in here."

Her statement was reinforced by hammering against the door as the two Infected continued their attempts to get in.

Eric looked pleadingly at Huang. "The storm will only get worse. Ships like this are not designed to–"

"They stay open," Huang snapped.

Eric looked at Markus, but the Greek clearly was siding with the women. Eric sharply stood and jabbed a finger towards the door. "And how do you propose we get out of here?"

A gunshot blast startled him. Eric spun around as the

booth's observation window shattered and driving rain blew in.

"We swim," Markus stated, sliding the shotgun through his belt. "Go left," he indicated. "There is a ladder midway along the pool. The door directly ahead of it leads below deck to the environmental lab. Swim hard. Don't stop. And once you are out, run like the devil is chasing you. Because he is."

Markus clambered onto the control panel and didn't pause as he dived into the moon pool. Maya recovered from her surprised and vaulted onto the desk.

"I wouldn't swallow any water either," Maya warned the others before cannonballing out of the window.

The cold water was no longer a shock to her system, but she immediately felt her waterlogged clothing weigh her down. Vision all around was shot to hell with particles and fungal strands drifting past. It was like swimming through sewage. She tried not to think about that as she kicked out in the ladder's direction.

She was a strong swimmer, but the days of sleep deprivation and exertion were taking their toll and with every stroke she felt herself inching downward. Eyes stinging, she searched for any sign of the moon pool's walls, but saw mass of floating fibers.

Nothing was recognizable. Each stroke was pulling her deeper into the void.

Had she swum through the pool's open doors and into the ocean?

Her heart pounded. Panic mounted as she searched for the surface. Direction became meaningless and the first signs that she was running out of air burned her lungs, yet she refused to panic. Thoughts of home had kept her going this far, and she was aware of her body's limitations. She wasn't there yet.

The desire to take a breath was merely her body's panic reflex. During a salvage expedition on a World War II bomber off the coast of Borneo, she regularly got drunk with a free diver who had taught her the secret of holding one's breath lay in tricking the diaphragm. The body held more than enough oxygen to at least double the average person's time underwater. The theory was all very well, but in practice...

She willed her stomach to relax, mentally calming her diaphragm from wanted to action a much needed breath, which would cause her instantly drowning.

An odd calmness washed over her. Was it working? Or was it the lack of oxygen playing tricks on her brain? She'd read drowning was like going to sleep. Maybe this was it...

The moon pool wall suddenly resolved itself in the murk – and by some miracle, directly in front of her was the ladder. A jolt of adrenaline surged her towards the rungs and she half-climbed, half-swam upwards. It was impossible to judge how far she had sunk and the ladder seemed impossibly long.

Then the surface suddenly appeared less than two meters above. Her feet found the rungs, and she powered from the water as fast as she could, inhaling a deep breath.

With stinging eyes, Maya blindly rolled onto the deck and enjoyed the rain and wind biting her face. She pushed herself upright and gazed across the pool. Huang was effortlessly powering through the choppy waters with her satchel strung to her back. Eric had been the last to leave and was doggedly struggling meters behind her. There were no signs of the other infected and she hoped they were still moronically pounding the booth door.

She yelped as a hand suddenly hooked under her armpit and pulled her to her feet. It was Markus. He briefly studied her with concern. Maya's numb fingers folded into an 'OK' sign, but she couldn't find the breath to speak. Markus pushed her towards a short building at the side of the ship. The building door was open, a set of steps beyond led below deck.

Maya could no longer feel her legs as she stumbled for safety the door. A strong gust of wind almost pitched her over. She grazed her knee on the deck, but ignored the blood as she stood once more and headed for relative safety.

She didn't look back until she reached the door. Markus was now help Huang up the ladder and there was still no sign of the infected.

Despite everything, she suddenly had an unexpected feeling of optimism. They had continued to defy the odds, no matter what hell was thrown at them. She hoped Scott was having similar luck as he headed towards the lowest levels of Point Nemo.

FORTY-TWO

ONCE CLEAR OF the moon pool doors, the Mowgli submersible lurched into the open ocean. Vasilis edged the thrusters up – a mistake as the clouded water suddenly cleared revealing huge branches of fungal growth, some the size of freeways and so entangled it was like flying through the boughs of an enormous tree.

He wrestled the control joystick as they descended straight towards a massive horizontal spar. The thrusters reacted sluggishly. High-pitched collision sensor screeched as the sub tilted forward, rolling the flooded water from the floor to a quarter-way up the canopy, before the gyros could level the craft.

It wasn't enough to avoid collision.

The dull scrape of the acrylic's port side sent waves of fear through Vasilis and Scott.

"Starboard thruster two is intermittent," growled Vasilis as he wrestled the control. "Something is gumming up the blades." The clothing from the attacking Infected was the most obvious culprit. He banked the Mowgli away from the growth, and they could see the scratches left on the canopy. They didn't look deep, but any defect could be catastrophic under pressure.

Vasilis hesitated. Scott gave a half-hearted nod, what else could they do? Crossing himself, Vasilis continue their decent, weaving Mowgli through a gap between immense spars, like diving through a femur bone.

At the last moment, Scott glanced up to see a tether that had connected them to the crane's jib hadn't detached. It had knotted in the water and now trailed thirty feet above them. As he watched it snagged on a forking piece of growth.

"Halt!" he yelled.

Vasilis reacted instantly, slamming the thrusters in reverse – but they were not quick enough.

The nylon strap pulled sharply taut, and both men were crushed back into their seats with a spine-jarring yank that splashed the pooled water on the floor up into their faces. Mowgli ricocheted upwards – straight towards a flattened trunk of growth that now loomed above them like a horizontal skyscraper.

"Impact!" Scott yelled.

"Release the tether or we'll bounce again!" Vasilis struggled upright in his seat and attempted to tickle the thrusters to life. Too much and the cable would bounce them back, not enough and they'd slam into the growth with enough force to fracture the already weakened canopy. Collision warning alarms trilled.

Normally the cables would be cleared by the support team, but an internal lock allowed them to be released in an emergency.

Scott clambered onto his seat, wet boots sliding on the slick material. He opened a panel built into the hatch revealing a pair of manual release levers: one would release the tether, the other unlock the hatch which would no doubt buck open following another impact.

"Scott!" Vasilis's hand trembled on the thrusters. The growth now filled their entire view above them. He snapped the throttle forward, deciding it was better than another impact.

The engines responded listlessly, failing to reverse their direction.

Scott gripped a lever and yanked it down, praying it was the correct one.

He was rewarded with a metallic clunk, followed by the cable snaking away in the water. At that moment the thrusters responded, and the Mowgli pitched downward, almost jarring him from his chair. They missed collision by centimeters as the sub began to sink once more.

After a drawn-out moment, the collision alarms disengaged, and the Mowgli was filled with the gentle hum of the engines and gentle whirl of the air conditioning.

Clear of the surface scum, the water at this depth was crystal clear and the true expanse of the growth was revealed. Nestling under the hulls of the stricken fleet it looked more like an enormous pale root structure. A submerged alien island that had no right to exist on this earth.

Scott's sense of scientific detachment had worn down to sheer awe, which was rapidly replaced by a wave of defeat. The irresponsible Russian experiment was clearly out of control. He was convinced that, whatever their intentions, the Russian's had assumed the parasite would burn up in the atmosphere, thus destroying all evidence. That was not to be. Fortune had dropped the surviving infection in the most desolate part of the planet, and hubris had resurrected it.

Vasilis remained silent, tense with concentration as he weaved the sub between the ever-thinning tendril. It was a difficult job with the weakened thruster, but he was compensating for the Mowgli's erratic behavior.

The invasive superstructure soon thinned into long jellyfish strands that extended for twenty meters before the submersible was completely free.

Without the RVs they have previously used to relay communications, the Mowgli should have wandered in radio isolation. However, these Tritons had been kitted out for just such an occasion.

"Launching communication buoy." Vasilis hit a switch. With a dull hiss of air a spherical pod was released from the rear roof housing. They watched it rise two meters before a skirt erupted around its circumference, stabilizing it in the water. Selecting an option on the computer, Vasilis pinged an ELF test beep to the buoy. The extremely low frequency signals were used by Navy's around the work to communicate with their submarine fleets. It might attract Russian interest, but it was vital if the surface team needed to update them on events.

"It's sending and receiving. But until somebody tunes in on the surface, I cannot say if we're getting through." If they had any hope of maintaining surface communication, then they would have to deploy another two buoys before they reached the seafloor.

Through the transparent floor beneath their feet, darkness greeted them. Vasilis flicked on the exterior lights and they dropped deeper into the black heart of Point Nemo.

FORTY-THREE

CREEPING through the Ventura's corridors had been tense, but ultimately Markus had led them safely without further drama. Conversation had been nothing more than a few harsh whispers in which he confessed he doubted there was a single other survivor amongst the thirty-strong crew, most of whom he had sailed the world with over the last seven years. They shared adventures, made valuable scientific discoveries and bonded closer than most families. Now they were dead. Or worse.

The hum of machinery starting up rippled throughout the lab as Huang hurried between pieces of equipment, activating each in turn. Half a dozen computers chimed as they booted up. She ran her hand over a spectrometer so new it still had transparent packaging stickers over the controls.

"This is quite a set up," she said approvingly.

A sheaf on the wall was filled with beakers, Petri dishes, a variety of acids to breakdown samples, cleaning solutions, and preservatives.

"We were doing Antarctic research," Markus said

sullenly as he peered through the hatchway, alert for the slightest movement in the corridor beyond. Eric had insisted they close it, but Markus had no intention of trapping them inside. He had instructed them to flee at first sign of trouble. His shotgun was useless, a token weapon. Flight was their only chance. "We abandoned that expedition in favor of this. Dropped the science team in Sydney so we could come and die here."

"Bacteria research?"

Markus shrugged. "I'm a mechanic. I don't touch that." He waved a hand at the machines before turning his attention back outside, a firm sign the conversation was over.

Maya helped Huang unpack her samples from the satchel. She held up a vial of the water they had extracted from the moon pool.

"Do we have everything we need?"

"No. But I hope it will we enough if Dr Bowers provides the missing data."

"If?"

Huang opted not to expand her doubts. She nudged Eric and indicated to a radio set in the corner. "See if you can raise him, or the American woman." She busied herself loading the water samples into the spectrometer.

The set hummed to life as Eric powered it up. He cycled through the channels to the frequency Alanis had given them and keyed the mic.

"Ventura to whoever's out there, come in."

White noise answered.

"Ventura to anybody out there, come in. We are survivors from the USS Gerald R. Ford and the Liaoning. Is anybody listening? We have sent a sub to the seabed to retrieve the Tiangong's data pod. We need assistant. Please come in–"

Maya's fist struck the mute button, startling him. "What the hell're you doing? The Russians'll be listening in!"

"If they get us off this crate, what does it matter?"

Her voice dropped threateningly. "It matters to me. You just told them what we're doing! Stop talking. Just listen you jerk!"

Eric considered arguing back, but her expression carried more than a hint of violence.

Huang broke the tension. "If you stop bickering, the spectrometer is now running." She sat in a chair and positioned herself to watch the monitor as the results slowly assembled.

Eric looked nervously at the Greek guarding the door, but he had little interest in what was happening inside the room. A squelch of static on the radio caught his attention. He watched the digital waveform tremble with background static... but it didn't repeat itself.

"Look at this," Huang said with a hiss, leaning into the screen as data began to piece together.

To Maya the result where meaningless, but Eric, now leaning over Huang's shoulder, watched in fascination.

"Polymers?"

Huang nodded, her brow knit in concentration.

"So there's synthetic crap in the water?" said Maya. "That's not exactly a surprise. Scott said plastic contamination had been found even as far out as here."

Huang tapped a peaked point on a chart forming on-screen. "This in particular. This is not all random plastic waste. Some of this has a specific chemical composition."

Eric tried to catch Markus' attention. "Markus, that Antarctic expedition, what did you do to your ship?" Markus gave another Hellenic shrug. "Vasilis told us the hull had been treated."

"Oh, yes. A special paint was supposed to stop ice from attaching to the hull."

"Did it work?"

Another shrug. "We didn't stay long enough to find out."

Eric and Huang exchanged an excited look and gave a rapid exchanged in Chinese.

Maya picked up on the sudden energy. "What?"

"That's the reason the growth hasn't got past the hull of this ship. And maybe the reason why it is breaking away! The polymer is tearing the phytoplankton apart."

"What did Bowers call it? Floccy..." Eric tried to recall the term.

"Flocculation," said Maya with a smile. "What was in that polymer?" She leaned over her shoulder, desperate for more information.

"A breakthrough..." Huang said as she hurriedly saved the results.

Eric crossed to Markus. "What did they tell you was in it?"

"We have barrels in the hold. We painted it on. They said it had some thermal properties, but I didn't ask."

The radio suddenly crackled to life, drawing everybody's attention to it.

"Ventura, this is Alanis. I read you."

Maya motioned for the radio – but flinched as a loud bang filled the room. Her blood ran cold as she turned to see Markus' headless body slump to the floor. Blown off by his own shotgun.

Eric held the stock and had pulled the trigger. He twisted the strap from Markus' arm as his body dropped.

With the Greek's fresh blood splattered across his face, Eric looked deranged as he trained the shotgun on the others.

"I hate people who are not curious." His voice was cold, lethal. He fished his USB thumb drive from his pocket and tossed it to Huang. She let it clatter on the floor and made no motion to retrieve it. "Copy your results onto that."

Maya eyed him with hatred. "I reckon we found our spy."

"It's nothing personal. I needed the money." His lip curled as he glanced at Huang. "The Russians pay more that China. I didn't know what they were planning when I sold them the Tiangong schematics. When Frisco Dynamics approached me, I wasn't in much of a place to turn down more money to report on your progress."

"You did all of that, just for money?"

Eric pulled a face. "I don't care about politics or military one-upmanship. It doesn't pay the bills and Shanghai is getting to be an expensive place to live. But right now, all I want to live. And that data is my ticket out of here."

Huang sneered and insulted him in Mandarin. She must have hit a nerve.

The shotgun's barrel barely moved as he pulled the trigger – and a scream filled the air.

FORTY-FOUR

ALANIS STARED AT THE RADIO, willing a response.

None came.

She felt the gaze of the young Spetsnaz officer bore into her. She called again, praying for any sign the others were still alive, before finally giving up and clipping the radio back to her belt. She registered fear in her companion's eyes, but he looked away, too proud to let her see it.

Through the basics of pointing he had introduced himself as Borya and had decided, like her, that it was better to fight side-by-side against a common enemy. She suspected that the Spetsnaz special forces unit hadn't been fully briefed on what to expect when they arrived, and doubted they even knew the extent of the mismanaged experiments.

She had no doubts she'd be treated as a Guinea pig in the Russian's hands, and it seemed as if Borya felt the same. From what she knew of the fearsome Spetsnaz, elite fighters forged for pure courage and loyalty, Borya knew he had no future now he was infected.

The explosion in the hangar had resulted in painful

burns to their backs. Alanis's neck stung every time she moved her head and guessed the skin was red-raw, but fear forced her not to focus on it. Borya's hazmat suit had melted in parts to his uniform underneath. The flamethrower on his back had grown hot to the touch, but the liquid inside failed to ignite.

They had crawled to another deck as superheated air seared their lungs and sucked the oxygen from the passageway. It was blind luck they stumbled through a hatch and out onto an observation platform just beneath the flight deck.

The driving wind and rain had rapidly cooled them off, before soaking them to the sink and chilling them. Taking an external stairwell onto the flight deck, they were dismayed to see the growth now covered the Liaoning's prow, tendrils grasping over the edge of the tilted ramp like giant talons.

The bow was a wall of dense smoke and intense orange flames licking from the flight elevator, which had collapsed into the hangar below. Out to sea, black clouds swallowed the fading sun as the murderous storm approached – inevitably now washing the Gerald R. Ford's toxic cloud from across them. By the time the smoke reached them, it was nothing more than a noxious scent and acrid tasting air. Alanis knew what they were inhaling.

"Reactor." She mimed an explosion with her hands. Borya nodded gravely. That one word he understood well enough.

Shielded by the bridge, with the wind howling around them, Alanis found herself numb. What were they fighting for? The Russian fleet, lost from view in the storm, was not coming to their aid. What would kill her first? Radiation from the reactor or the fungal growth dormant in her body?

She hoped it was the radiation.

During training, they had been given training on reactor leaks and the consequences of exposure. It had been a grim education, yet bleeding from sores and vomiting one's own insides seemed like a carnival to the mindless hijacking of your mind and soul. During training they had all decided a bullet to the head was better than suffering radiation exposure.

Now faced with the reality every survival instinct in her demanded she complete the mission she had set for herself. Get to the bridge. See if Jordan made it there alive. The bitter prospect of dying in his arms outweighed terminating things now.

With a trembling hand she pointed to the bridge, only lights coming from the ship.

"We need to go there." Her lips trembled as she shivered.

Molded in Siberian winters, Borya didn't react to the cold. He studied the bridge then gave a curt nod.

"*Da.*"

Despite everything, the simple word brought a sad smile to Alanis's cold cheeks. "*Da,*" she echoed.

It wasn't much, but it was a bond between them that would only be broken by death.

THE ELEVATOR DOORS were buckled from behind, warped by the fungal mass beyond. The growth was everywhere within the ship's command island. The stairwell was covered so thickly that it was now nothing more than a spiral tunnel ascending upwards. A warm breath of air issuing from it ruffled Alanis's damp hair as she shone the flashlight into the darkness.

"It can't be a suicide mission if we're already dead, right?"

She motioned to take a step, but Borya nudged her back and unleashed a stream of napalm up the tunnel. Flames sloshed around the curve giving a brief crackling light before the roar subsided and faded to black. If anything had been caught in the flame, Alanis doubted it would have been harmed. She took a step inside, boots slipping on the moist surface and only just finding purchase on jagged knots and bumps within the growth.

With the flashlight in one hand, she was forced to use her other hand to help the slick ascent. Midway up the tower and the humidity was sapping what little strength remained. Her mind became a fugue, yet she had just enough presence of mind to ensure each step was secure before putting her whole weight on it. One slip and she would slide down the rough surface, twenty meters back down to the flight deck level. Only the occasional soft grunt from Borya confirmed he was close behind.

Still she persevered until, at last, she saw light reflecting from the curved wall. She traded her flashlight for a pistol. Well aware that it was useless, the warm steel in her hand excreted a calming reassurance.

Almost at the top her foot slipped, and she slid backwards – only to be quickly stopped by the Russian's firm grip to her thigh. He pushed, helping her recover traction. The deck was now forty meters below them and she didn't possess the energy to attempt the climb again.

Taking each step with care, Alanis emerged on top the command deck level. The hatchway into the secure bridge was open, held in place by curled growth. She helped Borya up, then stepped through the portal and onto the bridge.

Any hope of finding survivors was extinguished the moment she saw inside the bridge. The windows were mostly smashed, others covered by growth. It crisscrossed the deckhead and floor, forming stalagmites and stalactites that occasionally had formed into pillars with such swiftness they had impaled crew caught in the act of abandoning their stations.

The dying daylight revealed faces masked in a thin veil of phytoplankton. Some had their eyes pushed out as the infection expanded within them. The Admiral was hunched over a control panel, half melded with metal and plastic controls. He still wore his hat even as the infection expanded within his head so viciously the back of his skull had cracked open, the growth suspending bone fragments in place like a gunshot exit wound frozen in time.

All of this was emotionless weight that ebbed Alanis's spirit.

The collection of Western faces huddled in the corner told her the rest of the story. Some of her crew had sought refuge here. But it hadn't been worth it. Two were encased beyond recognition, only their uniforms giving their identities away. Another two had taken matters into their own hands and blown their own brains out rather than endure whatever hell the others had experienced. A tiny corner of her mind registered the fact the growth had largely ignored those already dead, instead seeking the warmth of the living.

Not that it that mattered. What did matter was one of the dead was Jordan. His handsome features shattered when he had thrust the muzzle under his chin and pulled the trigger.

Alanis took in the sad sight with resignation. The emotional hammer she had feared failed to materialize. It was an expected outcome and her body was too exhausted to waste energy on emotions like grief. She had just enough strength to raise her own firearm to her temple.

All their plans. The excitement about the future; the stress of a Naval board of enquiry into their personal life and the life that had stretched before them had been snatched in a moment.

It wasn't the fragility of life that despaired her. Looking at the infection, it was the aggressiveness of nature. Survival of the fittest, and humans were clearly just another disruptive weak parasite in nature's cycle.

She couldn't feel the trigger under her numb finger as she squeezed it. Didn't she not even possess the last drop of strength to end life on her own terms?

A cracking noise from above caught her attention. The growth was slowly stirring to life, as if only just aroused by the fresh human presence. She willed herself to pull the trigger–

Then felt Borya yank her arm away. He blasted the deck-head growth with a bout of flame and shoved Alanis towards the captain. The burning growth stopped moving, but otherwise didn't seem harmed. It was Borya's excited spiel in Russian that focused her foggy mind away from Jordan. He was gesticulating to the control panel under the Admiral's hand.

Alanis shook her head, not understanding. All she wanted to do was die.

Borya tapped the panel with renewed urgency, demanding she look at it. All the controls were labelled in Mandarin, and only a few essential systems were still drawing power. Borya tapped the label with the tip of the flame thrower, careful not to touch the thin veil of growth over it.

She stared at the Chinese characters, her basic knowledge struggling to transform them into something eligible.

Then they did.

The Admiral had inserted a key into a slot, but had died before he had the chance to turn it. The three simple characters screamed in her mind.

Warhead.

FORTY-FIVE

FOR THE JOURNEY DOWN, the Mowgli had been running with no lights to conserve batteries. The only illumination came from the ghostly glow of the control panel. The near darkness was mesmerizing. Occasionally Scott thought he saw a flicker of light, bioluminescence perhaps... or just his mind playing tricks.

The eczema on his arm was playing up, and he scratched it for relief. Checking Vasilis wasn't paying him any attention, he checked himself for any signs of infection. There wasn't enough illumination to see anything other than the rough patches of skin. A mental health check couldn't decide if his motor functions were a little sloppy, or just victim of the punishing physical torment he had endured.

Vasilis was slumped motionless in his chair. Scott feared he was dead until a small snore escaped his throat. There was little point in waking him; it wasn't as though there was anything to collide with and if anything malfunctioned, they'd be dead instantly.

Scott busied himself by sending another few test transmissions on the ELF system after sending the last two replays out. Still no answer came. It was all very well retrieving the data from the seabed, but he was uncertain if he could interpret it by himself. He needed Huang's help if they were to stand a chance. He hoped she and the others were safely bunkered in the Ventura's lab as planned.

With nothing at hand to occupy him, his mind wondered to the inevitable – Ruth and their baby. Would she be worried that he hadn't reported in for... how long? Days blended into one another in a seamless mass... Probably not. He had been on plenty of expeditions with limited communication, so even two weeks of silence wouldn't be unexpected.

However, back then the stakes had never been higher.

The thought of the infection spreading unheeded around the world was suddenly more of threat than his own demise. Apparently with the advent of fatherhood, his perceptions had shifted with no conscious intervention.

He was not out to save himself, nor the world. He was out to save his child. That unborn, unformed concept burned in him like a supernova.

The sonar warned of seabed contact long before the dull plumes of the submerged volcanos became visible.

It was enough to rouse Vasilis who yawned and activated the powerful floodlights, revealing the superheated volcanic plumes stretching from them. With the dangers now visible, he carefully guided Mowgli between the smokers and towards the Tiangong's crash site. He was right on the money.

The hyper-grown coral lay smashed where they had left

it. Although they lacked the powerful additional search lights used when raising the craft, it looked as if nothing had moved. The infection down here had died and vanished when they'd removed the space station.

"Nothing left." Scott imagined a potential lifecycle of the infection. His conclusion was bleak. "Perhaps it only thrives on human contact."

"You were right then. It was a biological weapon."

"Experimental warfare that got out of hand."

"Why would any nation wish this?"

"Warfare without the collateral damage. What's the point in conquering a city if you have to sack it first? The military's dream biological weapon kills the victim, leaves the environment intact, then fades away without a trace." He had been hired by more than one think tank to hypothesize about such things and he realized his contract with Frisco Dynamics, the very one that landed him out here, was one such thinly disguised project. "Let's find this Mercury module shall we?"

Vasilis activated the scanner and keyed in the radio frequency Huang had provided. The computer gave a friendly ping to simulate that the inaudible signal had been sent. Scott watched the scanner for any hint of an acknowledgement. He tried again.

"It could have it burned up on re-entry," said Vasilis, leaning back in his seat and rubbing his cramped thigh.

It was the most logical outcome, but one Scott refused to accept as he tried again.

Vasilis closed his eyes as he relaxed back in his seat. "Or caught in a smoker and destroyed."

"Raise us five meters. It will extend the scanners range."

It took a moment for Vasilis to nudge the throttle, but he reluctantly did so and they rose almost imperceptibly.

"Down here is not such a bad place to die." Vasilis gazed at the flickering magma peeking from the nose of the nearest smoker. "Beholding such sights most mortals would never see."

"All things considered, I plan not to die down here." Scott was surprised by his own conviction. "Have you heard the English expression, keep your work and personal life separate? I never wanted to die on the job."

He sent another ping – and this time he was answered.

Scott pointed. "Thirty-six degrees port."

Suddenly rejuvenated, Vasilis delicately spun Mowgli around as Scott fished for another response. The Mercury pinged back.

"Hundred and three meters forward." He looked up from the screen. They were pointing right at the tallest smoker.

"That will bring us right up to the base," Vasilis warned.

"The Mercury must be still intact."

"Maybe. But the heat on the canopy..." Vasilis traced a finger along the scratches on the acrylic. The water around them was frigid, but would rapidly climb as they neared the vents. Such a dramatic change could have fatal consequences on the protective dome.

"Keep her low. Glide slowly in and we might keep out of the thermals."

Vasilis gingerly lowered the craft until the proximity alarm warbled as they reached the seabed. He killed the warning, his eyes glued to the descent readout – only stopping Mowgli five centimeters over the floor. The thrusters kicked up a trail of silt as they cruised forward.

Scott's gaze flicked between the scanner as they drew towards the pod and the temperature gauge as it nudged upward by a degree.

Fifty meters in and the outside temperature was a relatively barmy fifteen degrees. Both men flinched as a low crunch came from the sub's metal chassis as it fractionally expanded. Vasilis held them in place for a few moments, allowing the temperature shock to settle across the craft.

After a full minute, they edged forward.

The volcano loomed above them. A dark shadow against a tenebrous sea, crowned by a demonic flowing black vapors. This close they could now see small scars opening up along the flank. The bright red magma inside hissing with black searing sulfide particles that formed the 'smoke'. They lasted seconds before heat sealed the incision once again. Occasional bits of displaced rock lazily rolled down the flank.

"Twenty-one degrees," Scott reported as another shimmy shook the sub. His gaze was drawn to the scratched on the sphere. Had they grown, or was it a trick of the light?

"Okay, three meters and I don't see it." Vasilis brought Mowgli to a stop. He scanned the field of volcanic rock before them. They were both so engrossed that they failed to spot a chunk of glowing rock the size of a soccer ball roll down the flank above them and silently land within arm's reach.

"Christ," intone Scott. Then he spotted something amongst the rocks, just beyond it. "There! I see it."

Vasilis steered, abandoning the instruments in favor of Scott's directions. The Mercury pod stood almost vertical, snagged between jagged rocks. Its aluminum surface reflected the sub's lights. It appeared to be in one piece and was free from any signs of growth.

Scott activated the robotic arm and carefully reached for it. The Mercury slid free from the rocks on the second try. He was so focused on bring back the prize he didn't notice Vasilis had drifted them sideways to avoid another smoldering chunk of rock that bounced down just a couple of meters away.

"I think the volcano is angry with us for stealing its treasure," Vasilis remarked as a third, larger boulder rolled down further away.

Scott waited until the Mercury pod was in the safe confines of the sub's specimen net before he breathed again. "I don't care what it thinks – it's ours now. Let's get the hell out of here."

Vasilis nodded and reached for the throttle - just as the sub's sonar screamed. There was a new arrival. Something shot past them an struck the side of the volcano – exploding in a mass of rock and bubbles.

Vasilis had slammed full reverse as debris clattered from the bubble. The cracking of the hull as it reacted to the sudden drop in temperature convinced them the Mowgli was about to collapse.

Yet the plucky sub held together.

They watched a superheated jet blast diagonally out of the volcano's side from where it had been hit. Had they been any closer or higher in the water, then the new jet would have instantly liquidized them.

The shock of the near miss had drowned out the sonar's warning. Something was still out there, circling them. Something massive.

Vasilis spun them around, the floodlights glancing off the black hull of a huge submarine passing ten meters overhead. The engine screws were each four times bigger than the

Mowgli as they powered the newcomer around the white smoker.

Scott had seen the craft last time he was down here.

The hundred and two meter long black submarine banked in a tight turn to hunt down its tiny target. The Russians had brought a jackhammer to swat an ant.

And there was nowhere for Mowgli to run.

FORTY-SIX

MAYA STARED at the smoking remains of the radio, relieved the bullet hadn't been meant for her, but angrier than she'd ever felt before.

"You son of a bitch. You warned them about Scott, didn't ya?"

Eric twitched the shotgun between her and Huang with nervousness of somebody not used to holding a firearm.

"If anybody can synthesize a cure, it's our Russian friends. And they will need every byte of data they can get."

"You're a fucking moron," Maya spat. Rage made her unfazed by the danger. "You don't seriously think they'll cure us do you?"

"We're the perfect subjects to test any cure on. And every minute we waste onboard this junkyard is killing us!"

"And you're saving our lives? They'll cure us. Then they're gonna get rid of any evidence this ever happened. Which includes us."

Eric shook his head. "You're wrong."

"And you've drunk the cool aide if you think you're of any value to them."

The reference was beyond Eric, but he understood it to be an insult. "Shut up!"

"Or what? You're gonna shoot me?"

"Yes."

Maya gave a low mocking whistle. "There are three of us still infected. Each one you kill is a test subject away from perfecting your cure." Eric's scowl made her smile. "Ah, now it dawns. You're not as dumb as you look."

"That doesn't mean you can't slowly bleed," he snapped back.

A chime from the spectrometer caused Huang to swivel towards the screen. Eric took a cautious step to see what was on the screen, but he was too far away.

"Copy the data." He indicated to the USB drive he had tossed over. Huang reluctantly retrieved it from the floor and inserted it into the computer. "What does it say?"

Huang stared right back at him. "I have to study it. And waving a gun at me doesn't aid concentration." She began copying the data to the USB drive.

"How are the polymers weakening it?"

Huang considered her answer for a moment, then gave a casual gesture to the screen. "See for yourself. We know the growth is evolving with each iteration. Without recovering the data from the Mercury it is impossible to make a comparison to its first phase of evolution. What we perceive as a weakness maybe a strength. I need to analyze the growth itself." She rested her hand on the sample jar containing the fragment she had taken from the stern.

Keeping the gun raised, but aimed to the side, Eric positioned himself closer to the monitor displaying a full spectrum breakdown of the components. He didn't see Maya's swift move.

With one hand she snatched a glass container from the shelf close to her and charged forward, using her free hand to push the shotgun barrel towards the floor, fearing Eric would indiscriminately discharge it.

She smashed the container across Eric's face with all her strength. Glass shattered, the sulfuric acid inside pouring from his forehead and down his cheeks. He forced her hand back, and she felt molten pinpricks of pain as acid splashed her forearm.

Eric fell to his knees, his screams turning high-pitched as he clawed his melting face. The reek of corrosive burning scorched their nostrils. The gun clattered to the floor, sliding under the table. Huang ejected the USB drive and hopped over the writhing man. Maya was already at the hatchway, beckoning her to follow.

"Come on!"

Purposefully ignoring Markus' bloody corpse, they gave a last unsympathetic look at Eric, kicking wildly as he clawed his face. His left eye was nothing more than a glob of jelly, bonded to the waxy flesh of his cheek. Some of the flesh itself had dissolved, puncturing holes into his mouth.

The woman instinctively sprinted down the corridor, back the way they came and stopped at the stairwell leading up to the deck.

She panted, catching her breath. "The Russians will find here us, eventually." She held up the USB drive. "This is our only bargaining chip. We need to get to the bridge and contact them." She sagged at the reluctance on Maya's face. "It is the *only* way we will get off this ship alive."

Maya thought for a moment, then an idea stuck her. A bad idea.

"No. It's not the only way."

FORTY-SEVEN

THE ONLY ADVANTAGE Mowgli possessed over the huge Victor-class Russian attack submarine was agility. That was not much of an advantage when the only objects to hide behind were volcanos. They needed distance to evade the specialist hunter-killer, but with open ocean in every direction and limited range and speed, that was not an option. The Russians didn't even have to destroy them, all they had to do was pin them down until they ran out of oxygen.

The Mowgli shook as a pair of sonar whistles washed over it. The Victor no longer had to run silent. Flushing its prey was now a priority.

"We're a small target," Vasilis said, guiding their sub towards the ground and accelerating towards the nearest black smoker. "With luck we'll blend in."

Keeping the growling smoker to port, Vasilis kept a wary eye on the molten lava balls tumbling down the slope. The Victor sunk in the water, passing dangerously close to the smoker's flanks. So close that rivets and barnacle growth could almost be touched. A barrage of sonar screeches caused the Mowgli to tremble.

"They're ensonifying the area!" Vasilis said as he sped towards a field of boulders, each larger than the Mowgli. Full reverse brought them to a sudden stop. "They can't pick us out from the background clutter. If we stay put, there's a good chance we won't be spotted."

"Torpedo!" Vasilis yelled as he watched the sonar screen. A fast-moving target separated from the Victor and sped in their direction. Rapid sonar pings echoed through the Mowgli, each shorter than the last as it sped nearer.

Scott twisted in his seat and caught sight of the fast moving torpedo as is arced overhead, through the floodlights, and slammed into the volcano's flanks. They anticipated another blast of superheated water, but the explosion dislodged a huge collection of rock, creating a landslide that gave way in slow motion, although visibility was rapidly consumed by thick sediment.

"This may be our only chance to make a break for it," Scott said firmly.

Vasilis barely hesitated. He swirled the thrusters and began a rapid ascent. Splinters of rock that had been hurled in the explosion now sank sinking back to seabed, clattering like hail from the acrylic dome.

The submersible shuddered and lurched sideways, splashing the pooled water halfway up the dome before Vasilis could level out.

"Second port thruster is offline!"

Scott craned to see, gripping onto his chair for support. "I think a rock struck it." He was about to say more when Vasilis let out a loud gasp and spasmed in his seat, arms and legs outstretched, crucified in agony.

"Vasilis!" Scott's first instinct was that he was having a heart attack. He pushed himself forward, slipping in the pooled water. He spun the pilot's seat around to help Vasilis – and pulled back in alarm.

The Greek's eyes were open and staring. His jaw fixed wide in a silent scream. His skin was pallid, the veins in his neck pulsing. Scott took Vasilis's wrist. It was cold and clammy and the limb would not bend.

The bulges in his neck expanded. They were not veins – it was the infection swelling inside him. Scott watched with morbid fascination as white tendrils punctured through the thin skin of his neck, spreading up to the head.

Like watching time-lapse footage of a growing tree, more roots crawled from Vasilis's mouth and nostrils. Only his eyes still moved, opening wide in silent pain as they focused on Scott. Then, like a rubber sack, his skull lost integrity as it expanded with the audible crack of bones – and a fist-sized fungal appendage punctured through his forehead.

The Mowgli shook as more detritus struck it. Scott fought for his balance and realized they were still arising. A loud bang from the rear quarterdeck send up a curtain of bubbles. Scott didn't need to see the oxygen level on the control panel plummet to know one of the tanks had been punctured.

The hull cracked as the water temperature increased and they were suddenly clear of the debris cloud as rising up the side of the volcano, dangerously close to the cone and the funneling clouds of superheated particles – into which the Mowgli's current trajectory would take them.

Instinct overrode fear. He booted Vasilis's mutating body from the pilot seat and took command himself. His hands hovered over the controls, similar to every other sub he'd been in, but now the slightest mistake would kill him.

Just behind, Vasilis's slumped across the cabin and splashed in the pooled water which was just deep enough to submerge half his distorted head. He jerked as the water frothed and bubbled as it dissolved the fungus. Scott didn't have time to dwell on that. He twisted the joystick back, to avoid the volcano.

The damaged thrusters didn't respond as they should and the Mowgli awkwardly corkscrewed backwards. Scott was almost pitched from the seat as he vied for control.

The volcanic glow was the only reference point he had in the Stygian blackness. The sub's floodlights scythed through the surrounding murk – bringing the side of the Russian Victor in sharp relief. A sheer wall of black steel displacing over seven thousand tons of water cut across his path.

The Mowgli's collision alarms went crazy. He stabbed a control to silence them before the Victor could lock onto the sound.

Tumbling out of control, Scott was thrust back in his seat as he was flipped upside down. Behind, Vasilis's twitching corpse pinballed through the cabin, flailing as more water splashed over him.

The Mowgli glanced from the massive steel superstructure like a wayward baseball. The resulting clang sounded almost comical, but the sudden flood of system failure alarms was far from it.

The Mowgli was plunged into darkness as it lost power.

"No, no, no..." Scott whispered as he thumped the control panel.

Without power the air couldn't pump. Without heating he would freeze - or boil to death as Mowgli drifted into the thermal currents. Already he could feel the tug of the currents as it drew the tiny submersible upwards towards the plume. The glow from the volcano throbbed like a lighthouse luring him to his doom.

Panic would consume most men. Scott was stricken by an almost paralyzing inertness. His *alexithymia* was now a strength, repressing fear so that cold logic could prevail.

Survival depended on restarting the systems. If the collision had jarred a connection inside, then he had hope. If not, at least death would be swift.

In the darkness, every sound was amplified. He could hear the popping of flesh and mycelium from Vasilis's body. As far as he could judge, there was little movement suggesting the threat had been neutralized for now. The veil of water rising from the busted O_2 tank voiced a constant hiss. The bass-heavy thrum from the volcanos could be felt to the bone.

Working blind, he ran his fingers under the console. Forcing himself to concentrate on every notch, bolt, wire and screw, he built a picture of the components. The darkness enhanced his sense of touch. He felt small droplets of moisture still dripping from the components. The pooled water must have sloshed across the control short circuiting it.

Scott unzipped his Chinese flight suit and stretched it to wipe the underside of the panel. It was almost a fruitless gesture as his clothing was sodden, but it might be enough to prevent another short circuit. On the other hand, the system might not be retrievable.

With a final shake of the panel to dislodge any droplets, he unplugged the thickest cable on the assumption it was the power cord. A screeching whistle pinged through the cabin as somewhere out in the void the Victor attempted to get a lock on its target.

Condensation was forming inside the canopy, blurring the volcanic glow. His skin prickled from the increasing heat and sweat beaded on his forehead. By touch alone, he lined up the power and thrust it in place.

It resisted going in.

Carefully feeling the tip of the plug he felt a notch designed so it could only be plugged in one way. A difficult task in the dark. He slowly rotated it, pushing the plug each time until, after the fifth attempt, it inserted with a satisfying click.

For the eternal length of a heartbeat, nothing happened.

Then the panel flickered to life, and air con whirled into action. External spotlights grew in brightness – filling his entire field of view with the flank of the volcano. Multicolored coral swept past. He caught glimpses of crustaceans swarming the surface, feeding on minerals; three-meter long tube worms swayed in the currents. An entire unexplored ecosystem lay just beyond his grasp.

Then every warming sensor in the sub rose in an angry chorus, distorted by the water-logged speaker. The temperature gauge shot up to forty-seven degrees. He pulled back on the controls but it took seconds for the thrusters to respond. With one out of commission, and another barely responding, Mowgli turned almost ninety-degrees and smashed through delicate coral. Several tube worms were shredded as the remaining thrusters eventually rose to full power to nudge the sub away from the volcano, causing it to rotate helplessly.

Another sonar ping screeched across the Mowgli – and was instantly joined by constant whistle.

Another torpedo had locked on.

Scott didn't have time to think. His actions were purely automatic.

The very range of his spotlights glinted from an enormous black sphere. He was looking at the Victor head-on. It had slowed before deploying the torpedo – which was zeroing in on him with an increasingly rapid series of pings.

His hand slammed the ballast tank control. It responded, instantly filling to dragged Mowgli down like rock.

Seconds away from impact the torpedo was confused by the trail of bubbles leaking from the oxygen tank. The torpedo's onboard sonar locked on to the mass, and the weapon's heat lock didn't veer from the volcano.

It shot over the Mowgli and blew a sizable hole in the volcano's peak.

The Victor submarine was running blind, guided only by precision sonar. Perfect for navigating well-mapped irregular submerged landscapes, but lackluster when dealing with sudden environmental deviations - such as a direct scolding blast from the volcanic eruption.

Caught in Mowgli's spotlights, a high pressure tongue of molten minerals whipped sideways from the peak, engulfing the front of the Russian submarine as it attempted to steer around the smoker.

The Mowgli was caught in the turbulent wake as the Victory smashed into the volcanic flank– obliterating the unique ecosystem. Sheer tonnage meant it could not stop as it punctured deep into the brittle volcanic rock. The black hull glowed cherry red as it suddenly became superheated, broiling the crew inside.

Scott urged the Mowgli forward, constantly compensating the damaged thrusters to keep it straight. He set the sub into a rapid ascent as the seabed before him lit up in daylight as the submarine exploded in the thermal vent. Seconds later the violent shock wave struck the Mowgli, pushing him into the pilot's seat and giving the sub an extra kick to the surface.

As pitch darkness folded around him once again, he crumpled in the seat as exhaustion finally caught up with him. The oxygen levels told him he didn't have enough to reach the surface. No matter how hard he stared at them, they refused to change.

Tired, he killed the alarms and closed his eyes, listening instead to the sharp cracks and creaks that teased through the sub. As sleep took him, Scott wondered what would kill him first —being crushed like a can as its structural integrity collapsed, or asphyxiation.

Either way, he wouldn't be conscious to experience it.

He lapsed into a dream about Ruth. Ruth and his *daughter...*

FORTY-EIGHT

THE THEORY WAS SOUND. Getting in should be just as easy as getting out.

In practice, nothing was ever that straightforward.

Maya and Huang crouched on the stairwell, poking their heads just above the hatch to peer across the moon pool. Night had fallen, and the storm was driving harder than ever. Light from the control booth and bridge was the only disruption to the darkness. Rough seas would normally be pitching the Ventura violently around, but still cradled by the mass, there was very little movement. That didn't stop enormous waves from crashing over the deck as they were pounded, or dangerous swells from punching through the moon pool. The wind was so fierce that, at times, rain came in horizontally.

Their prize lay across the pool, close to the broken windows of the control booth: the Baloo.

The Triton swung in its harness. Gusts were so strong that it occasionally impacted the jib holding it a meter above the water. That was their ride off the Ventura.

"We're likely to drown before we make it," commented

Huang as she watched violent waves swell across the moon pool and out over the deck. Their plan to swim back to the control booth window was looking impossible.

"I still haven't seen any infected," said Maya. They had been watching for several minutes.

"Perhaps they were washed overboard? In which case we can just take the door."

Maya shook her head. "Perhaps. But just in case, to face them without a weapon... no. That's out way in." She lay a comforting hand on Huang's shoulder. "We don't have a choice. The moment this storm passes the Russians will be swarming the ship. That might be a day from now. It might be in the next thirty minutes. Either way, I don't wanna be around to find out."

Huang had stopped listening. She nudged Maya and indicated to the control booth.

One of the infected had made it inside.

"Now that's just fate shafting us." Maya searched for something, anything, that would prove to be a functional weapon. Then she saw it and indicated her find to Huang. "And I say we fuck fate in the face." Noting the apprehension on Huang's face she tried to summon a comforting smile. "Don't worry. I know how to use one. You just get ready to run."

Before Huang could complain, Maya crouch-ran across the deck – towards the three jet-skis secured to the side of the moon pool. She made it without attracting any attention. Orange nylon ropes bound the machines to a custom frame that kept them in the water and secure during transit, although the violent surface of the moon pool was hammering them into the side. The fiberglass hull of one was already cracked.

She pulled at the cords, but the damp knots had tightened, and her fingers slipped from them. Digging her teeth in, she pulled a strand free and the bowline effortlessly unraveled. Maya tightly held onto the cord as the jet-ski viciously bobbed. She jumped onboard just as it was already drifting from the poolside.

So far, so good. She stabbed the starter button and squeezed the throttle lever. The jet roared to life and edged forward. Maya leant her body weight as she turned the craft to face the control booth. The meter-high waves in the pool were already flipping the nose of the craft dangerously upwards. At speed she risked ramping straight out of the pool or bouncing from a wave and colliding with the steel superstructure either side of the broken observation window. Yet she had little choice.

The engine screamed above the angry storm, capturing the infected's attention. It leapt onto the control desk, but hesitated from throwing itself into the water.

A last second adjustment to Maya's course allowed her to hit a rising wave at just the right angle. She hunched low in the saddle as the jet-ski stuck the wave and skipped from the water. Twisting her body, she rotated the jet-ski in the air until it was almost horizontal. Flying snugly through the broken window and crashing into the Infected.

Maya was thrown from the vehicle as it ricocheted from the control desk. The contoured jet-ski hull struck the Infected, snapping an arm and its head clean off - before slamming the body hard against the wall, crushing the rest of it. The fiberglass machine shattered against the bulkhead, exposing the metal chassis. The jet engine continued to scream and started to burn, as it sucked in nothing but air.

Maya rolled off the control panel, her shoulder sending

out fiery message of pain. Either dislocated or broken, she didn't have time to reflect. Petrol from the jet-ski's ruptured tank mixed with the inch-deep layer of saltwater that had blown in. It might not ignite but the fumes were overpowering.

She was relieved to see the computer system was still up and running as they had left it.

Outside, Huang was sprinting to Baloo. A roped lobbed over one arm bounced from her precious laptop satchel with each step. The submersible swayed from the crane's jib like a wrecking ball as the wind took it, forcing Huang to slow down. She paused to counter its motion – then jumped from the pool edge, feet just landing on the narrow running board; hands grabbing around a thruster. She held on tight as the pendulum arc swung her back over the pool.

Maya hit the crane release.

The sub crashed into the water with a splash hard enough to dislodge Huang. For a moment, Maya couldn't see much as a wave spun the pod around and froth through the window stung her eyes.

Another wave twisted Baloo – and she was relieved to see Huang was still holding on. She climbed up the back of the sub as it tried to buck her like a rodeo. Determined, the plucky Chinese scientist clambered to the hatch, limbs splayed as she hugged the plexiglass. Maya flinched as Huang almost slipped off as she freed a hand to turn the hatch screw. She held her breath as Huang slipped again... but managed to open the hatch and slid in headfirst.

Maya climbed onto the desk and crouched in the window frame as Huang reappeared from the hatch and slung the end of the rope around her head, tossed it the seven meters to her. Catching it, Maya wasted no time in hauling

Baloo in. The waves resisted her, but she eventually pulled the sub over. It bumped sharply into the wall.

Standing on a passenger seat, Huang stood half out of the hatch and reached for Maya, pulling her onboard. Maya's boot squeak and slipped on the acrylic dome as it wildly bucked in the water, forcing Huang to use all her bodyweight to pull her through the hatch.

Just as a gunshot snapped, and the glass around the hatch starred centimeters from Maya's thigh. She threw herself into the craft headfirst. Huang pulling the hatch closed behind. As another shot scarred the dome.

Rain marred visibility through the canopy – it was Eric staggering across the deck. The distortion in the glass amplified the hideous scarring on the side of his face as he fired again – the acrylic glass scarring as the shot glanced off.

No words needed to be exchanged. Maya sat in the pilot's seat and powered the Baloo up.

"Hold on!"

She flooded the ballast tanks and the sub quickly submerged in a cloud of bubbles as Eric aimed again. Through the flurry of water curled over the dome, they just saw another figure grapple Eric from behind. The fourth infected crewman.

Caught in a monstrous bearhug, they watched Eric lifted from his feet and heard the shotgun report as something jagged punctured through his chest cavity–

Then they were submerged. Maya guided the sub through the murk, and out through the open moon pool doors.

"Wow... look at that!" she exclaimed as the colossal network of the growth revealed itself.

Huang was so astonished, she almost failed to notice the steady trickle of water down her back.

"We have a leak."

Water was seeping through the gunshot cracks around the hatch.

"We can't go any deeper," Maya said nervously. "That'll shatter. We have to surface."

The hope of a clandestine getaway had been snatched from them. Maya pushed the Triton to its top speed until they cleared the mass of the Ventura above. Then she reluctantly surfaced, wending Baloo between the massive trunks of growth.

Huang stood next to her and activated the radio, hoping that Scott could deliver them some much needed good news. She tuned it into channel thirty-three and was about to key the mike – when Alanis's voice came over the speaker.

"–Attempt to board us will result in immediate action. I repeat, this is Yeoman Alanis Sanchez, last surviving member of the USS Gerald R. Ford. I am onboard the Chinese aircraft carrier Liaoning with Spetsnaz officer Barya. The last two alive. I have activated a nuclear warhead and will detonate it in one hour. That might give you enough time to avoid the blast radius... but I'm no expert. Any attempt to board us will result in immediate action."

Static replaced her voice.

Huang and Maya exchanged a look. At their top speed of five knots, could they get far enough away? Especially as they would now have to run on the surface through impossible waves.

Alanis's voice came through again. "I repeat, this is Yeoman Alanis Sanchez, last surviving member of the USS Gerald R. Ford..."

FORTY-NINE

TURGID NIGHTMARES HAUNTED a dark sleep that refused to retract its talons from Scott.

One moment he was wading through knee-deep growth that choked the tropical Maldivian shoreline, the creeping menace expanding around the luxury ocean villa. Wood cracked and shattered as the tendrils contracted, collapsing the building into the clogged ocean. Ruth stood on the balcony, reaching for him as she was pulled into the destruction. Words were drowned, but terror was all-too clear on her face.

Every step Scott took marred him deeper in viscous phytoplankton that tugged at his knees. Three more steps and he was waist deep. The growth reached up and tangled around his neck, pulling him backwards.

Darkness swamped his vision, and he became light-headed. The desire to fight seeped from him. Even breathing was an unnecessary chore.

He understood this is how death must feel.

Icy water stung his face and seeped into his mouth forcing him awake.

Scott shook his head, blinking at the flashing lights close to his face. His mind was fuzzy, so starved of oxygen it took several seconds for anything to start making sense.

The lights were from the control panel his head rested upon. What was left of Vasilis's body had crashed into him, but flesh and bones had all but melted into a sickly cloth-bound slime.

Mowgli had rolled in the water, bobbing at a forty-five degree angle as the ballast and air tanks finally short-circuited. The engines had died but that no longer mattered. Against the odds he had reached the surface.

Mustering all his strength, Scott crawled up the wet dome and struggled to open the hatch. His arms trembled from the effort. He had to put his shoulder into it to inch the wheel around. With a hiss the hatch popped open, filling the cabin with cold fresh salty air.

Scott scrambled half-out, gulping deep breaths as he took in his new situation. It was night, and the storm had passed. Stars twinkled above but as he tracked them to the horizon, he saw the tail of the storm was still raging. Lightning stabbing the distant ocean.

Mowgli wasn't bobbing in the water, it had struck something and was held stationary. The ambient light was too dim to discern anything, but it looked like he had hit land.

It was impossible to have drifted thousands of miles... and yet he was definitely beached on a huge mass. He stretched down and ran numb fingers over it; it was solid enough. After a few seconds a burning sensation penetrated the numbness, not unpleasant, it put him in mind of a medical deep heat rub.

Scott dragged himself out of the submarine and lay flat on the land, heaving long deep breaths as he stared at the sky. Tears of relief flowed unchecked down his cheeks.

After an interminable span of time, he gradually felt motivated to move. He raised his head, relieved to see the Mercury data pod he had recovered was still clutched the Mowgli's sample net in the front of the sub. On all fours, he crawled to it, delicately retrieving the metallic pod. At two feet in length it weighed almost nothing, yet inside lay the secrets to his survival.

Again he laid back, hugging the precious treasure.

The rhythmic lapping of waves on the shore segued into whispering voices. He tried to blot out his fevered imagination, but they did not relent.

Mowgli's radio had latched on to a signal.

Flooded with the irrational desire for human contact, he crawled headfirst through the hatchway, an easier task now it was inclined. The radio was just within reach, although he had to be careful not to put his hand in the putrid remains of Vasilis. He pulled the handset as far as the spiraling cord would allow, which meant he could stand back out of the hatch.

The voice had faded into silence. With trembling fingers he keyed the mike, his voice coming as a hoarse croak.

"Say again, over."

"To the huge vessel two miles north of our position, please identify yourself."

The voice was faint and awash with static. Scott looked around for any signs of a large vessel. The distant storm filled the horizon in one direction, behind, the rising landmass obscured his view.

"I don't know what vessel you are referring to. My name

is Scott Bowers. I was aboard a submersible and now... I don't know where I am."

Silence. Then the voice excitedly broke over the static. "Scott? It's Maya!"

Scott could barely reply. He looked around for any sign of the fleet. Now he understood where he must be.

"I surfaced near land. I can't see the fleet..."

"I think we have you on sonar. I'll flash the external lights."

Scott scanned the horizon. In one direction stars. In the other flickering lightning from the receding storm. Then he saw it a regular pulse in the darkness between him and the storm. It was impossible to judge distant or speed, but it had to be Maya.

"I see you."

"We're heading your way. We've been running full power for nearly an hour so the thrusters are overheating. We'll limping in."

For the next twenty minutes, Scott could do nothing but sit and hug himself for warmth as Baloo drew nearer. Maya didn't use the radio again, preserving every amp of power for the engines.

Feeling returned to his hands as the gentle burning sensation spread up his arms and stung his cheeks and the back of his neck. Was this the onset of infection? He toyed the Mercury pod cradled in his arms. The answers... were they coming too late?

As Baloo hove into view, its floodlights illuminated Mowgli and he saw how lucky he had been to reach the surface. Three rear thrusters were black and charred, missing several blades. The acrylic canopy was mottled with cracks;

it was a miracle it hadn't shattered. But what really surprised him was the island he was standing on.

Mowgli was surrounded by a thick soup of floating plastic, sheets, soda bottles, and unidentifiable trash from six continents. Caught in a gyre, the junk had congealed into a floating mass of trash, compacting into an immense floating superstructure, so large that sonar saw it as an island. Ordinarily such floating garbage patches were of such low density that they wouldn't even show on satellite imagery.

Scott's heart sagged. It was clear the collective plastics clogging the ocean were at an unprecedented scale that not even the harshest survey had predicted.

He knelt and gently rubbed the uneven ground. A deck of plastic detritus mashed together under terrific pressure, perhaps forged in the heart of violent storms; the artificial hallmark of mankind's self-destructive stamp on the planet.

Yet, caught in the beam of Baloo's lights he saw something impossible. The curves of a wooden branch. At first he thought it a piece of driftwood caught in the mash, but as he limped closer he was amazed to see green leaves fluttering in the breeze. It was alive; the roots reaching down into the plastic.

Life found a way.

He dropped to his butt and laughed at the irony as his fingers burned and the truth dawned on him.

His skin was reacting to the plastic. He held his fingers up for closer inspection as Baloo drew closer. There was just enough light to see his fingertips were streaked with red welts from touching the mass. Was the dormant infection inside him reacting to the plastic polymers?

Maybe the plastic plague choking the oceans was saving them from an even greater contagion induced by man?

With a soft crump, Baloo was snagged by submerged trash and fell into the island's embrace. Huang already had the hatch open and eagerly jumped to the ground, collapsing to her knees as the effects of violent motion sickness from the storm passed through her. Despite this, she still managed a smile when she saw the Mercury data pod in Scott's hand.

"You found it." She patted her satchel. "We have hope."

Maya hopped from the submersible and looked around, overwhelmed. "Sonar reads this at over three hundred square miles. That's about half the size of London!" The sorrow on Scott's face dispelled her wonder. "Vasilis?"

Scott nodded towards Mowgli. "The infection took him. I think it's taking me too." Despite the promise of Huang's inhibitor, he was certain the infection would claim both women soon enough.

Life found a way; it just depended on *what* life won the struggle.

He opened his mouth to speak—

Then the entire horizon lit up in a spectacular flash of such intensity he saw the storm clouds ripped apart like smoke as a blazing mushroom cloud punched for the heavens.

Then utter darkness swallowed the nuclear blast, leaving nothing more than an image burnt on the retina.

Maya and Huang dropped next to him, both too exhausted to stand. They all peered into the darkness.

"The fleet..." Scott began.

"Gone." Maya assured him. "The infection with it. Thanks to Alanis."

Scott's thoughts jumped to Ruth and his unborn child.

The encroaching danger that threatened to swallow the

world had just been obliterated because of the selfless actions of one woman.

They would live...

Huang smiled at him. "We picked up a radio message. There is a British frigate heading towards us. It should reach us by dawn." She lay her head on his shoulder and sobbed with relief. "We're saved! Once onboard we can synthase a cure."

Scott looked at his hand. Then at the top of Huang's head.

Not quite saved.

It could still find a way...

Life always did.

THE END

ALSO BY ANDY BRIGGS

EPICENTER

Majestic Files 1

SOME THINGS ARE BEST LEFT UNDISTURBED...

An **earthquake** strikes - and with it several bizarre murders.

Something is emerging from beneath the earth – leaving behind destruction and carnage.

A terrible **secret** has been disturbed.

And now it's poised to trigger a disaster that will **destroy** the world...

CHEM

Majestic Files 2

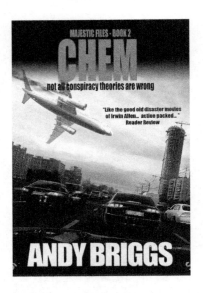

Not all conspiracy theories are wrong...

Aircraft vapor trails slice through the skies around the world. A harmless side effect to international travel. Until aircraft investigator Sam Dwyer discovers something bolted to the wing of a fatal crash. Something that shouldn't be there...

He stumbles into a global conspiracy to lace the skies with chemtrails – chemicals designed to alter the population's behavior. It's an intricate plot with global ramifications – and it's happening in plain sight!

With his life on the line, Dwyer races to expose the syndicate behind it. But their resources are vast. There is nowhere to hide...

PHANTOM LAND

Majestic Files 3

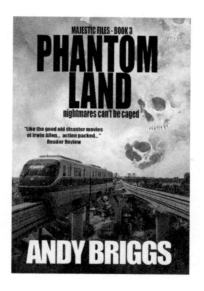

NIGHTMARES CAN'T BE CAGED...

Ghosts, wraiths, phantoms... science has just proved they are real animals from another dimension. So what better way to exploit the discovery...?

Las Vegas' new glittering jewel is a zoo with a difference. Come face-to-face with **specters**; watch **phantoms** soar through their enclosures; or dare to walk through the **banshee** tunnels. The world of the supernatural has been contained so you can confront your darkest fears...

It's a popular attraction – until a radical group of animal extremists try to liberate the beasts during the unveiling of the new star exhibit: An Angel of Death... and hell is unleashed.

Lowly zookeeper, Wes Talasky becomes the last line of defense. Forced to face his darkest fears so he can save the children of the woman he loves...

Blending science and horror into a rip-roaring adventure!

Printed in Great Britain
by Amazon